CW00702526

BEST WISHES

SHADOW OF THE SWASTIKA

Billy Yull

SHADOW OF THE SWASTIKA

First Edition

In this work of fiction, the characters, places and events are either the product of the author's imagination or they are used entirely fictitiously

Published by Shanakee Multi-Media Ltd
Printed by Lightning Source UK Ltd.
Copyright Billy Yull 2005

I know my fate.

One day my name will be
associated with the memory
of something tremendous.

A crisis without equal on
earth.

The most profound collision
of conscience.

A decision that was conjured
up against everything that
had been believed,
demanded, hallowed so far.

I am no man. I am dynamite.

Friedrich Nietzsche.

Feldkirch Town
Austrian-Swiss Border.
May 16TH 1945.

White knuckles clasped the attaché case handle in a vice-like grip, as the two rear occupants of the vehicle tensely watched fleeting images of Gothic buildings melting together like an endless snake of bricks and mortar.

The whining roar of the engine accompanied the distant murmuring of thunder, engulfing the silent occupants in an envelope of sound, while the heavens rumbled like a disgruntled lion with toothache.

The figure in the front seat turned to face the two rear occupants. English in a heavy German accent no matter how softly spoken, carries an unsettling undertone, especially when you're American officers, not wearing uniforms, and unofficial guests of the SS.

'Cigarette?'
The figure in the front held out a silver cigarette case.

The first figure's hand slowly stretched out to take one, while the other figure remained motionless, his hands still gripping the attaché case.

With his hat perched on his knee the older American took a long pull on the cigarette causing the end to glow bright red. The flame from the lighter that illuminated the car was allowed to exaggerate the thinning ginger hair flecked with grey. Hair lovingly slicked down, emphasising his moon-shaped face and the faded freckles that once covered the skin, a welcome gift of middle age, unlike his portly physique.

The second figure remained motionless, his hat still on his head, hiding most of the face. An exceptionally ordinary face, almost forgettable. It was the face of a man in his late twenties with mousy hair, dark eyes, accompanied by the lack of distinguishing features. In fact he would have to be stark naked amongst a group of nuns to stand out in a crowd. A chameleon, a man in whose company you could spend an hour, and a month later, you would struggle to remember what he looked like.

Slowly the flame returned towards its owner as he lit up his own cigarette. The flame took on a life of its own bathing the car with a strange sinister glow, forcing the emblem on his collar to stand out like a three-dimensional headstone; the insignia of a Major in the SS, an emblem of death.

His face glowed strangely under the flickering flame, waxen, sinister. It was not the face that made the rear occupants shuffle uneasily in their seats; it was the eyes.

No more than a fleeting second did they hold the Americans captive, but it was enough. Eyes, ice blue, cold and mean. The eyes glanced at the older, American, then to his white-knuckled nondescript companion.

'Relax. We are all friends this night.'

The SS officers softly spoken voice carried with it a treacherous undertone.

A thought pierced the younger American's mind. A sharp, terrifying thought as the flame was snuffed out, plunging the car once again into darkness. Lucifer means giver of light, and, facing him, was an angel of death!

The SS Major returned to his forward-facing position. A slow smile crept across his face as he glanced at the two Americans in the central mirror.

The older one peered anxiously out of the rear window at the trailing car, while the younger one remained inanimate, head bowed, gripping onto the case, afraid to look up. Afraid he may have to look into those eyes.

The vehicles slowed to a halt outside a dark, imposing, 18th century house silhouetted against a snow-laden sky.

No sooner had the occupants from the first car alighted, then, as if on cue, the large door to the front of the house opened, bidding them to enter.

A storm-trooper stood rigidly to attention holding back the door for the entourage to pass. Beside the SS Major, and his two American companions, a further five Americans, a man and four women, alighted from the trailing vehicle.

Stood waiting to greet them, in the grand entrance hall with marbled pillars and a sweeping staircase, was a smartly dressed young German woman. She smiled and bid them to follow.

She was five feet six with strong attractive features, emphasised by golden blond hair that swept upwards to form a bun on the top of her head. Her posture was elegant, with a gait that oozed sexuality. A gait she had used in the past, to her advantage.

She led them towards an open double door and into a large sitting room that should have been filled with the finest Rococo furniture and trappings. Walls that once held the Renaissance paintings were now bare and empty, with only faded imprints on the walls where the paintings once hung.

All that was left in the room was an ordinary old desk and several uncomfortable chairs. The one item of luxury was a drinks cabinet stocked to the hilt.

'Please be seated.' The woman smiled warmly as she spoke.

The Americans did as she instructed. The one gripping the case felt even more vulnerable as the SS Major preferring, to stand, towered above them.

He was the ultimate Aryan. Six foot two, square jaw, blond hair, blue eyes and a strong athletic frame. A role model, and a perfect specimen, as far as the Nazis were concerned.

The sound of footsteps could be heard approaching the room. Two officers entered. One a Colonel of the Waffen SS; the second wore the long black leather coat, the unofficial uniform of the dreaded Gestapo.

The Colonel held out his hand. A small, fat, podgy, hand connected to a small, fat, podgy body, with a red-and-purple-veined face, the result of excessive rich food and drink.

"Colonel Fritsch." He bowed and clicked his heels together as he spoke.

The older American stood up to take his hand.

"Colonel John Makin and this is," pointing to the, man gripping the case, "Lieutenant Quint."

Fritsch motioned towards the drinks cabinet.

"Brandy, gentlemen?" He asked

"No thank you. We would prefer to keep this as brief as possible." Colonel Makin replied.

Fritsch smiled before responding.

"Of course."

Fritsch nodded to the Gestapo Officer, who without showing the slightest gesture of recognition, strode out with long, slim legs towards a door at the far end of the room.

Both Americans were wondering what they had let themselves into. First a six foot plus blond giant with the eyes of a killer, now they were being led into another room by a tall, slim-framed, feminine-featured, member of the most feared arm of the Third Reich, the Gestapo.

Fritsch held out his podgy hand, beckoning them follow.

"This way gentlemen."

The two Americans obeyed Fritsch, following the Gestapo officer as he led them towards the door.

The SS Major lit another cigarette and smiled at the American women, ignoring the lone man who remained seated. A smile that flirted yet sent a shiver down their spines as the Gestapo officer opened the door and stood aside. Flanked either side of the door stood a Storm-trooper. Gingerly, the American Colonel entered the room.

Colonel Makin straightened his back and stared in amazement at the sight, before glancing at his companion, who was also transfixed. Breaking their trance the SS Major bust into the room, ready to take centre stage.

"Well gentlemen, are you so in awe that you cannot speak?" His voice was sharp, excitable.

"What is it you Americans say? Cat got your tongue?"

Both Americans took in a deep breath as they gazed upon the results of the Nazi culture. Years of experiments trying to achieve the ultimate dream in genetic perfection. Thirty blond-haired, blue eyed children, ages ranging from two days to six years, accompanying them their ten mothers. These were not just ordinary blond Aryan children, these were the sole reason for the American's presence. A true race of super beings, specially bred not only for their appearance but also for their abilities. Abilities that the Germans feared would fall into the wrong hands, namely, the Russians.

The mighty Third Reich was on its back foot. All of Hitler's dreams looked to be crumbling before their eyes. These children were all that would be left of Himmler's legacy. The perfect beings. The Master Race. The Children of the Herrenvolk.

Colonel Makin turned to Fritsch.

"We have no need for your women. We have our own."

Fritsch nodded in agreement, signalling for the troopers to bring the American women.

The SS Major beckoned one of the mothers. She was holding a new-born baby in her arms. He took it from her.

"Yours?" he asked.

The mother dared not look into the Major's eyes.

"No sir," she replied.

"Who is his mother?" He looked around as he spoke.

"She is dead sir." She sheepishly replied.

The smartly-dressed German woman quickly interceded.

"Do you not recognise the child?"

The SS Major smiled before answering.

"Should I?"

The smartly dressed woman stroked the child's head, before looking into the SS Major's eyes

"He is special. Very special."

The Major accompanied her by gently stroking the baby's face.

"Ah yes." he smiled." Special you say. If he is so special, then you shall personally take care of him."

He removed the child from the woman's arms and handed it to the smartly dressed young woman.

Colonel Makin instantly responded.

"Sorry Major but we are taking no extra baggage."

The SS Major's eyes fixed themselves upon Makin.

"With respect Colonel, the doctor is not baggage. She is and has been an intricate part of the programme from its conception and will be of enormous help to you. Secondly, the child's mother is dead, as will be the child if he is not fed and looked after. The doctor has herself recently lost a child and therefore still carries milk in her breasts. Thirdly, if she does not go then none will go."

Makin turned towards Fritsch who shrugged his shoulder, forcing Makin to ponder for a moment before responding.

"What about papers? She will need papers."

The SS Major's voice grew smug as he replied.

"But you have her papers do you not? I assume that the attaché case your Lieutenant guards so intently has the necessary documentation for one Ida Kroll?"

Makin looked to Quint, who nodded.

"Okay." Makin replied. "Her, and only her."

The SS Major bowed his head.

The American women began to lead the children out of the room. Some of the women were crying as they watched their babies being taken from them. One woman refused to release a child, begging the SS Major to let her go with it.

The child, a girl of six, clung to her mother, arms wrapped around her neck, legs around her waist, like the tentacles of an octopus.

A trooper prised the child away. Picking her up in his arms he walked towards the door. Suddenly, the screaming child clasped her hands either side of his temples.

At first the trooper stood motionless, then his body began slowly to shake. Initially it was not a violent tremor, more like a person suffering from Parkinson's disease. Then the shaking grew and grew until the trooper cried out in pain before slumping to the floor, dropping the child with a thud.

A faint trickle of blood ran out of his tear duct and down his cheek, followed by bleeding from the nose and ears. The child, unhurt, rushed back towards her mother's waiting arms, as the American contingent stood motionless, mouths agape.

The SS Major briskly walked past Quint, who was still holding onto his case. With a smile he gently lifted Quint's lower jaw.

"Best keep out the flies," he sarcastically sneered.

Walking over towards the child, he slowly prised her away from her mother. The child instantly accepted her fate as she was led hand in hand by the SS Major to a petrified American woman.

"Please, take her hand. She will not bite. She may have faults, but biting is not one of them."

The SS Major gently kissed the child on the cheek before wiping away her tears. The young girl offered no resistance as she slipped her hand inside the American woman's, who recoiled slightly before leading the girl out of the room to join the rest of the children.

Fritsch motioned for one of the German mothers to help the trooper who was slowly coming round.

"Come, gentlemen, we have business to conclude. There is a bus waiting outside to transport the children and your staff to the border. To ensure your safe passage our colleague from the Gestapo will accompany you, once we have satisfactorily finalised our deal."

The two Americans and the three German officers closed the door behind them and returned to the sitting room. Fritsch stood in the centre of the room, hands on hips, looking more like Mussolini than a Nazi.

"Well, gentlemen, shall we press on?" He rubbed his hands together.

Makin nodded for the attaché case to be opened, forcing Quint to speak for the first time. His voice was high-pitched and broken, like a schoolboy in the early stages of puberty.

"All the passports and papers you require," Quint responded.

"And the money?" Fritsch's tone rang of greed.

Makin interceded.

"In a Swiss bank, all will be transferred once we are safely across the border. Details are inside."

Fritsch's face grew more highly coloured as he spoke.

"Come now gentlemen, trust, where is the trust? You ask us to trust you, but you do not trust us." Fritsch's voice carried an air of frustration.

Makin rose from his seat as he spoke.

"Surely Colonel, you did not think us foolhardy enough to hand everything over without some form of assurance."

Fritsch's face glowed as he tried to suppress his anger.

"What I see, gentlemen, is not assurance, but a display of American, what is your expression? Double dealing?"

Instantly the SS Major interceded.

"Come, let us not quarrel. There is a simple solution," he said.

Fritsch sarcastically responded.

"Ah! Behold the man with all the answers. Well Herr Major, do not keep us in suspense. Enlighten us?"

The SS Major's eyes burned like ice on fire, as he glared at his commanding officer.

"If my Colonel will allow me to continue, I will hopefully solve our little dilemma. Colonel Makin will accompany the children across the border, leaving Lieutenant Quint on the Austrian side, along with his precious attaché case. Once Colonel Makin and the children are safely across the border, Colonel Makin will release the money.

As we already possess all of the passports and necessary travel documents, we only need confirmation of the money transfer. Doctor Kroll will be able to confirm that. Once this has been achieved we will release the Lieutenant."

Quint's voice rose at least two octaves as he spluttered out his words.

"That means I will be trapped, on German soil."

The SS Major smiled as he responded.

"Austrian soil to be precise. As for trapped, hardly a word to use among business partners. Well Colonel?"

Makin looked at Quint before replying.

"Okay."

Quint, terror written over his face, pleaded with his eyes to his commanding officer.

"You will be fine, Quint. They have nothing to gain by killing you," Makin reassured him.

The SS Major moved closer to the American Colonel; his face no more than an inch or two away from Makin's. His cold eyes held the American as he spoke softly.

"That is true Colonel. Still. A word of warning. Just because you are across the border, it does not make you safe, especially if you do not keep your part of the bargain. The little exhibition, the one you witnessed with the child. Nothing. It was nothing. What the British would call a pantomime. No more. Nothing compared to what I will do to you if you misplace our trust."

There was cold venom in his voice, and it had the required effect, sending a shiver all the way down Makin's body before earthing itself like an electric current.

Colonel Makin left the room to join the rest of the party on the bus, leaving the SS Major to turn his attention to Quint.

"Well, Lieutenant, aren't you the lucky one? A personal bodyguard, and a member of the Gestapo. You will drive together in the staff car, to the border where you will wait for the all clear regarding the transaction. Once it is satisfactorily completed you will be released. Unharmed."

Quint was about to leave followed by the Lieutenant in the Gestapo, when the SS Major caught him by the arm.

"The case." the SS Major held out his hand.

"Time to give your knuckles some colour other than white."

Quint reluctantly handed over the case before following the Gestapo officer out of the room.

The SS Major smiled at Fritsch as he walked towards the drinks cabinet.

"Brandy?"

Fritsch had a troubled look on his face as he spoke.

"Do you think it wise?"

"What, having a drink?" smiled the SS Major

Fritsch's face grew angry at his sarcastic response.

"You know what I mean, allowing that American to cross the border without transferring the money."

The SS Major smiled in only the way he could. A smile so cold it sent a chill thorough the body of the recipient.

"I trust him." The words hissed through his teeth. "He has a trustworthy face. The face of a man who will keep a promise, as he knows I will keep mine."

Austrian Swiss Border Post.
May 16TH 1945.

The German border guards were perplexed having never before been presented with so many crossing the border at one time. But they were still soldiers of the Third Reich, disciplined in unswerving acceptance of orders, especially when they came from a Colonel in Waffen SS, and were delivered by a Lieutenant in the Gestapo; orders any soldier of the Third Reich would act upon without question or hesitation.

The snow was falling think and heavy. Flakes as large as English muffins steadily began to build up a barricade of white on the windscreen of the car. While the occupants of the bus, the driver and two storm troopers decided to take a well-earned nap.

Quint sat alone in the rear of the car with the Gestapo officer and the driver in the front.

"Mind if I smoke?" Quint's words fell on deaf ears.

"Cigarette, anyone?"

Quint tapped the Gestapo officer on the shoulder, who turned to look at him without showing any emotion.

Quint offered him a cigarette.

"Smoke?"

The Gestapo officer turned his back on Quint without replying.

"Guess not?   "Quint continued. "Mind if I do?..... No?...... Then I will.....Speak to your Goddamn self, Quint. "

Quint's attitude had changed; he looked upon his fate as being out of his hands and in the hands of the enemy. He may be a member of the O.S.S. Office of Strategic Services, and knew the mission was a dangerous one. But he was certainly no field operative, he was a psychologist employed in the intelligence core. He was only here for the ride. His job was to ascertain that the Germans had actually bred a group of children with psychic ability.

The demonstration by the girl was enough proof for both he and his commanding officer. What the American's were unaware of was that not all the children were bred for their psychic abilities. Some were the result of selective breeding between physicists, biologists and chemists. Germany and Austria had been scoured for the top Aryan academic minds and had been used to breed what Himmler would eventually claim to be the descendants of the Herrenvolk.

"Speak English?" Quint tried once more to communicate "Do you speak English?"
Neither German replied.

"Guess not." He continued. "No good, fucking goose-stepping arse bandits."

Quint sat back in the seat taking long pulls on his cigarette while muttering to himself how he hated all arrogant fucking Germans, who are even worse than that other Saxon lot, their stuck up tight arsed English fucking cousins. If the truth was known Quint didn't like anybody, including himself.

House, Feldkirch Austria. May 16TH 1945.

The operation, for obvious reasons, had been conducted in secret relying on staff the SS Major could trust. Excluding the mothers in the other room and two storm-troopers, in the house there were a further two troopers and a woman, the Colonel's private secretary.

The SS Major gathered the remainder of staff in the house together while they all sat around in the room waiting for the telephone to ring with confirmation that the transaction was complete.

This would come from the Gestapo officer at the border. After Kroll had used her pass to cross back into Austria to collect Quint, Fritsch would be informed by telephone from the border post that the transaction had been successful.

Each of the troopers had changed into civilian clothing. Their guns and uniforms lay piled in the far corner of the room as they sat around chatting and laughing. Each was offered a drink of one kind or another.

The informality was something they weren't used to. Something they had never experienced before, especially in the company of their commanding officers. Only the Major and Colonel remained in uniform.

The atmosphere was so light-hearted that the SS Major insisted that they all joined the mothers in the other room, taking their drinks with them.

As they were about to enter the room the telephone rang. It was confirmation that the transaction had been completed.

Fritsch clapped his hands before rubbing them together and announcing the good news.

"Well gentlemen," The Colonel paused, "and ladies. This time tomorrow we will all be on our way to South America."

A loud cheer went up. Even the sobbing mothers in the other room managed to force a smile of relief as the SS Major ushered the remaining stragglers into the other room, with the exception of the Colonel and his secretary.

"Come, pass round the drinks; as of this moment we are all civilians. Come, let us celebrate." The SS Major smiled as he spoke.

The troopers did not waste a second as they filled up their glasses for a toast. The Major held up his hand.

"Wait, what we need is something special. You wait here; I have just the thing. A little surprise."

He closed the doors behind him, leaving the troopers singing as they tried to get the women involved in the merriment. They could hear a record being placed on the phonograph. It was the "Ride of the Vakyries" by Wagner. Happy faces were replaced by sombre ones, as some of the children's mothers sensed all was not well.

At that the doors burst open. Standing in the doorway was the Colonel and the SS Major, with machine guns in their hands.

Within a blink of the eye, blood, bits of flesh, and bone where decorating walls and furniture. Bodies writhed as bullet after bullet ripped through flesh and shattered bone. All to the sound of Richard Wagner accompanied by two SS officers on machine guns.

The floor was awash with blood. The carpet, unable to soak any more of the crimson liquid that flowed freely from the mass of writhing bodies, formed a small lake in the centre of the room.

Machine guns emptied. The SS Major motioned for the Colonel to take one side of the room while he took the other.

Each removing from their holsters a Luger pistol, they clinically placed a bullet into the head of any form that twitched or showed signs of life.

One woman, miraculously, was only slightly wounded. Curled up in a ball in the corner of the room, she slowly lifted her head at the figure towering above her.

Large blue eyes begged the SS Major, as the mouth opened in a vain attempt to plead for her life.

A flash emanated from the end of the Luger, as a red hot bullet pierced one of her large blue eyes, shattering the back of her skull into a thousand fragments. Grey tissues mixed with blood splattered against the wall behind.

A fountain of blood spurted out of the wound like an unattended garden hose. What seemed a lifetime for her, was in reality no more than three or four seconds.

Death in this manner was not an unfamiliar scenario to either of the men. Men who had witnessed, and in the SS Major case, had personally performed executions on a far greater scale. As for Fritsch, it was the first time that he had been the one to pull the trigger.

The moaning had ceased. Bodies no longer writhed in pain. Even the music had stopped. Fritsch looked over towards the SS Major who was still looking at the lifeless body of the woman. A woman the SS Major knew intimately, a woman who in the past had borne him two children. Her reward was having her brains decorate a wall where a priceless work of art had once hung.

Slowly Fritsch lifted his Luger. The gun was aimed directly at the SS Major. The SS Major's head turned, his cold eyes looked down the muzzle of the gun.

"Greed, Fritsch. Is money your God?" the SS Major hissed at his would-be assassin.

Fritsch moved closer to his prey before speaking.

"Don't bother raising your gun. I listened and counted your shots, your gun is empty. You wasted your last bullet on your ex-bride. As for money being my God, I prefer mine to Himmler. At least mine will give me the life I long for."

The SS Major smiled and bowed. A split second later the crack from the muzzle of a small pistol sent a bullet ripping into the chest of Fritsch. In a flash the SS Major was upon him, like a spider upon a fly.

The SS Major gave a fleeting glance at a small, petite woman of twenty, with dark brown hair and soft hazel eyes, standing in the doorway holding a gun.

Fritsch was on his knees with both hands gripping the wound in his chest. His gun was lying on the floor.

Fritsch looked up at the woman, his eyes wide with shock and pain.

"Why?" He cried out.

She walked over towards him, gun still pointed at his fat body.

"Why? I'll tell you why. Night after night I lay in bed beside you, crying myself to sleep as I looked upon your grotesque bloated face. Night after night I had to endure your puffing and panting as I almost blacked out under your weight, as you relieved yourself on my body."

She was about to shoot him again when the SS Major snatched the gun from her hand.

"No! Leave him to me," he insisted. "You go and pack. I will join you shortly."

The secretary left closing the door behind her. Fritsch tried to slide his hand towards the gun he had dropped when he was shot, but the SS Major kicked it away before speaking.

"Naughty. Naughty. You avaricious old toad. I knew a share would not be enough for you."

Fritsch's voice was cracked as the pain in his chest intensified.

"And you. You have it all now."

The SS Major gave a small laugh.

"Money." He retorted. "You think I did this for the money? Then you are a greater fool than I thought. This was for the future. What we did today will help fulfil the greatest prophecy of mankind. I did this not for the money. I did this for the Fatherland, for our Fuhrer.

Our divine destiny lies in the legacy we have sown, once the Children of the Herrenvolk inherit the earth."

Throwing his empty gun away, the SS Major clasped his hands either side of Fritsch's head. Fritsch tried frantically to free himself from SS Major's grasp.

Fritsch's eyes, wild with terror, slowly turned upward in the sockets as his body began to shake followed by an epileptic convulsion. Blood poured out of his nose, ears, mouth and anus. His head shook from side to side, his eyes turned red as the blood surged into each eyeball until they could expand no more, finally bursting, splattering crimson spray over the SS Major's face.

Fritsch's body grew limp, as the SS Major finally let the lifeless hulk slide to the floor, a new addition to the slaughterhouse.

Before leaving the SS Major surveyed the room and smiled at its tangled mass of lifeless, bloodstained mannequins.

Austrian Swiss Border Post. May 16TH 1945.

A sharp rap on the driver's side window by the border guard startled Quint. The guard informed them that a woman was waiting at the boarder post.

The Gestapo officer climbed out of the car before opening the rear door allowing Quint to climb out also.

Quint looked towards the border post. He could see the shapely figure of Ida Kroll waiting outside. Without a word he set off in her direction. Suddenly his heart missed a beat along with his stride, as a soft almost effeminate voice called out in broken English.

"Goose-step you arrogant tight-arsed bastard before I change my mind and stick a bayonet up it.

Quint dared not look back. He knew who had called out to him. His heart pounded in his chest as he watched the border post draw nearer and nearer. If only he had kept his big mouth shut.

"You stupid big mouth son of a bitch!" he whispered to himself." Should have known he'd be able to speak English."

Reaching the post, documents checked, Quint and Kroll crossed once more into the Swiss sector and safety.

The Gestapo Officer signalled for the bus to start up and follow as he climbed into the rear seat of the car. No words were exchanged as the car tentatively manoeuvred down the hazardous path back towards the town. The snow was falling thicker than ever and the road was becoming increasingly treacherous. Suddenly the Gestapo officer gave the order for the driver to stop.

The puzzled driver did as he was told, forcing the bus driver behind to do all he could to avoid hitting the rear of the car and pushing it off the road down the side of the mountain.

The driver of the car was about to turn round and ask why they had stopped, when he felt a sharp stabbing pain that shot up from the nape of the neck and into his brain.

The passenger in the rear slowly removed a long silver dagger with the death's head insignia from the nape of the driver's neck, allowing the driver's head to loll on his neck like a slinky spring.

A small push was all that was needed to allow the head to slump forward, thudding against the windscreen.

The weight of his body pressed down against the horn in the centre of the steering wheel, shattering the icy silence as the Gestapo officer wiped the knife clean with a white handkerchief.

Climbing out of the car the Gestapo officer was greeted with the running figures of two of the storm-troopers from the bus. Remaining calm, the Gestapo officer called out to the troopers.

"You two. See what is wrong with him."

Without questioning, the two troopers headed towards the front of the car. The minute their backs where turned, the Gestapo officer drew his pistol and shot them both in the back of the head.

The driver on the bus, quick off the mark, rammed the bus into gear and headed for the Leather-clad officer. Three shots through the windscreen sent the bus crashing into the mountain side, crushing the front end and almost killing the Gestapo officer who miraculously managed to dive out of its path.

Slowly he rose to his feet to survey the wreckage. The driver, although shot, was not dead and managed to grab hold of his rifle. A shot rang out as a bullet whizzed past the Gestapo officer, smashing the rear window of the car.

Keeping low, he returned fire. Both men exchanged shots, the driver bleeding badly from a wound in his chest.

The Gestapo officer, crawling backwards in the snow, tried to make his way to the car. He was out of ammunition and needed to get one of the trooper's weapons. A bullet hit him in the foot as he turned to make a dash for a rifle, causing a shooting pain to run up his leg towards the brain.

This was instantly blotted out by raw adrenaline, allowing him to roll over in the snow and grab one of the dead trooper's rifles.

Hidden behind a rifle, a head popped up inside the bus. Before it had a chance to exchange another shot a bullet smashed its way through the window and ripped into the occupant's forehead.

Still blotting out the pain, the Gestapo officer dragged the bodies of all three troopers onto the bus and restarted it, before sending it plummeting down the side of the mountain into the ravine below.

A smile of satisfaction crept across his face. He knew it would take at least a day for a rescue team to get to the mangled pieces of scrap, if indeed they could be found beneath the snow.

House, Feldkirch Austria. May 16TH 1945.

Three loud raps echoed in the empty hallway, as the secretary opened the door allowing the bleeding Gestapo officer to limp into the entrance hall. Holding onto his arm she helped him towards the staircase. His face grimaced in pain as he forced out the words.

"I can't climb them."

A voice called out from above.

"There will be no need. Dress the wound downstairs. Your case is packed. You can change down there."

The Secretary helped the Gestapo officer into the library. Sitting him in a large leather chair, she left the room to get some bandage and treat the wound. Returning, she helped him off with his boot. Fortunately the bullet had passed right through. Unfortunately it had broken the ankle on its journey.

The wound dressed, the Secretary helped the Gestapo officer out of his clothes.

The door behind them opened. Standing in the doorway, dressed as a priest, was the SS Major. Draped over his arm was another black priest's suit. The Secretary was about to take the clothes to give them to the Gestapo officer.

Instantly she recoiled. Hidden under the clothes was the very gun she had used to shoot Colonel Fritsch.

The Major smiled as he pointed the gun in the direction of the Gestapo Officer and the woman.

"I am sorry but you are a liability."

The woman looked at the Gestapo officer's expressionless face as his eyes locked onto those of his commanding officer, before returning her gaze once more to the SS Major.

The muzzle of the gun exploded twice. Blood poured from two wounds; one in the throat and one in the chest. A third explosion ended the matter ripping into the centre of the forehead.

"Come along, Father, get dressed. We have to attend mass in the morning," the SS Major laughed aloud at his joke.

The Gestapo Officer showed no emotion as he watched the SS Major using the gun as a priest would a cross muttering in Latin over the lifeless body of the young woman.

A smile was on the SS Major's lips as he looked at his companion.

"Just practising. Just practising."

Austrian, Swiss, Border Post. May 16TH 1945.

The border guard examined the documents of the two priests. He was about to question them further when one of the guards recognised the Gestapo officer. Afraid to confront him as he might jeopardise a possibly secret mission, he took over from his colleague, allowing both priests to pass unchallenged.

Suddenly a loud explosion followed by a further two, echoed up the mountain. A red glow illuminated the sky above the town of Feldkirch.

The result of three bombs and several incendiary devices, all carefully timed, all carefully placed and all carefully planned by two men of God.

Christine's House
Durham England.
October 29th 1969.

A bright moon, subdued by the stained-glass window on the first turn of the staircase, tentatively illuminated the hallway, as particles of dust trapped in its sombre glow danced a polka in the moonlight.

The grandfather clock standing proud and erect in the hallway played its customary tune, followed by eleven single loud chimes. The last chime faded melancholically away into the empty hallway, allowing the loud rhythmic tick, like the beat of a heart, to reign supreme in the still of the night. Tired timbers groaned and cracked, as all old houses do. Familiar sounds the occupants become accustomed to.

A dull thud shattered the metronomic beat, followed by the sound of slow heavy footsteps climbing the stairs. With every step a small expulsion of air was let out, as if each tread of the staircase was an effort.

Step by step phantom feet climbed their way up the stairs, past the stained glass window and past the dust particles that continued to dance undisturbed in the moonlight.

With the last tread reached, the footsteps halted directly opposite a bedroom at the top of the stairs. To the left was a long dark corridor leading to a bathroom, another bedroom and a second flight of stairs. To the right there was a short corridor and another bedroom that had its door ajar.

A thin yellow beam of light cut into the darkness. A chink of light emanated through the crack, no more. Just enough for the occupant inside to listen in fear, in fear at what was about to take place.

In the bedroom on the edge of the bed sat a pretty young woman nineteen in years, with dark hair, and blue tearful eyes that stared wildly at the door. Her head was cocked to one side, allowing her ears to be ready, ready to pick up the slightest sound.

She swallowed hard. Her hands trembled as the last footstep reached the top of the staircase. Her eyelids closed as she waited for what she feared most. On cue from out of the darkness came a pitiful little voice, a voice that filled the empty corridor.

"Please let me go home, please. My mummy will be worried. Please."

The young woman on the bed raised her hands to her face and began to sob. She had heard it all before, and she knew what would come next. That's why the door was ajar. She had to be sure her mind wasn't playing tricks on her.

Suddenly the young woman jumped up from the bed and slammed the door shut with such ferocity that the frame shuddered with the force, in a vain attempt to blot out the piercing scream that was to follow. A scream that ricocheted off walls as it ran unabated throughout the house.

Her back pressed against the door the young woman sobbed and sobbed, deep meaningful sobs that came from within the soul. Eventually her head turned to look towards the window and the bright visitor that peered in from outside. The moon full, bold ominous, like a luminous undertaker, hovered silently in the night sky.

St Oswald's Church Underwood Kent. October 29th 1969

Perched high on a hill, the ruined remains of a once-proud castle, stand like a lone sentinel overlooking an even older Saxon church, as a pale moon shrouded by the clouds, casts its eerie light on this lonely place of worship. A little country church, a mile, no more from the village and prying eyes, hidden behind a stone wall, and two small wrought-iron gates.

To the right of the iron gates is a small kissing gate, the type that will admit only one person at a time, by pushing the gate one way before standing to the side to allow it to swing back to it place of origin. An entrance that admits all be they an inquisitive tourist, devout worshipper, or those with intentions of a more sinister nature.

Even on the sunniest of days this churchyard carried an aura of finality, more a place of mourning, than a place of worship. And when the night falls a sinister atmosphere attaches itself to all that look upon it, or dare to venture inside its grounds, grounds where the dead rule supreme.

Like guards of honour, yew trees line either side of the path, their branches like fingers stretch upwards and across, interlocking with their brothers on the opposite side, forming a dark tunnel that blots out even sunlight, let alone the watery glow of a full moon.

To the left, at the end of the tunnel, stands a small tower. All that is left of a once larger place of worship, with a stone arch linking it to a quaint little chapel. A chapel used occasionally for special events.

An owl hoots in a distant tree, as a bright light scatters the shadows from among the tombstones. Another flash of soft light illuminates the stonework beneath the arch, causing the creatures of the night to scurry for safety back into the shadows. Including the owl, who flees on silent wing, leaving the moonlit ritual to continue unobserved and undisturbed. For two, three seconds at the most, absolute silence reigns supreme.

The night becomes still, with no wind to rustle through the trees and no owl to hoot. Engulfed in a vacuum of silence, the moon slips behind a cloud, drawing a veil of blackness over the churchyard.

" Forgive me, my God. Forgive me. "
The repetitive plea is followed by a solitary sob. One sob leads to another, followed by a high-pitched wail like a vixen crying for its mate, shattering the still of the night.

As if to see what all the noise is about, the moon comes out of hiding, bathing the landscape in its cold light. Below the arch a figure kneels with arms outstretched, begging for forgiveness, like a wolf baying at the moon.

Bolly's Flat, Edinburgh Scotland. October 30th 1969

Bang, bang, bang. The door rattled in its frame at the weight of the raps.

Below a poster of Jimi Hendrex, pinned to a plain blue wall, were a jumble of sheets and the outline of a body.

Slowly a head poked out, like a tortoise from its shell. Half-open bleary eyes, searched for the bedside light, as the nicotine-strained voice, cracked and hoarse, muffled a jaw-breaking yawn.

"All right. All right. Hold your horses."

Grudgingly the figure wearing a rugby shirt three sizes too big made its way towards the door and the communal telephone in the hallway. The hunched figure of a young man in a dressing gown trudged back to his own room, grumbling about being woken from his slumber. Bolly placed the telephone receiver to her ear.

"Yes"

The voice on the other side was hysterical, forcing Bolly to overcome her sleepiness as she quickly brought the conversation to a conclusion.

"Jesus, Christine! Calm down. What! You're joking. Okay, I'll come. Explain it to me in the morning."

Bolly replaced the receiver and let out a sigh, as her back flopped against the wall.

"The kid's lost her marbles," she whispered to herself.

Christine's House Durham England. October 30th 1969.

The rusty hinges on the wrought-iron gate grudgingly gave way as Bolly stepped onto the Victorian paved path that led towards her aunt's house.

It was a large dark and sombre Victorian property, with leafless ivy and barren climbing roses that clung to red engineering brickwork like strands of dried-up spaghetti.

Its dark-green-painted doors and windows made the house look dreary, standing in its own grounds of an acre and a half, especially on this dank miserable day.

Silhouetted like a refugee from a monastery, Bolly's face showed no sign of emotion as she pulled the hood of her duffel coat tighter around her small pixie-like face. It was a pretty face, with large blue eyes, a turned-up button nose, and a mouth that courted an impish smile. Features that were all proportioned in a petite five-foot frame. Good things came in little parcels. A saying she constantly used.

Standing inside the front porch Bolly rapped on the door several times with the highly-polished brass lion's head door knocker. A small puddle had formed beside the porch where the guttering was missing. She stared vacantly, watching drip after drip as they plopped into the water sending circles rippling outwards to the edge of the miniature lake.

Bolly give small shrug of he shoulders as she muttered to herself.

"Don't know about it being haunted. But I do know is It's bloody falling apart."

The door finally swung open. Standing before her was the young woman who only the night before bore witness to a horror that was to become the catalyst for the most incredible series of events that would change their lives forever.

Christine threw her arms around Bolly's neck not giving her the chance to enter the house.

"Steady on, girl. Sisterly love's all well and good, but you're breaking my bloody neck," was Bolly's response.

The grandfather clock chimed the quarter hour as Christine lead Bolly out of the hallway and into a wood-panelled study, that was obviously a man's room. A man who's hobbies were shooting and fishing, judging by all of the dead animals. Badgers, otters, foxes, whole or heads severed from the body and mounted on wooden plaques. Above the fireplace was a picture of a gamekeeper and his master returning from the shoot with their dogs, overseen by a bright winter's moon.

Alongside the fire was a pipe-rack, tobacco and a pair of well-worn slippers. All neatly presented waiting for their master to return, a master who would never return, who could never return.

Bolly give a shudder as she stood in front of the fire.

"Jesus! Why this room?" she exclaimed.

"I don't want Aunt Ivy to hear," was the reply.

Bolly removed her wet duffel coat, and let it fall to the floor as she warmed herself before the fire.

"Hear what?" Bolly asked.

Christine drew closer before replying.

"About the house. About it being haunted." Bolly made no reply. "Did you hear what I said? Christine asked.

Bolly smiled.

"Yes, the house is haunted. I was just thinking it's better than you being pregnant."

"It's not funny." Christine snapped.

Bolly tried to suppress her amusement.

"I'm not laughing. Well, not yet."

Christine tried to control her emotions.

"I knew when I asked you to come you would think I was either hallucinating or nuts."

"Nuts. I'll go along with that," Bolly sarcastically replied.

Christine flopped down onto the sofa, running her hands through her hair.

"Bolly I've seen him."

"Him?" Bolly asked.

Christine's voice began to tremble.

"Him and.... "

Bolly's facial expression took on a countenance of concern. The lack of frivolity was noticeable in her voice as she asked the question.

"And what?"

"And the children." Christine began to cry.
Bolly sat besides her sister and placed her arm around her shoulder.

"Look I know you're not mad. Well, not completely. But make sense."
Christine gripped her sister's hand.

"It's terrible, Boll. Their little voices crying, begging, and then....then the scream."

Bolly sat in silence, and tenderly attempted to comforting her sister. Lifting Christine's face to hers she looked into her eyes.

"Tell me all about it. And I mean everything. If we're going to talk about the dead," she looked about her. "Then this is the room for it."

Christine was about to begin her story when the door opened and in walked their aunt. A tall slim woman with sharp features, small thin lips that were over shadowed by a long nose, shaped like a paper dart. She looked at Bolly.

"Arabella!" she exclaimed
Bolly nodded in acknowledgement.

Their aunt lifted Bolly's coat from the floor and looked at Christine.

"You never mentioned your sister was to pay us a visit. Just passing by, is she?"

Christine intervened before Bolly had the chance to reply.

"No. She is staying for a few days. If that's all right with you?"

The coolness between Bolly and her aunt went back a long way. Back to Bolly's childhood when at the age of three she cut the tails off the goldfish with a pair of scissors.

"Of course, of course," Their aunt replied." Your sister will be made welcome. After all we no longer possess any goldfish. Just two rules. I would be obliged if you would refrain from smoking in the house."

Bolly was quick to reply

"And the other?"

Their aunt drew in a short intake of breath before replying.

"Please use the sitting room for your socialising. Not this room." Aunt Ivy held Bolly's duffle coat in the air. "I will hang this where it belongs."

Bolly smiled, before sarcastically replying.

"Thank you for being so caring."

Their aunt was about to leave the room when Bolly's question stopped her in her tracks.

"Oh, by the way. Have you seen or heard these ghosts?"

The aunt turned slowly, fixing her eyes on Bolly.

"So that is the reason you are here."

Christine stood up placing herself between the women.

"I had to ask her to come. You never hear anything and, and."

She began to cry. Aunt Ivy instantly placed her arms around Christine pulling her closer to her.

"Come, come now my dear."

Bolly standing next to the two women, persisted with her questioning.

"Well, have you?"

Ivy kissed Christine on the forehead before replying.

"Of course not. Do you think for one moment that I would let her suffer like this? Ghosts., ha! No such things, just superstitious poppycock."

"Poppycock. Is that a botanical sex organ?" Bolly retorted

The older woman glared at her niece.

"I see you have still retained your rudeness."

Aunt Ivy turned and walked out of the room closing the door behind her.

Bolly poked out her tongue.

"Old bitch.

Christine flopped down onto the sofa.

"Please Boll try not to argue with her. I'm under enough stress as it is without world war three."

Bolly's hands rubbed her backside as she let the fire that blazed inside of it, warm her nether regions.

"Listen kid. The sight of me in my rugby shirt will put the shits up anything living or dead."

Christine forced half a smile before a frown appeared above her eyes. Slowly she pointed to the hunting picture above the fireplace

"It will come tonight. It always happens when the moon is full."

Felton Village
Kent England.
October 30th 1969.

The slow hypnotic sweep of the windscreen wipers beat time like a metronome to the piece of music on the radio, Gustav Mahler's 'Adagietto' Symphony number five.

In the distance the little figure of a child could be seen, umbrella held high as little red Wellington's refused to pass a puddle without the customary leap into its centre. With the entrance to the village shop a few feet away, she carefully lowered her umbrella before entering.

The car slowed to a halt some distance from the shop, as the driver sat patiently waiting. Slender fingers drummed a tattoo upon the steering wheel, as the thin anaemic bottom lip was gently nibbled by the upper set of teeth.

The music on the radio changed to Pia Jesue. The fingers no longer beat. They slowly removed the spectacles, giving them a wipe with a handkerchief, before returning them to their rightful position, so the cold blue eyes behind could watch and wait.

Inside the shop a local woman and the shopkeeper were indulging in the usually daily ritual of gossiping. The child placed the umbrella down to open her little purse, the one with a rabbit's face. The purse that was a present from her grandmother, with a whole pound note inside she would often remark. That was the best Easter she had ever had in her short little life.

"A pint of milk please."
The shopkeeper heaved her more than ample frame to the milk crate and handed her a bottle before asking,

"How is your grandmother, haven't seen her for weeks."
The child excitedly replied.

"She's taking me to the pictures. Were going to see 'The Lady and The Tramp'."

The woman smiled as she handed the child the change.

"That'll be nice."
Milk purchased, the child hurried out of the shop, her mind racing with excitement at the forthcoming treat. Noticing the umbrella, the shopkeeper picked it up.

"Look at that. All excited about the pictures. She leaves her umbrella behind. Forget their heads if they weren't screwed on these days."

The shopkeeper waddled to the door; opening it she stepped outside to call the child back. There was no sign of her. An expression of puzzlement crept over her face.

"Couldn't have run that fast," she whispered to herself.

In the gutter was a broken bottle of milk, with its diluted contents mixing with the rain to form a river of grey-white before drifting silently into oblivion.

Christine's House
Durham England.
October 30th 1969.

Endless cups of coffee, accompanied by Bolly's persistent interrogation, left both girls sleepy. Bolly glanced at the clock high on a shelf in the kitchen it was 10.45 pm.

"Sod it. I've drunk that much coffee it's coming out of my ears. Look, you go to bed and I'll join you once I've had a smoke."
Christine quickly jumped to her feet.

" Don't smoke in here. You know what she's like."

Bolly gestured with her hands, to calm her sister down.

"I know, I know." She rose from her seat. "Come on kid, off to bed. Leave the cups until the morning, you need some sleep."

Christine obeyed without question, following her sister into the hallway, who quickly ushered her off to bed.

Bolly waited by the front door, and watched Christine wearily climb the stairs, passing the stained-glass window that was not sinister under the glare of a brightly-lit chandelier.

With Christine out of sight Bolly pulled open the front door to stand in the porch. The night was clear and fresh.

Several hours had passed since it last rained, leaving a sharp nip in the air. Sharp with an autumn freshness, that carried a faint hint of frost that caressed the lawn with its slender icy fingers.

The door behind her was left open, with the light from the hallway illuminating the immediate area where she stood, a comforting friend, especially after Christine's supernatural ramblings. If the truth was known, Bolly on the surface appeared to be sympathetic, but she found it hard to believe a single word.

Striking a match, she lit up her Woodbine. The smoke from the cigarette formed a small genie as it slowly spiralled its way outwards, mingling with the shadows before disappearing into the night. She drew once more, puffing out smoke tainted with heated breath.

A faint shuffling sound behind her caused her to hold in the remaining smoke as goose bumps crept over her skin. Slowly she turned her head to look into the hallway.

A small explosion of smoke was released as Bolly called out into the empty hallway.

"Is that you, Chris?"

There was no reply.

Still not sure, she took a small step into the hallway to look around. There was no one there. It was empty. Returning to her position in the porch, she mumbled to herself.

"Letting it get to you kid."

Suddenly the light in the hallway went out as the door behind her clicked shut, while the moon like a dagger drawn from its sheath slipped from behind a cloud, a silent observer.

Bolly's lips neither closed around the cigarette nor drew on it as a cold chill swept through her body. Her heart raced as she slowly turned her head. Head half turned with eyes widening by the milli-second, she saw what no one should be made to see.

The smouldering cigarette slipped from between her fingers as she stood transfixed. Her breath came and went in short rapid breaks as she stared at the doorway and the lone figure of a child. A little girl, no older than three years, in a little pink party frock standing inanimate, glaring into Bolly's ashen face.

Melting from out of the shadows the figure of a man emerged through the door. A man with cold callous eyes, hidden behind gold-rimmed spectacles that stared into Bolly's eyes. They showed neither emotion nor recognition to the young woman. It was as if he was looking straight through her.

Gently taking the child by the hand, they silently passed through the door, leaving a paralysed woman whose hands neither trembled nor twitched. It was as if Bolly was carved out of ice.

A second or two passed. Bolly had no idea of real time; it was as if time had been suspended. Suddenly a rush of blood forced it way upwards, charging through her body, bursting into her head, forcing her mind to try to comprehend what she had just witnessed. She tried the door; it was locked. Frantically she began to bang on it with both hands, which was followed by her kicking and calling out.

"Chris, Chris, let me in, let me in!"

A light shone through the window above the door, and was quickly followed by footsteps running down the stairs. Suddenly the door was flung open. Standing in the hallway was the welcoming sight of Christine.

"What is it? What's happened?" she asked.

Calming herself down, Bolly quickly entered the hallway. Taking hold of her sister's hand she looked her in her eyes.

"I've seen them, Chris. I've fucking seen them." Bolly shook her head in disbelief. "Jesus I don't believe it. But I've seen them."

Christine bursts into tears, which was quickly followed by a laugh of relief.

"Then I'm not going insane. You have no idea what a relief it is."

Bolly ran her fingers through her hair.

"Oh wonderful! Doctor Boll cures your madness and my own constipation."

Christine had no time to smile as the lights dimmed, leaving the hallway lit only by a lunar glow that filtered through the stained-glass window.

The young women stood motionless as a sweet sickly smell almost overpowered them. It was a strange mixture. A surgical smell mixed with perfume. They gripped each other tight as the shuffling sound returned. Only this time it was beside them.

Bolly moved Christine behind her as out of the shadows the figure of a man emerged. He ignored the women and headed towards the foot of the stairs.

Bolly recoiled in horror at the little bundle in his arms, it was the limp body of a child.

With deliberate step he carefully climbed each stair one by one, with dark heavy footsteps that took on an acoustic life all of their own, echoing throughout the house.

Terror either freezes one, or makes one's adrenaline flow to the point of rashness. In Bolly's case it was the latter. Forcing her fingers free from Christine's grip, and without thinking she followed the figure up the stairs, past the stained-glass window that formed a sinister pattern across her face.

The closer she got to the phantom the more the nauseating odour engulfed her, clung to her, causing her to retch. Suddenly the figure disappeared.

Bolly momentary stopped to regain her composure before climbing the last remaining stairs. Her breath came and went in short spasms and her heart beat so fast her lower jaw doddered as she fought back her fear.

Standing alone on the landing she was about to call for her sister to join her when suddenly her eyes where held by the sight of a young child of about nine. A different child to the one outside, and certainly not the one being carried up the stairs.

Dark terrified eyes begged and pleaded as small lips slowly parted, allowing the mouth to form words the eyes had already spoken.

"Please let me go. Please, my mummy will be worried. Please let me go."

Tears ran down Bolly's face as she instinctively held out her hand to the figure before her.

An icy chill ran through her body, paralysing her soul as from out of her body the outstretched hand of the man emerged. She convulsed with fear as the form of the man passed through her body, grabbing the child, who clung onto the door handle of the room opposite.

The man, arms were around the child's waist, as he yanked at her little form, forcing from her a piercing scream that sliced into Bolly's ears, causing her to clasp her hands either side of her head.

Bolly watched helplessly as tiny little fingers finally give way to brute force, and released their grip on the door handle.

With flaying arms and legs the child was unceremoniously carried off along the corridor towards the bathroom and the stairs towards the second floor, before both figures finally melted into the shadows, like snowflakes on the hand.

Bolly still motionless watched as the door before her opened on its own. Sitting on the edge of the bed, head in hands, was aunt Ivy. Bolly could feel her temper rising as she glared at the figure before her.

"You bastard. You fucking cow. Chris, Chris, come quickly!" she called out to her sister.

Aunt Ivy slowly rose from her bed. Before she had time to reach the door Christine was standing beside Bolly, who was pointing at their aunt.

"Look Chris, do you see. The old cow knew all along."

Aunt Ivy raised her hands in a pleading gesture.

"Please let me explain."

Bolly pushed their aunt away from Christine.

"Explain. Get away from her. You knew all along. You mean old bastard. Come on, Chris."

Bolly forcibly pushed Christine backwards along the corridor, towards her own bedroom, with Aunt Ivy in tow. Reaching the room, the door was firmly slammed in the older woman's face and locked.

Ivy called out several times begging for Christine to let her explain.

"Please let me talk to you."

Christine ignored her aunt's pleading before finally screaming at the top of her voice.

"Will you just fuck off."

Christine's House Durham England. October 31st 1969.

The rain beat its now familiar tattoo on the windowpane, accompanied by the scraping of a knife on toast, a duet of sound that seemed oh so far away. An indistinguishable collection of noises that the brain with far more important things to deal with refused to separate as they intermingled with Christine's voice, faint, distant, unrecognisable.

"Boll."

The voice seemed tiny, Lilliputian.

"Boll"

Frustrated at the lack of response, Christine resorted to stealth.

"Arabella."

Bolly, melancholy gazing into her cup of coffee suddenly snapped out of her dark brooding catalepsy.

Like most people when ones Christian name is used in full, it usually means you're in trouble. She instantly responded.

"Sorry. What did you say?"

Christine gently stroked her sister's hair. She knew what she was going through. She knew the thoughts that would dart and race throughout her brain, like a laboratory rat in a maze searching for the way out.

Two months had elapsed, two terrifying months since she had first come to live with her Aunt Ivy. She remembered the first day she arrived in Durham, an exciting time for a young girl, striking out in the collegiate world as a university student. And who better to stay with in a strange city than your own aunt?

Christine was a shy, studious polite girl. Unlike Bolly, who was the tomboy of the family, or of what family remained. Their parents had died in a fire some years previously. In fact the same fire had taken the life of Aunt Ivy's only child, Simon.

After their parent's deaths the girls were brought up by their grandmother, who duly sent Bolly off to a convent school. Unfortunately she had a far too rebellious attitude, forcing the grandmother to spend more time apologising for her behaviour than she cared to remember.

After Bolly had run away for the second time the grandmother decided to send her to the nearest suitable school, and left it at that.

Not wishing to make the same mistake with Christine, she allowed her to remain at home until she was old enough to attend the same school as Bolly. Neither girl missed out and both were given a more than adequate education. Where Bolly was undoubtedly more intelligent than her sister. Christine always tried to please by hard work and diligence.

At the ripe old age of eighteen, Bolly left home and went off into the big wide world. Hitchhiking from town to town, working in one job or another, but never in a position of authority.

After all, if she were to be a dropout then the last thing she would want was responsibility.

The truth of the matter was, she was a fraud. She was never really a dropout. She tried to be, but hated the so-called hippie culture. In fact, free love was something she tried to avoid especially after a Canadian she met in Reading had given her crab lice and scabies. It could have been worse she could have contracted gonorrhoea or syphilis.

She even experimented with drugs, smoking cannabis or taking the odd trip on L.S.D. Pot she liked, but one bad trip on acid was enough for her. In fact, when Christine telephoned, she was working in an antiquarian book shop in Edinburgh, hardly the place for an anarchist.

If only last night had been a bad trip, she thought. But she knew it wasn't and she had to face up to the reality that the most horrendous of creatures one could possibly imagine haunted the house. A child murderer.

The door to the kitchen opened. Standing in it was their aunt.

"May I join you?"

Bolly completely ignored her. As for Christine she made a half hearted gesture of annoyance by shrugging her shoulders.

Aunt Ivy sat down at the table alongside Christine. Her hand gently touched the back of the young woman's, who instantly pulled it away.

"I'm sorry." Aunt Ivy pleaded. "I truly am. Christine, darling, I love you dearly. I always have, and when you decided to stay with me I was overjoyed."

"At last I thought this big old house would not feel so empty with a vibrant young thing like you around. I had no idea that this abomination would rear its head again."

Christine's eyes widened.

"What do you mean, again?"

Aunt Ivy's eyes filled up with tears as she held Christine's hand.

"I only lied because I hoped it would go away, like before."

Bolly raised her head. The coffee cup no longer held her undivided attention. Sitting back in the chair she lit a cigarette, blowing the smoke arrogantly upwards.

Her aunt ignored her and continued to speak.

"It has been over fifteen years. Simon was only a child, and he was the first to see it. We took no notice. We assumed it was a nightmare, nothing more. But he persisted in his story until one night we all witnessed it, including your uncle. Whatever it was he saw only God knows. But he was never the same again."

Aunt Ivy drew in a deep breath to steady her trembling voice before continuing.

"He took a week away from work almost digging up the whole of the garden. He even called in a priest to bless the house. None of it worked. To save Simon we decided to send him away to boarding school. It seemed to work. Once Simon had gone the haunting ceased. That's why during the holidays when the moon was full he would stay with you and your grandmother in the Yorkshire Dales. "

Aunt Ivy lifted Christine's hand to her lips, tenderly kissing it.

"I'm so, so sorry. Please find it in your heart to forgive me."

Christine kissed her hand back, before giving her aunt a hug. Aunt Ivy hugged her tight and whispered in her ear.

"Bless you dear, bless you."

Suddenly banging the table with her fist, Aunt Ivy sat upright in the chair.

"That's it! " she shouted." I will sell the house. It's far too large. I did intend to pass it on to you, as there is no one else to inherit it. But no, I will sell it. You will still get an inheritance."

Bolly stubbed the cigarette out in the saucer.

"That's not the solution. All it means is that some poor bugger is going to inherit not only the house but this, this thing whatever it is. Just as you possibly did. No, it is wrong to leave without even trying to get rid of it."

Christine for once was in total agreement.

"Bolly is right, we should at least try."

Aunt Ivy sighed.

"All right. Try if you must, but I will be contacting my solicitor to make the necessary arrangements for the house to be sold."

Bolly was on a high. This was now an adventure.

"Right who's got any suggestions?" she excitedly asked.

Christine pondered for a moment before replying.

"Well, it seems pointless calling in a priest as that has already failed. I suppose we could call in a psychic."

Bolly slapped her sister on the back.

"Cracking idea. Still, the last thing we need is some amateur making things worse."

Aunt Ivy removed Bolly's coffee cup and saucer from the table. The sight of the used cigarette and ash made her feel physically ill. Clearing the saucer into the kitchen bin, she turned to look at the girls.

"There is someone who may be able to help. After you've asked your grandmother for permission."

Bolly looked puzzled.

"Gran? Why Gran?"

Aunt Ivy returned to the table.

"Do you ever listen to the radio?"

Bolly screwed up her pixie-like nose.

"Of course."

Aunt Ivy clasped her hands together resting her elbows on the table.

"Not your regular pop music. Stories late night stories. Stories from the Shadowman."

Christine shook her head.

"Gran won't like it."

Bolly shook her head in disbelief.

"Like what? For Christ's sake cut the double talk and get to the point."

Christine looked her sister in the eyes.

"The point is, my dear sister, that the man who writes the Shadowman series is called Calvin Dane and he lives in the old gate house."

Bolly was still none the wiser.

"What's a writer got to do with psychics?" she asked.

For the first time in Bolly's recollection Aunt Ivy actually smiled at her.

"That's precisely it. After the story the listeners are invited to write in with their problems regarding the supernatural. Some of the replies, providing they are not faked, make fascinating listening. It's as if he can see into their souls."

Bolly was sceptical as she responded.

"If this Calvin Dane is so good then why isn't he on the television, or more famous?"

Christine shook her head.

"Because no one is supposed to know who writes the stories or who replies to the letters."

"You do and Aunt Ivy does." Bolly retorted.

"Yes, because we are family, and Gran told us."

Christine's reply angered Bolly

"Thanks. So now I'm not family?"

Christine held her hands out in an apologetic gesture.

"No, silly, you're never at home, so how would you know. Mr Dane has an agreement with B.B.C Radio that his identity remains a secret. All dealings are through his agent."

Bolly stood up.

"Right kid. Get your coat, we're off to see our dear grandmother. By the way, what does this Calvin Dane look like?"

Christine shook her head.

"I have no idea. No one ever sees him. He keeps himself to himself and refuses visitors."

Bolly smiled.

"Not any more."

New Scotland Yard England.
October 31st 1969

Another cigarette butt topped an already over-flowing ashtray, as a weary faced policeman leant back in his chair, rubbing his face with both hands. Dark shadows encircled tired, heavy eyes; the result of too many cigarettes, accompanied by too many glasses of Scottish malt, accompanied by long sleepless nights.

There was knock at the door. Before he had time to answer, in walked his superior, Superintendent Gann, a large robust man with a bald almost polished pate. The few hairs that still clung to the top of his head constantly fell down like spindly spiders legs dangling over his ear.

Detective Chief Inspector Paul Ray stood up.

"No need for formalities Paul," was the response.

Ray instantly returned to his seat as Gann drew up a chair sitting opposite his junior.

"How are you Paul?" he asked

Ray viewed his superior suspiciously.

"Oh. So-so," was the reply.

Gann smiled.

"Busy?"

Ray removed a fresh pack of cigarettes from his pocket before replying,

"When am I not?"

Gann held out his hand.

"Got a little job. Need you to spare me a couple of your men, your very best men."

Ray lent across the table offering his superior a cigarette.

"What is it?" Ray asked.

Gann removed one from the packet.

"Nasty little job I'm afraid." was the reply.

Ray remained motionless, still leaning over the table arm, outstretched pack of cigarettes in hand.

"Nasty. In what way?"

Gann waved him to sit back before replying.

"Missing children."

Ray drew a small intake of breath.

"Felton?"

Gann nodded.

"Yes and three others."

Ray lit his own cigarette, drawing the smoke deep into his lungs, which was allowed to emanate freely out of his mouth as he spoke.

"I thought D.C.I. Banks was in charge?"

Gann lit his own cigarette, drawing in only enough to make the end glow red.

"He is," Gann replied." That's why you will work independently from him and his team. You report directly to me. I'll keep Banks informed on a need-to-know basis."

Ray was puzzled at the request. After all, it was common knowledge that he and Banks were sworn enemies. Banks was an up-and-coming star, a whiz-kid, a socialite who learnt to kiss ass before kicking it.

Whereas inspector Ray was a conscious, solid old-fashioned policeman. A plod, as Banks once referred to him. A plod he might be, but he was a damned good one.

A divorcee and loner without the chance of ever re-marring. Not the type one invites to social evenings. But definitely the type to get a job done and done well.

"Why fragment the investigation." Ray asked

"Nothing will be fragmented?" was the reply

"I'll see to that. Banks plays it by the book. He's only in charge due to politics, not because he's the right man for the job."

Ray sucked once more on his cigarette.

"And I am?"

Gann avoided the question.

"You've been working on the case of the missing girl from Kepple in Essex?"

"Yes," Ray nodded.

Gann smiled that same cunning smile that Ray hated when he knew he was being used.

"Then you have the perfect excuse. If Banks should contact you, all you are doing is checking the details of other missing children in case there's a link."

Ray had by now caught the gist of the matter; he was unofficially to pull Banks out of the shit. Gann didn't give a rats arse for him. He was only concerned about the bad publicity that Banks, the blue-eyed boy of the force would bring, if he were unable to find the missing children or, God forbid, the killer, if that became the scenario.

Ray chewed on his bottom lip as he replied.

"There's only one problem. It's common knowledge that the farmhand who committed suicide is thought to have abducted her. He even left a suicide note more or less admitting guilt."

Gann's steel grey eyes locked onto Ray's.

"Has a body ever been found?"

"No," was the reply

Eyes still locked onto Rays, Gann rose to his feet.

"Then the case is still open. Find out what's happened to these children and let me worry about D.C.I. Banks."

Gann stubbed out the cigarette, and left without another word.

Calvin's Cottage Litton Village England. October 31st 1969

Bolly's ramshackle old Morris Minor pulled up outside the gate house. A stone-built cottage adjoining a churchyard and the entrance to the estate of Lady Winspear, the girl's grandmother.

It had a small stone wall that skirted the churchyard then swept around the rear of the cottage, giving it and the small garden some semblance of privacy.

Bolly remembered the cottage that stood in the shadow of the tall county church with a grand tower and a large blue clock face, but she had never been inside. If her memory served her well, it was occupied at the time by the church verger a mean thin lipid man with yellow teeth and foul breath.

The clock chimed the quarter hour. Ten forty-five a.m. to be precise. The sound of the mechanism cranking itself up ready to chime brought back fond child-hood memories of how she and some of the other village children would play in the churchyard, frightening one another with ghost stories.

If only she had known then what she knew now, little Jimmy Pierce would have urinated himself with fright, a task that was never too hard to achieve.

Both girls alighted from the car at the same time, making a quick dash through the torrential rain towards the cottage door. Three sharp raps on the door by Bolly's hand would hopefully have the desired result.

Christine was apprehensive as usual.

"Perhaps we should have spoken to Gran first."

"Nonsense," was the reply.

The handle on the door turned, allowing it to creak open, before them stood a tall slim woman with mouse-like features. Bolly and Christine instantly recognised her.

Mrs Thirkell, or as Bolly once christened her, old sourpuss. She had worked for their grandmother for over thirty years. Never married, never had a fiancée, and possibly never wanted to.

"Mr Dane is out," she snapped.

Bolly never liked the woman, and had no intention of returning by invitation only, pushed passed her.

"No problem. We'll wait," she arrogantly snapped.

The hallway was small and compact with a door to the left, and a short flight of stairs, directly ahead was a small passageway leading to another door and the kitchen.

Bolly with an apologetic Christine in tow, entered the lounge, with its large welcoming fire roaring in the hearth.

Above the stone fireplace was a rough wooden mantle that hoarded numerous artefacts and memorabilia relating to the war, especially the Nazis era.

And above the mantle on the wall hung a lone crossbow and a shape on the wallpaper where its partner should have been.

Bolly stood warming herself, back to the fire.

"When's he due back?" she asked.

Mrs Thirkell, trying to restrain her obvious anger reluctantly answered.

"I'm not sure. But he doesn't like visitors."

"He won't mind us calling," Bolly cockily replied." Tell you what." Winking at the woman.

"Why don't you make my sister and I a nice hot cup of tea?"

Mrs Thirkell controlled her anger as she left the room. Had they been anyone other than Lady Winspear's granddaughters, she would have sent them on their way tails tucked firmly between their legs.

Bolly lit up a cigarette and sauntered around the room.

"Poky hole!" she exclaimed.

Christine faced her sister, hands on hips.

"Bolly! There was no need to be rude to her."

Bolly smiled.

"No harm done. Never liked the old sow." Her eyes settled on the bookshelf at the far end of the room. "Hey, look at all those books."

There was a small archway leading to another room. It was small just large enough for a desk, chair, typewriter and telephone. The rest of the space was taken up with bookshelves.

Bolly strode over towards the books, pulling one out.

"Jesus Chris, look at this. Devil worship and demonology."

The book was colourfully illustrated

"Shit. I wouldn't like to bump into that in the dark."

Christine was becoming nervous.

"Boll, I think we should go."

"Why?" was the response.

"It's not right barging in uninvited. And you were so rude."

Christine was making her way towards the door as Bolly called out.

"Who to? That old cow. Sod her, she was always telling on me to Gran."

Christine gave a half-laugh.

"And you never deserved it? Saint Arabella!"

Bolly blew the smoke from her cigarette arrogantly upwards.

"Flippancy, my dear sister does not become you. Never mind her, what do you think this Shadowman fella looks like?."

Christine walked back towards her sister, took the book off her and placed it back where it came from.

"Oh I don't know." she replied. "Tall dark Latin type, with satanic eyes and a fetish for sheep, wearing black stockings and suspenders."

Bolly laughed out a loud.

"Good for you girl. Better than my fat old fart with a goatee and leather patches on the elbows of his jacket. Fetish for sheep is it? What have you been up to while I've been away?"

A strange sound attracted their attention. Both girls spun around to face the window. Visibility was nil as the rain had now reached almost monsoon proportions. But the sound was undoubtedly the roar of a powerful motorbike drawing up outside.

The door to the room opened simultaneously as the roar of the engine ceased. In walked Mrs Thirkell tea-tray in hand.

"That will be Mr Dane."

A second or two latter the door to the front of the cottage opened and closed. The girls waited for the mysterious Shadowman to enter.

Almost filling the whole of the open door frame stood a leather-clad young man of twenty-four years.

His white shoulder-length dripping wet hair hung like rat's tails over his American flying jacket. In one hand he held a crossbow and the other a brace of hares.

Sunglasses covered his eyes, which both girls considered strange, especially as the chance of any sunlight penetrating the dark thunderclouds that threatened even more rain, was nil.

Slowly the man removed his sunglasses, glaring at the intruders. Both women were visibly shocked at the eyes that glared at them. Eyes like they had never seen before. It was not the glare that shook them. It was their colour, red. Calvin Dane was an albino.

Mrs Thirkell was quick to try and save her skin.

"These are Lady Winspear's granddaughters. I told them you never allowed visitors, but they ignored me and barged in, almost knocking me down"

Bolly sarcastically responded.

"Still dropping us in it."

Calvin looked at the tea-tray in Mrs Thirkell's hands, before speaking in a Bostonian American accent.

"No need for that. They're not staying."

Without another word he placed the two dead hares on the tray, knocking the cups over. It was all Mrs Thirkell could do to stop the cups falling to the floor.

Calvin took his flying jacket off and laid it over the back of a chair. Crossbow still in hand he turned to the girls.

"Still here?"

Christine tugged on Bolly's arm, dragging her to the front door.

"Come on, Boll."

Calvin bowed his head.

"Good day, ladies.

Bolly was about to walk back and square up to him, but Christine refused to let her go.

"Arrogant bastard!" she cried out as she was pushed through the door by Christine.

"Born one. Die one." Was his reply as he hung the crossbow back on the wall.

Calvin's Cottage
Litton Village England.
October 31St 1969

LATER THAT EVENING.

The flickering flames from the fire formed mysterious shapes on the white plaster walls of the cottage, as Calvin lounged in a throne-size armchair. A chair large enough to take all of his six-foot-four frame.

Rich embers in the grate warmed his bare feet, causing the toes to glow red. The heat caressed tense muscles that readily submitted to the warm ambience of the room, while the logs on the fire competed with one another as to which could make the most noise, or the most fluorescent of colours. Greens, blues, purples, yellows and reds danced hypnotically to the soulful voice of Peter Green, Fleetwood Mac's 'Man Of The World.'

The remainder of the body was also in a state of sublime relaxation. His arm in a lever-like movement slowly raised a large brandy-glass to the lips. To be followed by a long effortless pull on a fine Cuban Partagas, allowing rich plumes of grey smoke to billow upwards towards the dark, beamed ceiling like the spirits of the dead rising from their graves on the day of judgement.

Calvin let out a large sigh as he closed his eyes, tranquillity was king, his body slipped into a state of partial drunkenness, cushioning the mind, allowing it to forget the dark secrets it held.

Several loud knocks on the front door shattered the tranquillity. Remaining seated, Calvin let out a sigh of annoyance.

Bang, bang, bang. The knocks sounded louder now the music had ceased. He grated his teeth, as he knew he would eventually have to answer the door. Three sharp raps almost shattered the glass window in the lounge. Even in the dark, Calvin could make out the face pressed against the glass.

Draining what brandy was left, he eventually ambled to the front door, allowing it to swing open. Without uttering a word he returned to the room, followed by a small, elegantly-dressed woman in her early sixties, with eyes that blazed on par with the fire. Calvin returned to the lounge to replenish his now-empty glass.

The instant she entered the room she switched on the light.

"Still sitting in the dark I see." Her voice was sharp and authoritative. "And I won't ask why you refused to answer the door."

The bright light hurt his eyes, forcing him to instantly whip his sunglasses on. The dark held no fears for him. In fact he found it comforting. Ignoring the woman he flopped down in his chair without uttering a word.

The woman stood over him.

"I know you have a right to your privacy, and my granddaughters should have asked if you would see them, instead of barging in. Still, a little civility on your part would not have come amiss."

Calvin continued to stare into the fire.

"Sorry. Ask them to accept my apologies," he replied in a sarcastic tone.

Lady Winspear positioned herself between Calvin and the fire.

"Look at me when I am talking."

Calvin raised his head.

"I'm looking,." was the response.

Lady Winspear continued to berate him waving her finger as she spoke.

"It's not your apologies they want. It's your help."

To Calvin's great amusement he could see that the heat of the fire was burning the back of Lady Winspear's legs. Trying not to smile, as he was enjoying her discomfort, he took a long pull on his cigar before replying.

"Help, in what way?"

Rubbing the back of her legs she quickly moved away.

"Damn that fire." she snapped.

"Temper, temper." He tried to hold back his amusement.

She was shaking with rage as she responded.

"You'll find out what a temper I've got if you don't show some respect and stand up when I'm talking to you."

All six foot four of Calvin obeyed, by towering over all four foot eleven of her.

"Oh. Sit down and listen." she snapped.

No matter how hard he tried, he could not hide the smile that crept across his face as he regained his seat.

Lady Winspear continued to speak.

"I'll get straight to the point. The house my granddaughters are living in is haunted."

Calvin sat up straight in his chair to look at the woman.

"Haunted? And you expect me to help? You must be out of your mind."

She bent forward, clasping both hands on the arm of the chair, her face no more than a few inches from his.

"Not quite, but I'm getting there," she retorted." Well, are you going to help?"

Calvin's countenance changed.

"In one word. No."

"Why?" was her reply.

Calvin sat upright, removing his sun glasses; his red eyes burned into the woman's.

"You know full well why. If I opened up just once, it would be enough. Enough for them to kill me"

She never flinched as she returned his stare. Finally he had to replace the sunglasses to protect his eyes. Seeing him back down, she continued to speak.

"Rubbish. Open up. If that were the case then they would have tracked you down long ago, change of name or not."

Calvin jumped out of his seat and walked over to the drinks cabinet to pour himself another large brandy.

"You have no concept of their power, have you?"

She shook her head.

"No. Only your word."

He stood motionless and drew in a deep breath before replying.

"Take my word for it. It's lethal."

She moved closer to him.

"If they are that dangerous, then dangerous as it is for you, it must be equally as dangerous for those around you. Perhaps you should look for another sanctuary."

This was not the response he had expected.

"You would turn me out, knowing who I am?"

She shrugged her shoulders before answering.

"It would upset me if anything were to happen to you. But as you have already refused my help"

"Help!" he let out a small laugh. " Oh yes, the old boy network, M.I.6, or whatever number it is. They would certainly help. Help me into my grave."

"Calvin"

He cut her short.

"Enough. Leave me alone. Please."

Lady Winspear shook her head as she made her way towards the door before turning to speak.

"Still afraid of your own shadow."

She reached for the light switch, flicking it off, leaving the room in semi-darkness, illuminated only by the fire.

"There, Mr Shadowman, dark enough for both you and your shadow to hide."

Calvin stood motionless. Hearing the click of the door as it closed behind her, he gave out a sigh as he made his way towards the fire, brandy glass in hand.

"Bastard."

The word roared out of his mouth at the same time as he flung the glass into the fiery inferno causing it to exploding into a flaming fireball, which in turn roared up the chimney like a dragon's breath.

Judge's House, Peel, Kent, England. October 31st 1969

A bright moon hovered in the clear star-filled sky. Its silvery hue outlined the grandeur of the large mock-Tudor property it silently watched over.

The torrential rains that had drenched the country, had finally passed, making way for the crisp chill of autumn to have its turn. Under a tree in the garden of two acres or so, silhouetted against the backdrop of a summerhouse, was the pitiful figure of a man. His body was slumped to the ground, shaking as it attempted to restrain the sobs that emanated from within, yet somehow they still managed to be carried effortlessly on the wind.

Slowly the kneeling silhouetted form of the man began to rock back and forth like a mother shushing her child to sleep. But the child in his arms would never awaken from hers.

Litton Manor, Litton Village, England. October 31st 1969

Bolly had difficulty relaxing as she paced up and down in the drawing room, while Lady Winspear remained seated opposite Christine, gently interrogating her granddaughter about the so-called haunting. Bolly, tired with the lack of progress, interrupted their conversation.

"No point going on about it. What we need is action."

Lady Winspear looked up at her granddaughter.

"And what do you suggest?"

Bolly walked over to face her.

"Well for a start, we can tell that arrogant Yankee to kiss our arses, and find someone else."

The older woman's face instantly rebuked her.

"Arabella, where have your manners disappeared to? You certainly were not brought up to speak in such a coarse way."

The quick rebuke caused Bolly to sheepishly hang her head.

"Sorry, Gran."

Before the conversation could continue, there was a knock on the door. In walked Calvin Dane.

Lady Winspear instantly rose from her seat to great him.

"Does this visit mean you have decided to help?" She motioned with her hand towards the sofa. "Please be seated."

Calvin shook his head.

"No need. I won't be staying." he replied.

Christine rose from her seat so she could face the visitor.

"Have you changed your mind, are you going to help?"

Bolly remained silent but Calvin could feel her eyes burning into him.

"I take it you've had the usual people around. Priests or some form of holy man?" he asked.

Christine instantly replied.

"Yes but it failed."

Calvin nodded as he responded.

"Okay, this is what I'll do. There's a spiritualist meeting tomorrow evening, in Middlesbrough. We'll get someone to help you there."

Bolly raised her arms before allowing them to slap noisily against her side.

"Bloody marvellous. That's a great help. We could do that ourselves."

Calvin turned to walk out of the room.

"Fine. Then you have the answer, no need for me."

Lady Winspear quickly intervened.

"Arabella, please do not be so ungracious. What Calvin can do is make sure whoever you get is not only capable but genuine."

Bolly looked suspiciously at them both.

"How can he do that?"

Lady Winspear could feel Calvin's eyes glare at her through his sunglasses.

"Let us just say he can and leave it at that. Now, shall we have some tea? What a pity we are not at your cottage, the girls would have loved your home-made scones. Calvin's quite a cook, you know."

Bolly, standing to the side of Calvin, pulled a face, poking her finger in her mouth before placing her hands around her neck as if she was choking.

Calvin looked towards her.

"A mouth that holds a tongue as poisonous as yours has nothing to fear from my cooking."

Christine burst out laughing, as Bolly for once was rendered silent.

Calvin turned to leave.

"Tomorrow."

Restaurant, Edinburgh, Scotland. November 1st 1969

The first few heavy droplets of rain crashed upon the large Georgian window of Bistro de Loire, causing the lone figure sitting at the table in the bay to raise his head from the opened book before him. Returning to his reading, as was his custom, he ignored the weather outside and the impending storm that was about to force pedestrians and the like to go scampering for shelter.

A waiter appeared beside him. No words were exchanged as the waiter retrieved the menu and the piece of paper with the order carefully written from the wine to the final course.

As was the custom, or should one say nightly ritual, no words where exchanged by either man. Strangely enough, the waiter took no offence at the lack of verbal communication.

To the owners of the Bistro the gentleman at the table was more than just a regular customer, he was considered a friend, an eccentric member of the family, greatly admired by the owner and the rest of his staff who assisted in the running of the family business.

Sitting at the same table at the same time every night, he would always be immersed in some paperwork or a book, and often during the course of his dinner would frantically scribble notes on pieces of paper that would be carefully folded up and placed in his pocket at the end of the meal.

He was always impeccably dressed in a pin-stripe suit with a white silk handkerchief in the top pocket and a small red rose in his lapel. He looked every bit the English gentleman, which was rather strange in the capital city of Scotland, and especially strange because he was not English but German.

Dr Hans Vogel, a former professor in Psychology and Eugenics prior to the rise of Nazi Germany, had been forced to flee the country of his birth after refusing to help Himmler in his quest for the master race. This resulted in him fleeing to England where Churchill was more than happy to use his scientific abilities along with his lesser-know darker talents. After the war he was awarded for services he had rendered, full British citizenship.

The waiter returned with the wine, and poured a glass out before placing the bottle carefully on the table. A young waitress also appeared at his side with the first course, soup. No words were uttered as both waited for the customary wave of the hand or nod of the head to assure the pair that everything was satisfactory.

Vogel lifted his eyes for the first time from the book. He took a sip of wine and nodded his approval. Picking up the spoon, he carefully dipped it in the soup. He was about to raise the spoon to his mouth when a flash of lightning illuminated the street outside, followed closely by a deafening clap of thunder.

Vogel instantly looked out of the window. His eyes widened in terror as the spoon slipped from his fingers back into the soup bowl, causing it to splash over his clothes.

Transfixed, he stared out of the window at the figure before him, a thin gaunt figure.

Another flash of lightening illuminated the figure. It was gaunt, pale face with a strange stubbed moustache and goatee beard. The split second the lightning lasted, seemed to him a lifetime as blue demonic eyes glared at him through the glass.

As quickly as the vision appeared it vanished. Vogel knocked the chair over as he jumped up from the table and rushed outside into the pouring rain, with the waiter and the waitress following in amazement.

Outside, the bedraggled figure of Dr Vogel looked one way along the street then the other as the torrential rain like a river rushed along the gutters.

The owner of the restaurant rushed passed his employees with an umbrella.

"What is it, Doctor? What is it?"

Turning to the waiter and the waitress, who were still standing in the doorway, he called out to them.

"Did you see him?"

They both look at one another and shook their heads.

Dr Vogel grabbed the owner by his waistcoat.

"He was here. I saw him."

"Saw who?" was the reply.

Grabbing the umbrella, Vogel rushed off in the direction of his flat, a mere five minutes walk from the restaurant.

"I must go home. I must."

"But your hat and coat!" the restaurateur cried out.

His cries where in vain as Vogel, in military fashion, marched briskly out of sight.

Spiritualist Church, Middlesbrough, England. November 1st 1969

Neat rows of stacking chairs filled the blue-painted room with where spiritualistic paintings of angels and Christ adorned the walls, giving a calming ambience to what was in affect an old, rundown building.

To the front of the church was a small stage with a portable lectern. Behind it was a table and three chairs, and to the right stood an artist's easel with a large sketch pad in place, as well as a fourth chair. This was for one of the members to sit while he played the accordion.

The church was obviously run on a shoestring, but still the place had warm feeling to it, and the flowers on the stage gave it a friendly atmosphere.

The church soon began to fill up with a congregation that consisted mainly of women of various ages. Some, desperate to contact their dead loved ones, and others just there out of curiosity. Then there were the true spiritualists, the ardent believers the ones who genuinely attended their church and treated it with the same amount of respect that religious people do everywhere.

Some jostled for the best seats, wherever they may be, some believed that if they sat near the front, close to the medium, he might pick them for a message. On Calvin's insistence, Bolly and Christine sat at the rear of the church.

Bolly shuffled around on her seat, and watched three people plus the accordion player, climb up onto the stage.

A fat man with grey hair, in his mid-sixties, introduced the guest mediums.

"Well, friends, it gives me great pleasure this night to welcome two very old friends of ours, David and Marion Wales. David is a highly respected clairvoyant and his wife Marion a psychic artist. So friends I would like you to send out your love and a warm welcome to David and Marion."

They sang a few hymns and said a prayer. Then the medium began by giving what is called the philosophy.

Bolly turned to Calvin and whispered.

"They're praying to God."

Calvin gave a slight shake of his head.

"What did you expect? Naked women dancing around a man dressed as a goat?"

Bolly screwed up her face and whispered under her breath.

"Arsehole."

After the philosophy was finished, Marion the psychic artist took her position next to the easel. Standing behind the lectern, her husband, the medium, took several deep breaths before removing from his top pocket a large handkerchief. Holding it theatrically in his hand, he pointed to an elderly woman with large winged spectacles and neatly-permed grey hair.

"I would like to come to you. I have a large man, ruddy-faced and slightly overweight. Portly is the word he would use. I also get the impression of a steel works. Can you take that?" The woman instantly replied.

"Yes."

Without waiting for the reply, the artist began to sketch a likeness of the spirit.

Bolly turned to Calvin.

"Is he the one?" Calvin shook his head. Bolly was confused. "Why not? He seems good."

Calvin had his eyes fixed on a young woman in the row of seats opposite to them.

Bolly repeated her question.

"What's wrong with the medium?

Calvin turned to her.

"He's weak. He's drawing his power from the rest of the congregation. No she's the one."

Calvin's gaze lead the two girls towards a young woman in her early twenties. She wore a long flowing hippie-style dress, with a crystal hanging around her neck. Calvin was about to say something when he stopped and turned his gaze back to the medium at the lectern. The medium had stopped in mid-flow and was holding his throat in an even more theatrical manner.

"No. Please stop. Take it away."

The congregation was hushed. The silence was broken only when the artist quickly turned to a clean sheet as the medium struggled with his words, continuing to clutch his throat, as if he were being throttled by an unseen force.

"She refuses to stop. I have a message for a Wolf. Does the name Wolf mean anything to anyone?"

The artist began to sketch a beautiful young woman with large dark eyes and long black hair. The medium continued.

"She says the message is for a young man a man called Wolf. Perhaps it is a nickname." He paused.

"No, she insists it is his name."

Both Christine and Bolly watched Calvin's body become rigid, behind his sunglasses his eyes darted first to the sketch then to the medium and back again to the sketch.

The medium continued.

"This young woman went tragically into spirit, brutally."

Calvin returned his gaze to the medium. Nostrils flared as he slowly removed his sunglasses. His red eyes were burning like the fires of hell, as he concentrated all the venom he could muster at the medium.

The medium at the lectern began to sway, as he raised his hand trying to wipe away a faint trickle of blood that ran out of his nose onto his lips. Two other small rivers of blood began to flow from the tear-ducts down the cheeks, followed by blood from his ears, as his legs give way.

Suddenly his body slumped over the top of the lectern crashing off the stage. The congregation rushed forward to help, with the exception of Christine and Bolly, who remained rooted to their seats, eyes fixed on their

American companion who rose from his seat without saying a word, and left the church.

The night was cold and damp as Calvin's legs straggled his Harley.

A finger and thumb bridged the gap across his nose and wiped the tears from the corner of his eyes, before he started up the powerful machine to speed off into the night, silently watched over by the two young, mystified women.

Dr Vogel's Apartment, Edinburgh, Scotland. November 1st 1969

Oblivious to being soaking wet, Dr Vogel, with shaking hands, rattled the bottle against the glass as he poured a very large brandy. Two gulps and it was gone, only for it to be refilled as quickly as the first.

Still trembling, he removed his clothes while muttering to himself as he slowly walked towards the bathroom to take a shower.

"It must have been a trick of the light. Yes, that was what it was. Come now, Hans, get a grip of yourself. It was a trick of the light."

Removing the rest of his clothes, he entered the shower. It felt good, warm and comforting.

With his body relaxed, his ego slowly began to convince his mind that what he had seen was nothing more than a subconscious vision from the past.

Leaving the shower and drying himself off, he dressed in his favourite navy silk pyjamas and royal blue smoking jacket before slipping his feet into soft matching blue suede slippers.

He was now feeling hungry he needed a quick meal, something substantial, not too fussy. Cooking for himself was something he had never done for years. Although he had a kitchen in his flat he was low on food, as his habit was always to dine out.

The larder was bare, with the exception of a selection of cheeses, and garlic pate plus the usual accompanying assorted biscuits and bread. Not exactly a feast for a king; still it would serve its purpose.

With a plate of pate, cheese and biscuits placed on a table beside him, he settled down in front of the fire for his feast.

His body jumped as the telephone gave what seemed to be a louder-than-average ring. Calming himself down, he walked over to it and raised the receiver to his ear.

"Yes."

The voice on the other side sounded faint.

"Dr Vogel?"

"Yes." was the reply.

The voice on the other side was the voice of a young man, an American.

"Dr Vogel, you don't know me, but I attended one of your lectures recently, in Boston."

"Yes." Vogel was mystified.

"I'm sorry to disturb you and I do apologise for ringing you. But the strangest thing happened to me today."

Vogel interrupted.

"How did you get my number"

The voice on the other side trembled like a child who was about to be scolded.

"I have a friend who works for the university that arranged your trip. I persuaded her to supply your number. Please don't report her; she'll lose her job."

Vogel was annoyed.

"That's as may be, young man."

The voice on the other side interrupted him.

"Please Doctor, listen, to what I have to say before you decide," the young man begged.

"Continue." was the response.

Vogel could sense the nervousness in the voice on the telephone as it continued its story.

"As I said, the strangest thing happened no more than an hour or so ago. I was in the library trying to study, when suddenly I found myself no longer there, but in a street."

A frown appeared over Vogel's eyes.

"A street?" he interrupted.

"Yes," The voice continued. "I was standing in the pouring rain in a street, looking through the window of a restaurant."

Dr Vogel felt the hairs on the back of his neck rise as a shiver ran through his body.

The voice continued.

"I was looking into the restaurant, looking at you. Suddenly there was a flash of lightening and you looked up at me. I obviously startled you, as you dropped your spoon into the soup, splashing your clothes."

Vogel straightened his back.

"And then?"

The young man's voice quivered as he replied.

"Then I was back in the library. I said it was weird. And I'm sorry to have bothered you, but something compelled me to telephone you, and now I feel a right jerk."

Dr Vogel's hands trembled as he wiped the sweat from his brow.

"What is your name?"

"Adrian. Adrian Hoff sir," the voice replied.

"And where are you telephoning from?" Vogel asked.

"From home."

"And where would home be.

"Boston, Massachusetts," was the response.

Dr Vogel reached for a pencil and pad.

"Please give me your telephone number and I will call you back immediately."

Adrian Hoff supplied him with the number. Before dialling back Dr Vogel sat behind his desk running his hands through his hair.

Slowly he retrieved a key from a secret drawer in the desk. He then lifted a small rug up from under the desk to reveal a safe. Opening it, he removed a large metal box that was also locked. Inside was a large leather book and a small parcel wrapped in cloth. He carefully unwrapped it and took a deep breath before pulling back the last corner to reveal a selection of drawings and what looked like a small diary, plus a collection of postcard-size sketches. Slowly sliding one picture beneath the other, he finally stopped at one.

He closed his eyes, and once again drew in a deep breath before uttering the words.

"Please, God, let it not be true."

Holding one of the paintings in his hands, he telephoned the young American.

"Adrian Hoff." The young man's voice was the same.

Dr Vogel felt physically ill; he now knew that this was no hoax.

"Hello. Hello. Is that you, Dr Vogel?" he enquired.

Dr Vogel stared at the painting, the painting of a flaming spear signed by a struggling young student. Who's features even then stood out, pale, gaunt face with a stubbed moustache, goatee beard, and blue demonic eyes. Eyes that stared at him as he ate, one Viennese evening back in 1912. The painting was signed Adolf Hitler.

Calvin's Cottage, Litton Village, England. November 1st 1969.

The room was silent; even the fire was apologetic for its occasional outburst when one of the logs, whistled and spat.

Calvin sat, cigar in one hand, drink in the other, and gazed melancholy at a tattered photograph of a young woman. The same young women the psychic artists had sketched.

He leant his head back in the chair and closed his eyes. Suddenly a vision appeared before him. It was the shadowy figure of a man placing a plastic Guy Fawkes mask over the lifeless face of a little child; a child dressed like a guy, with the exception of her little red wellingtons.

The glass dropped to the floor. Calvin instantly sat upright. Beads of perspiration formed on his brow before running down towards his eyes.

He jumped up out of the seat, wiping the perspiration away, with shaking hand he threw the large Havana into the fire.

"Jesus no. What have I done?"

Normandy France
November 2nd 1969.

The audience was hushed as a hundred eyes watched and waited for a young man dressed as Louis the XIV, long pole in hand to make a move.

He stood motionless, patiently waiting for the signal to use the hook at the end of the pole and move one of the chess pieces that hung on the board. Opposing one another sat the mental duellists, heads bowed, oblivious to their surroundings.

The door at the far end of the great hall in the chateau opened allowing a small weasel faced character, dressed in sombre clothes, not unlike an undertaker's, to enter.

His movements were swift yet silent. Like an unseen phantom he glided towards one of the audience, a tall distinguished looking man, with a swarthy skin tone emphasised by his dark hair and greying temples.

The Undertaker whispered in the man's ear, as a gasp went up from the audience. One of the duellists had made a move. Dark brown eyes glanced first at the board, then towards his servant, who, having finished what he had to say, left as silently and as unnoticed as he entered.

Marquis De Jay rose from his position, making his apologies to the woman occupying the seat next to him, before leaving the great hall.

The door to the study was open as De Jay entered the room. The undertaker was as motionless as a statue awaiting the arrival of his master, telephone in hand.

De Jay placed the receiver to his ear.

"Yes."

The voice on the other side spoke swiftly yet calmly.

"Marquis. It is Vogel."

"I am aware who it is," replied the Marquis in a smooth French accent. "What is it that is so urgent?"

"The beast has returned," Vogel continued.

The Marquis remained silent, as Vogel repeated his statement.

"Did you hear what I said? The beast has returned."

"Yes. I heard." the Marquis's face showed no emotion.

"Tell me, why you are so sure?"

Vogel explained the episode in the restaurant and the young man Adrian Hoff, while the Marquis listened patiently, allowing him to finish his story.

"Well, if what you have said is true, and I do not doubt you are sincere in your beliefs, we will have to take action. First, I will have your young American friend checked out. You continue to communicate with him. While the order take the necessary precautions. I do not doubt your sincerity and have admired your ability for some years but surely it is too soon?"

Vogel's voice was more excitable.

"I understand. Why do you think I was so shocked? We always knew it would happen eventually. But"

The Marquis cut him short.

"Leave it to me. I will reconvene your group."

"Edinburgh, you live in Edinburgh do you not?"

"Yes." was the reply.

"If it is what you believe, I will assemble some of your old comrades plus a new face. One of my special acquaintances. Leave it to me. And may your God go with you."

The Marquis replaced the receiver. Lifting the lid on his silver cigarette box, he removed one and lit it up. A pensive look etched its way across his face, forming a frown above his dark, liquid eyes. Locked in thought he pulled hard on the cigarette, while his fingers drummed a slow tattoo on the desk. His countenance slowly darkened, as his eyes narrowed.

"To soon. It is too soon. Something else must be happening." He shook his head as he repeated the words. "To soon. God forbid we are wrong"

Christine's House Durham England. November 2nd 1969.

Christine and Bolly were in the sitting room, patiently waiting for the arrival of the young woman from the spiritualist church, the one Calvin had suggested they employ.

There was a loud knock at the door. Knowing their Aunt would answer, neither girl rose from their respective seats Christine on the sofa and Bolly in one of the chairs either side of the roaring fire. In less than a minute, the door to the sitting room swung open to allow their expected visitor to enter. Both girls' eyes widened at the figure that accompanied her.

"We met at the door," was Calvin's response to their obvious surprise.

"Didn't expect to see you again." Bolly replied sarcastically.

The corners of Calvin's mouth formed an excuse of a smile.

"Didn't expect to come."

Aunt Ivy offered the young woman a seat on the sofa next to Christine.

"Please take a seat, Miss Grainger."

"Lucy. Please, call me Lucy."

The young woman's voice had a melodic ring to it, as if she sang each word.

Aunt Ivy offered Calvin the vacant seat next to the fire opposite Bolly, before asking,

"Tea or coffee?"

Lucy's voice once again sang the words.

"Nothing for me thank you, not before a sitting. But I would be grateful for a glass of water. I like to ground myself."

"Ground or drowned?" Calvin's interjection was cutting.

Lucy stared at the tall America as he lounged in the armchair. He felt her gaze and slowly lifted his head before removing his sunglasses, locking his eyes onto hers. Like a current of electricity passing through the body Lucy gave a jump and instantly looked away. Aunt Ivy, oblivious to the little exchange of minds, was still offering refreshments.

"Would you like anything to drink Mr Dane?"

Calvin replaced his sunglasses and smiled at the elderly woman.

"No thank you. I'm just content to be here warming myself by your welcoming fire."

Lucy rose from her seat, eyes fixed firmly in the opposite direction to Calvin's.

"Would it be possible for you to show me around the house now, as I do have another engagement."

Christine and Bolly were startled by her sudden change of attitude.

"You can tell me all about your experiences while you show me around."

Christine rose from her seat

"Of course. If that's what you wish."

Christine and Aunt Ivy looked in the direction of Calvin.

"Sit this one out. If you don't mind?" he smiled at the women as he spoke.

Christine shook her head.

"Of course not. You coming Boll?"

Bolly's eyes darted from Christine, to Lucy, to Calvin, then back to Christine.

"No I think I'll stay and keep Calvin company."

The three women exited the room leaving Bolly and Calvin sitting in opposing chairs next to the fire. Bolly looked Calvin up and down, with him deliberately ignoring her.

A whole two minutes passed before Bolly final broke the silence.

"Arrogant bastard aren't you?"

Calvin smiled.

"Is that a question or a statement?"

Bolly continued to glare at him.

"I saw through you the first day we met. You're a fraud."

Calvin made no reply, he just raised one eyebrow and smiled.

Bolly continued her attack.

"The arrogance, lack of emotions, always acting as if you are superior, superior to us lesser mortals."

Calvin's smile turned into a smirk.

"You almost had me fooled." She glared at him as she spoke. "That was until the other night in the spiritualist church. It was then that I realised what you really are."

Calvin's expression changed.

"And what is that?" he asked.

Bolly projected her face forward, thrusting it almost into Calvin's.

"A liar, a fraud, and possibly something even worse, Mr Shadowman. Or should I call you Wolf".

Calvin sat upright as he glared into Bolly's eyes.

"You obnoxious little toad."

The words spat from his lips like the venom of a cobra.

"What are you and your sister up to?"

Bolly sat back in her seat.

"What do you mean?"

Calvin's expression hardened.

"You know exactly what I mean. This house isn't haunted. There are no ghosts, spirits, poltergeists, pooka's or hobgoblins - with the exception of you, in this house now - nor have there ever been. So why don't you stop wasting people's time and stop worrying your grandmother. If the house bothers you, then sell the Goddammed place."

Calvin rose from his seat, ready to leave.

Bolly instantly sprang to her feet.

"Go on then, Shadowman, leave. Talk about fooling people, what about you? I bet Gran doesn't know."

Calvin towered over her.

"Know what?"

Bolly, in her usual aggressive manner, strained her neck as she looked up into Calvin's face.

"About you, and that Maria girl. The one in the drawing. The one who died.

How did she die Wolf? Come, on tell me. How did she die? Do you know or, even worse, did you kill her?"

Calvin struggled to contain his temper; his eyes blazed with fury behind the sunglasses. Raising his hand he pointed his finger at Bolly, touching her lightly on the nose.

"Poking your nose into other people's business can seriously damage your health."

Suddenly Bolly's nose began to bleed. At first it was only a trickle, then the blood gushed out as if she has been punched.

Calvin turned and walked towards the door as Bolly frantically tried to stem the flow of blood that had now saturated her turtle-neck jumper. Standing in the doorway, Calvin smiled at his adversary before leaving.

The nose finally stopped bleeding, leaving Bolly looking as if she had just gone three rounds with Mohammed Ali.

The door to the room opened. In walked Christine and Lucy.

"My God, what has happened?" Christine exclaimed as she rushed over towards her sister.

"Nothing, just a silly nose bleed. Never mind me, did you find out anything?"

Lucy looked first at Christine, then at Bolly.

"Sorry, I could find nothing."

"Nothing, nothing at all?" Lucy was apologetic. "Sorry."

Bolly dabbed the blood from under her nose as she spoke.

"That's what he said."

"Who? Mr Dane?" Lucy replied.

Bolly looked at Lucy.

"How did you know I was talking about him?"
The melodic tone had disappeared as she answered.

"Let's just say, if anyone would know, then he would. In fact I was surprised you asked me to call, especially with him around."
Christine was puzzled.

"Do you mean, Calvin is a medium?"
Lucy shook her head.

"Best I don't comment as he's your friend."
Bolly laughed.

"Friend. You must be joking. We only met him the other day and I personally loathe the man."
Lucy drew in a deep breath before speaking.

"It's hard to explain. When I first came in I felt something about him. Using my psychic ability I tried, as they say to weigh him up. Unfortunately, he knew what I was doing and he gave me back more than I bargained for. In fact, of all the psychics I have met, none of them could do that to me.

"What did he do?"
Christine was looking at the woman as she asked the question.

"He retaliated. I can't explain how he did it but my head still aches. Calvin Dane is a psychic and a powerful one at that."
Christine turned to Bolly.

"Seems there's more to Calvin than we thought."
Lucy made her way towards the door.

"Sorry I was of no help. Just a word of warning, be careful, very careful. As good as I am."

Lucy pointed to Bolly's nose.

"I could never have done that."

Christine was so stunned she allowed Lucy leave without saying goodbye as she stared at the blood-soaked figure of her sister.

"He hit you?" Christine asked.

Bolly shook her head as she took her sister by the hand.

"No, he just touched my nose with his finger. It was so light a touch I could hardly feel it. Then my nose began to pour."

Christine's blue eyes widened

"My God. We have got to warn Gran."

Bolly squeezed Christine's hands.

"I'm going to warn her."

"No. We're going together." replied Christine.

Bolly shook her head.

"No. You're staying here with Aunt Ivy. I'm going to warn Gran. If anyone's going to get the satisfaction of seeing that bastard kicked out on his arse, it's me."

An Empty Field Outskirts of Kirby Kent England. November 2nd 1969.

The flames from the bonfire licked the evening sky as the wail of the fire engine drew closer and closer.

Three small, shadowy figures scurried towards a small copse of trees at the far side of the field. A perfect hiding place to watch the events unfold.

Calvin's Cottage Litton Village England. November 2nd 1969

Calvin stooped down towards the fire to light a taper, before raising the naked flame to a large Havana held between his lips. Three short intakes of breath were enough to make the end grow crimson. Before blowing the smoke upwards, as was his usual habit, he turned towards his guest.

"Called about your granddaughter?"

Lady Winspear's face held a stern countenance.

"Christine telephoned and said you attacked Arabella."

Calvin offered the woman a drink as he poured himself a large scotch and water. The woman shook her head.

"Well, explain yourself." she continued.

Calvin drew on his cigar before replying.

"Its simple. She accused me of being a murderer. In fact I'm sure in her eyes Jack the Ripper was a missionary compared to me."

Lady Winspear looked puzzled.

"She accused you of murder. Whose murder?"

Calvin took a large swig of the whisky before answering.

"Maria's"

"Maria's. What does she know about her?" Lady Winspear asked.

Calvin sighed.

"The other night at the spiritualist meeting. Some fucking medium got her through. "

"And?" she pressed him to continue.

Calvin straightened himself as he replied.

"And I overreacted, and rushed out of the church."

Lady Winspear moved closer to him.

"I still don't understand. How could they tie you into a message from a spiritualist? And what made them think you killed her?"

Calvin gave another slight sigh.

"The medium had a sidekick. She drew a sketch of Maria, an almost perfect likeness. They must have been drawing on my powers without me knowing. There's no way they could have done that on their own. They got the name Wolf and the drawing. When I saw and heard that, I just flipped."

"What did you do?" she asked.

Calvin poured himself another drink.

"I decided to shut him up so I gave him a little headache."

Lady Winspear cocked an eyebrow as she spoke.

"I thought you were afraid to open up?"

Calvin gave a little laugh.

"Too late. I did and now. A hornets' nest."

Lady Winspear poured herself a drink as Calvin flopped down into his chair. Lady Winspear drink in hand sat in the chair opposite to him.

"She thinks I killed her," he continued. "Jesus if only she knew. Killed her, I loved that woman and would have given my life for her."

"But it wasn't you who gave your life." She interceded. "It was her."

Calvin jumped up out of his seat.

"Don't you think I know?

He clenched his fists, before drawing in a deep breath, only to be exhaled slowly flaring his nostrils as he spoke.

"Do you have any idea how many times I go over it in my mind? How many times I wish I could change things. And then, then this little troll of a granddaughter of yours comes along and accuses me of killing her. I'm glad I gave her a nosebleed. The little shit."

Lady Winspear remained composed.

"Ranting and raving will achieve nothing. As for my granddaughter being a little shit, well she can be rather irritating at times."

Calvin laughed.

"Irritating! Jesus! That's an understatement."

Lady Winspear rose from her seat to stand next to Calvin, who was close to the window.

"Are you in danger?"

Calvin bowed his head.

"No idea."

Lady Winspear pondered for a moment.

"You need some help, let me contact Croxton," her voice rang with sincerity.

Calvin raised his hand.

"Whoa! Hold your horse, lady! I've told you before. I want nothing to do with your old boy network. M.I.5. M.I.6 or what ever number it is."

She tried to touch his hand.

"They could help."

"Help me into an early grave." he laughed. "If I'm going to go then it'll be by my own hand."

Lady Winspear once again cocked one eyebrow.

"Suicide?" she asked.

"Yeah. I've toyed, with the idea." was the reply.

She now laughed.

"No you haven't. You have a built-in sense of survival. That's why you buried yourself away. Survival, nothing more. The trouble is you have not only buried yourself and your identity, but the one thing that makes you different, special. Your mind."

Calvin ran his fingers through his hair.

"She said she loved me."

"Who?" She had a concerned look on her face as she asked.

"Maria," he replied.

Lady Winspear reached out once more to take his hand, only to be rebuffed once again.

"I'm sorry I ever got you involved."

"Yeah. Okay." he sighed.

There was genuine concern in her voice as she spoke.

"What happens now? Will they be able to trace you?"

Calvin shrugged his shoulders as he replied to her.

"I doubt it. Never opened up enough. Anyway, they're not that good."

She looked suspiciously at him as she asked the question.

"I thought they could track you down if you ever used your gift?"

Calvin's screwed up the corner of his mouth as he replied.

"Only if they're still looking for me. By the way, I'm sorry for what I did to your granddaughter. She can be quite amusing in a grotesque way." Lady Winspear gave a gentle smile.

"I will inform Arabella of your apology." Calvin glanced towards the window. Out of the corner of his eye something caught his attention.

"No need."

He nodded towards the window.

"How long?" Lady Winspear asked.

Calvin shook his head

"No idea."

Lady Winspear rapped hard on the window and called out.

"There is no point hiding out there. Get yourself inside immediately."

The sound of the front door opening was followed by as a sheepish looking Bolly. Lady Winspear was about to give her a tongue-lashing but was taken aback by the state of her bloodstained clothes. Regaining her composure she asked her granddaughter what she had overheard. Bolly hands stuffed in her duffel coat pockets replied.

"Most of it."

Lady Winspear folded her arms.

"Then you will apologise to Calvin."

Bolly looked astonished.

"What! Apologise after what he did to me?"

Calvin waved his hand in the air.

"Leave it. Let's forget who said what and who did what. Water under the bridge."

Lady Winspear took Bolly by the arm to lead her out of the cottage.

"Come along we will leave Calvin to himself, and get you cleaned up, my lady."

Bolly, following her grandmother, turned to look back at Calvin. As a parting gesture, smiling sarcastically, she poked out her tongue.

Litton Manor,
Litton Village, England.
November 2nd 1969

Upon their return to the manor Lady Winspear instantly dispatched Bolly to the bathroom. In the drawing room with Bolly out of the way, she made a telephone call.

A voice answered. A male voice, and very English. The type of voice one associates with cricket at Lords or the Henley regatta.

"Yes."

Lady Winspear instantly replied.

"Croxton?"

"Who is this?" he asked.

"It is Eve," she replied.

There was a momentary silence as the person on the other end of the telephone scanned his memory.

"Eve... Eve. How are you, my dear?"

His voice was high pitched, almost effeminate.

"I'm fine." her voice quavered as she spoke. "I have a small favour to ask. In fact I'm not sure that contacting you is the right thing."

"Well, why not run it past me, dear heart, and I will decide," was the response.

Lady Winspear paused momentarily before answering.

"There is a young man who is in need of your help."

"In what way?" asked Croxton.

"I think it is something we should discuss in private and not over the telephone."

Croton's voice rang with laughter.

"How mysterious one is."

Lady Winspear bit her lower lip before replying.

"It concerns a descendent of the Herrenvolk."

The laughter in his voice instantly disappeared

"One of Heinrich's?"

"Yes." was the reply.

The tone was now serious, deadly serious.

"I will call tomorrow, in time for lunch."

She gave a small sigh of relief.

"Thank you."

"On the contrary my dear, it is I who should be thanking you."

Croxton replaced the telephone. Pulling together his silk dressing-gown, he place a cigarette in a small slim ivory holder, and lit it up. His smoky grey eyes held a pensive look as he gazed out of his apartment window overlooking the river Thames.

"One of Heinrich's," he whispered to himself.

"How long I have waited for this moment."

Calvin's Cottage, Litton Village, England. November 3 [rd] 1969

Calvin sat staring at a sheet of virginal paper in an inanimate typewriter. He stroked the front of his brow with his forefinger as he tried in vain to force a worthwhile thought, an idea, anything out of his stagnated mind, while his eyes darted constantly to the newspaper folded no more than a few inches away from him. He had a strange feeling, that the newspaper was hiding something. He had read it from the front to the back, even the births deaths and marriages, nothing. Yet he felt it should have contained something; what, he had no idea. A knock on the door snapped him out of his dilemma.

Gladly leaving the typewriter he made his way to the front door and opened it. Bolly smiled.

"Sorry to disturb you."

Calvin looked at her.

"Why do I get the feeling, that line is a load of crap?"

"Because you're psychic?" she replied.

"No, because it came out of your mouth." was his response.

Bolly shuffled uneasily before him.

"I have a favour to ask."

Calvin's lips parted in a smile.

"This should be good. Ask away."

Bolly held her head in a cocky pose.

"May I come in?"

Calvin smiled as he replied.

"No. Your favour can be granted or refused just as easily here as inside."

Bolly drew in a deep breath, in an attempt to control her temper.

"It's Christine, she has just telephoned."

"And?" he asked.

"The man has just been to the house," was the reply.

"What man?" Calvin exclaimed.

Bolly sighed before replying.

"The man in the house, the one with the children."

Calvin looked suspiciously at her.

"So your sister's seeing ghosts again?"

Bolly was doing her best to keep calm.

"No, you don't understand. He has been to buy the house. The estate agent sent him round. She has fobbed him off and asked if he could call back later. That's why we must get through there as quickly as possible, before he returns."

"We. Why we?" His voice was suspicious.

Bolly turned to walk away.

"Okay, if you don't want to help, then."

Calvin held up a hand.

"Whoa. Never said I wouldn't help; I just find it strange that your ghost has suddenly become flesh and blood."

Bolly looked up into his face.

"No more than me. Well, will you or won't you?"

Calvin moved aside to allow her to enter.
   "Okay we'll go on my bike, its quicker. There's an old helmet under the stairs."

Christine's House Durham England. November 3rd 1969.

Christine was standing in the entrance porch, talking to a tall slim fresh-faced man in his late twenties.

His hair was blond and already thinning, brushed in a parting style that allowed the front of the hair to fall forward covering his right eye as it trailed over thin gold framed spectacles. Occasionally he would sweep it away from the face with a long slender hand.

A sigh of relief ran through Christine's body as she looked over the man's shoulder at the sight of both Bolly and Calvin walking down the path. Having endured the man's company for the past fifteen minutes as she showed him around the house had taken its toll on her, and her face showed it.

The moment she feared most was when she had to show him the upstairs rooms. At one time she left him on his own to look around as she rushed to the bathroom and was physically sick.

Bolly and Calvin reached the pair in the porch; Christine instantly introduced the visitor.

"Bolly, Calvin. This is Mr Meynell; he is interested in the buying the house."

Bolly made no response as she stared at Meynell, only Calvin responded by holding out his hand.

"Pleased to meet you."
Meynell was in the process of pulling his gloves on. So as not to be rude he passed his right glove into his left hand before shaking Calvin's hand.

They say a grip tells you more about a man than the spoken word. Unfortunately in Calvin's case it was far more. As his fingers close around Meynell's hands a vision, an image surged into his mind. The mental image of an effigy of Guy Fawkes being placed on top of a bonfire. It lasted a split second, no more.

Calvin was as startled as Meynell, whose hand he was still holding. He had not intended to pick anything up, but the intensity of the vision shook him to the core.

Meynell's face winced in pain as Calvin's grip tightened. Calvin, oblivious to what he was doing, was slow to react as Meynell tried to free his hand from his grip.

Snapping out of his trance, Calvin, not quite knowing what to say stooped down to retrieve Meynell's loose glove.

"Sorry. Didn't mean to squeeze so hard."
Still shocked, Meynell gingerly retrieved the glove, before turning to Christine.

"Will you please inform your aunt that I am definitely interested and will contact my solicitor."

Without saying another word he hurried away along the path, only turning to look back when he reached the gate.

Bolly, still silent, watched him leave, before turning to Calvin.

"What the hell was all that about?" Calvin gave no reply.

Christine interrupted.

"Its him. Isn't it, Boll?"

"Yeah, that's him."

Calvin shook his head.

"Let's get this straight. You told me the man who haunts the place was a lot older. This man is young."

Christine was about to interrupt but was stopped by a wave of Calvin's hand.

"Let me finish. If he haunts the place, then how in God's name can he be flesh and blood, and trying to buy the fucking house."

Bolly was quick to reply.

"How the fuck should we know? You're the fucking psychic"

Calvin nodded.

"Dead right, and my psychic vibes tell me to get away from you two loonies before I catch something."

Christine called out to Calvin who was already walking away.

"What do I tell Aunt Ivy?"

"Tell her you've got a buyer for the place and give us all some fucking peace.

Calvin's Cottage, Litton Village, England. November 3rd 1969

The rain, driven by a cold November wind, beat relentlessly against the windows of the cottage. Leaves that tentatively hung to the branches were ripped from their host, and flattened against the glass.

Calvin had still not managed to place pen to paper. The incident with Bolly and the mysterious Mr Meynell haunted his thoughts, causing him to finally throw in the towel as far as his writing was concerned. It was time for him to relax with one of his favourite pastimes, cooking.

The aroma of wood pigeon casserole wafted appetisingly around the kitchen, as Calvin checked to see if his masterpiece tasted as good as it smelt. Several loud raps on the front door caused him to frown.

"Fuck them."

The words were muttered under his breath as he lifted the spoon to his lips and tasted his culinary delight. The banging continued. Calvin, unperturbed, added a little more seasoning to the pot. Finally the intrusive knocking ceased.

With the casserole carefully replaced into the oven he was about to return to the lounge. Suddenly several more loud raps thundered against the kitchen door. Controlling his temper, he reluctantly opened it.

The bedraggled figure of Bolly, wellingtons full of water, stood before him, the result of stumbling into Calvin's wild life pond at the rear of the garden.

Calvin blocked the doorway without inviting her in.

"Yes?"

"What do you mean, yes? Are you going to invite me fucking in or not?" she retorted.

A slow smile sneaked across Calvin's face as he stood aside to let the rain-soaked figure enter. Her feet squelched as she walked across the floor, as the water pushed itself upwards and out of the tops of her wellingtons.

"Wet?" he sniggered.

Bolly ignored his sarcasm as she removed each Wellington in turn before pouring their contents into the kitchen sink.

"Very hygienic." he sarcastically commented.

"Stop moaning. If you'd answered the front door when I knocked then I wouldn't have fallen into that bloody pond."

Calvin couldn't contain his pleasure at Bolly's bedraggled state.

"Take your coat off and hang it over the back of the chair. Then go into the room by the fire, I'll be with you once I've cleaned up.

Bolly did as she was told, and a little more, by helping herself to a large whisky.

The fire was warm and inviting as she sat in the chair opposite Calvin's. Even she knew how far to go.

Calvin entered the room.

"No need to tell you to make yourself at home.
Bolly gave him a smile as she raised the glass.
Calvin sat opposite her.

"Okay, why are you here?"
Bolly lifted the front of her jumper up to reveal a
newspaper.
Calvin laughed.

"You've got a job as a delivery girl."
Bolly ignored him.

"Read this."
Calvin glanced at the paper without taking it
from her.

"Already read it."

"Not the late edition." she snapped. "Read the
stop press."
Calvin sat back in his chair.

"You read it for me. I'm sure you know what
you're looking for."

Bolly wiped away a large droplet of water that
was hanging off the end of her nose.

"You must have read about the missing
children. About the three young girls that have
all disappeared over the past months."

Bolly had finally grabbed Calvin's undivided
attention.

"Three? I thought there were only two?"

"There were." She continued. "That was until
the other day when a third child went missing."
"The police kept a lid on it trying to play it down,
especially after the other week when the police
and the army were out looking for a missing
child that turned out to be a hoax. All of the
children have gone missing at the same time of
the month. The time of the full moon. It must be
Meynell."

Calvin shook his head.

"How did you come to that conclusion?"

Bolly lifted the lower part of her jumper up to dry her face.

"You could have brought me a towel."

She finally had Calvin's undivided attention.

"Never mind that Sherlock," he grumbled.

"Let's hear your deduction."

Bolly continued.

"Don't you see; all the children missing are from Kent."

"So?" Calvin was still puzzled.

"So" Bolly cockily replied. "Meynell is from Kent."

Calvin rose from his seat and slapped the mantle.

"Of course Meynell must be the kidnapper. I don't know anyone else who comes from Kent. It has to be Meynell."

Bolly drained the whisky in the glass before answering

"All right. I know you think I'm overreacting and making something out of nothing. But I have this feeling. This gut feeling."

"Gas. You've got gas." His laughter incensed her.

Bolly flung the paper at Calvin.

"Here, read it for yourself. The child s body was found on a bonfire."

Calvin snatched the paper from the floor.

"Bonfire, where does it say bonfire?" he snapped

Bolly pointed to the stop press. His eyes quickly scanned the few lines in heavy black print before glancing at the clock. It was almost nine o'clock, time for the evening news bulletin. Grabbing Bolly by the arm, he lifted her out of the chair.

Oblivious to Bolly's protests, he frogmarched her out of the room and into the kitchen, before unceremoniously ejecting her out of the door flinging her coat and boots after her.

Locking the door, he returned to the lounge and switched on the radio as loud as it would go in an attempt to drown out Bolly's screams and accusations about his parentage.

Calvin listened intently to the opening highlights.

"The partially-charred body of a female child has been found on a bonfire in Kent. Police have stated that they are not giving any more information other that the November rain had prevented the body, which was disguised as Guy Fawkes, from being completely burnt."

Radio switched off, he slowly he made his way towards the fire.

"Shit!"

Was his only word before flopping backwards into his chair. Running his fingers through his hair, he closed his eyes.

"Fuck, fuck, fuck."

Cupping his face with both hands, he slowly rose from his seat and walked over towards the drinks cabinet, to pour himself a brandy. Gulping it down he banged the top of the cabinet.

"Fuck it."

Ignoring the glass, he picked up the bottle, gulping almost a quarter of its contents down in one go, before returning to the chair where he took another swig. Resting his head on the back of the chair, he closed his eyes.

Dr Vogel's Apartment, Edinburgh, Scotland. November 4th 1969

Dr Vogel sat in his chair by the bay window that overlooked a small square and shrubbery. Beside him was his usual cup of morning coffee, a packet of Capstan full strength cigarettes and two morning newspapers. A ritual he indulged in every morning at precisely 7.30.

The cigarette had been lit no more than a second when the telephone rang. Vogel rose from his seat and made his way to the desk where the telephone sat.

"Yes."

The voice on the other side trembled almost to the point of crying.

"Dr Vogel. You must help me. I beg you."

A frown formed above Vogel's eyes.

"Who? Is that you Mr Hoff?"

The voice on the other end of the telephone line replied.

"Yes doctor. Please help me before I go insane."

Vogel instantly responded.

"Why? What has happened?"

The voice on the other side began to break up in a vain attempt to answer.

"Compose, yourself young man." Vogel tried to calm the young American down. "Please. Now take several deep breaths before replying. Did you hear me."

"Yes doctor. I'm sorry." Hoff replied.

Vogel took a long deep pull on his cigarette before continuing.

"Now I want you remain calm and explain everything to me."

Hoff sighed before speaking.

"I don't know whether I'm going insane or not. In fact I doubt my sanity so much that this conversation may only be a figment of my imagination."

"It is not." Vogel reassured him. "Continue."

"I keep having blackouts, fits, whatever you wish to call them. Well to others they are fits." Hoff continued.

Vogel took another pull on the cigarette, blowing the smoke into the telephone as he spoke.

"Explain."

Hoff continued after taking several deep breaths to calm himself down.

"Yesterday during a tutorial I suddenly fell to the ground. Everyone assumed I was experiencing an epileptic fit, but I know it wasn't. I saw myself at a railway station. It was snowing as a train pulled in. Then the next thing I knew I was back in the classroom. My lecturer was helping me to a chair."

Vogel frantically made notes all the time Adrian Hoff spoke.

"Have you experienced this before?" Vogel asked.

Vogel could hear Hoff take in another steadying breath.

"It is becoming more frequent. The night I saw you I didn't fall to the ground. But just recently it has been getting worse."

"In what way?" Vogel asked.

"It's as if my personality is changing. I can no longer eat meat. The very sight of it makes me vomit. Then there are my mood changes. My mother has complained about my being moody and playing music too loud." was the reply.

Vogel tapped the end of his pen on the sheet of paper, making several blue dots with the point.

"Surely that is a normal stage of adolescence?"

Hoff sighed as he replied.

"The music I have been playing, I don't even remember buying."

"What music is it?" was the response.

"Wagner."

Vogel closed his eyes for a second before asking the next question.

"You have telephoned me now which must be 1.30am your time?"

"Yes." Hoff replied.

"What has happened to make you so frightened you call me now?" Vogel asked

Vogel could hear what sounded like Hoff licking his lips as he tried to lubricate his drying mouth, before answering.

" About fifteen minutes ago I had another fit, trance whatever. I saw myself in some passages. They were dark, yet I could see perfectly. It was as if all the paintings on the wall were luminescent. I walked along one passage after another; the drawings were strange. Drawings of winged soldiers dressed in German uniforms and knights of old. Suddenly I came to a large steel door. I was about to enter when I came out of the trance. It was then I noticed the blood."

"Blood?" Vogel could not hide the surprise in his voice.

"Yes my side was bleeding." Hoff continued." It was as if something had stabbed me in the side."

Vogel scribbled frantically as he asked another question.

"Were there any marks?"

"No, none," was the reply.

What had earlier seemed to be random dots were now slowly being joined together to form a name. He asked Hoff one more question.

"Tell me, in, your earlier vision you said you were at a railway station?"

A tone of puzzlement rang in Hoff's voice as he replied.

"Yes."

"Do you by chance know its name?" Vogel asked.

Vogel could hear Hoff draw in another short intake of breath before replying.

"Yes there was a sign above the ticket office. Linz."

Vogel stubbed his cigarette out in the ashtray and pondered for a moment, looking at the now joined-up dots that spelt out the name Linz.

"Listen to me very carefully." Vogel's voice held a serious tone. "I will arrange for some people to call upon you. Do not be afraid; they will be there to help you. Please explain this to your mother. I will contact you at approximately 11.00 am, your time. Please try and get some sleep and whatever you do, do not leave your house. Do you understand?"

"Yes." Hoff replied

"Good night, Adrian. And get some rest."

Vogel replaced the telephone. His mind was racing. As was his custom, he began to talk to himself as he paced the floor of his apartment.

"Surely, it could not be true. It could be some elaborate hoax. Why? For what purpose? Think, Hans. Think."

The coffee in the cup was now cold, and his newspapers held no attraction for him. Even the headline about a child's body having been found on a bonfire in Kent made no impact. He had other things on his mind, things far more important to him than the murder of a child.

Calvin's Cottage, Litton Village, England. November 4th 1969

Calvin's head ached as he raised it heavily from the back of the chair. His eyes opened slowly, allowing the bright autumn sun to pierce his pupils like red-hot needles, forcing him to crawl on hands and knees, desperately searching for his sunglasses.

Shielding his sensitive eyes from the light. He groaned, as he groped around like a blind man, until he found his trusty protectors. Adjusting to the morning's rays, he groaned once more at the empty brandy bottle on the floor visible through a thin layer of black smoke that hovered around the room.

His nose twitched at the foul odour that engulfed the room. Finally clicking his mind into gear, he rushed as best he could into the kitchen, which was filled with dense smoke.

"Shit!"

Whipping the door to the oven open, he winced and recoiled backwards at the sight and smell of the cremated blob that was once a gastronomical creation.

It was now the turn of the kitchen door to be flung open as he rushed outside with the cremated wood pigeons, dish and all.

The combination of the drink and the stench of what had been the wood pigeons caused Calvin to vomit with such ferocity, the back of his throat burnt as he added more liquid to the already overflowing wild life pond.

Litton Manor, Litton Village, England. November 4 [th] 1969

Bolly found it hard to sleep and pulled on her faithful and now dry old duffel coat over her nightdress.

Wearing a pair of her grandmother's slippers, she took an early morning stroll in the grounds. She was just about to turn the corner when something stood before her, causing her to jump with fright. It was the dishevelled figure of Calvin.

"Jesus! What the hell?" she screamed.

Calvin held his finger to her lips.

"Just shut the fuck up for once and listen."

Bolly was motionless and for once silent, as Calvin continued.

"I've been thinking. Thinking about this Meynell character and the children. Especially the children."

Bolly tilted her head to one side.

"And?" she asked.

"If Meynell lives in Kent, then why does he want a house in Durham?"

Bolly was still bemused at Calvin's outward appearance, and hesitated before replying.

"Because he's a bank manager who's been posted to Durham."

Calvin drew in a deep breath before speaking. His stomach was still feeling the effects of his night of indulgence.

"Then he might not be the guy we want." he replied.

"What do you mean?" she asked.

Bolly winced as Calvin drew closer. The stench of his vomit-ridden breath caused her to recoil. Calvin, noticing the affect his breath had on her, causing him to place his hand over his mouth in embarrassment as he spoke.

"If he's working in Durham, then he obviously couldn't have been at the other end of the county at the same time."

Bolly give a sigh.

"I know what you are getting at. I thought of that myself, but he looks just like the man. The ghost. So wouldn't it make sense for him to be checked out."

Calvin pondered for a moment.

"I'll get back to you."

Without another word he turned and walked along the tarmac driveway leading back to his cottage. The thought of children disappearing and the possibility of Meynell being the one, haunted his thoughts once again. He knew he should help but was afraid. Afraid to truly open up, in fear for his life.

A lot of the stuff he had fed Lady Winspear was bullshit and she knew it. But the fact that his life was in danger, if he were ever tracked down, was real.

The sound of whistling could be heard, as the newspaper boy made his way on his bike towards the Manor. Calvin held out his hand to stop the boy.

"Have you dropped my paper off?"

The boy looked bewildered. Then Calvin realised that the boy had never seen him before.

"I live in the cottage at the gate," he reassured the boy.

The boy instantly replied.

"Yes. Just delivered it."

Calvin reached inside the boy's newspaper sack. The boy didn't know what to do as he watched Calvin unfold the Daily Mail.

On the front page was the photograph of the little child, the one found on the bonfire. The one who had gone to buy her mother a pint of milk, wearing little red wellingtons. The one Calvin saw having a Guy Fawkes mask placed over her face in his vision. Without a word he folded the newspaper up and placed it back inside the sack, allowing the newspaper boy to continue his journey towards the Manor, followed by Calvin.

Bolly was there to greet the boy and take the morning papers. As the boy peddled back along the driveway Calvin called out to Bolly before she entered the Manor.

"I'll pick you up about noon."

Without another word to Bolly, he turned and walked away, muttering under his breath.

"Someone's got to nail that son of a bitch. And you're just the stupid bastard to do it. That's if you don't get killed first."

Children's Park, Durham, England. November 4 <u>th</u> 1969

Three young children played happily on the swings and small roundabout in the little park under the shadow of the castle.

One little boy's laughter was so loud it echoed across the river, as his mother pushed him on the swing. His laughter grew and grew, as each push with legs straight out sent him higher and higher in the air, all under the gaze of a solitary tall, fresh-faced watcher.

A watcher wearing thin gold-rimmed glasses, whose hair constantly flopped over his eye.

Meynell sat silently nibbling on a sandwich, his cold eyes following every movement of the swing, the child and the mother.

Slowly his eyes closed as his mind drifted back in time, back to his own childhood when it was he who was laughing as his mother pushed him on a swing.

A memory he continually replayed over and over in his mind. The one and only cherished memory it possessed. The rest of his childhood was swallowed up, engulfed by a large black hole that protected the mind and numbed his soul.

His daydream suddenly shattered as something hit him on the leg. Startled he looked down. There before him lay a multi-coloured ball. Picking it up, he handed it back to its owner, a smiling little girl.

A weak smile flickered across his thin lips as he handed the ball back to the child before touching her gently on the cheek with the back of his hand. Quickly the child turned and ran back to her mother.

Meynell wrapped the remaining sandwiches up, and placed them back into his briefcase ready to leave. Removing his glasses he gave the lenses a wipe with a handkerchief before placing them back over his cold eyes, eyes that neither remembered love nor knew how to receive it.

Mrs Fenton's House, Hartlepool, England. November 5th 1969

Calvin and Bolly had spent the previous day finding out as much about the house as possible.

He still found it hard to believe that Meynell could be the ghost, and the murderer. Patching together information from Aunt Ivy and contacting her solicitor, they managed to trace the address of the previous occupants of the house. They were in fact the only previous occupants.

Calvin and Bolly were led into the small but comfortable lounge. Mrs Fenton, a sprightly woman in her late seventies, bade them both to take a seat on the sofa.

She smiled, showing two rows of teeth that obviously spent more time in a glass than in her mouth. Her naturally grey-coloured hair was tinted blue, giving it a strange ultra-violet effect as she stood under the solitary light set in a small tiffany-style shade.

Both Calvin and Bolly sat in stunned silence as they were introduced to Mrs Fenton's sister Beth. Beth, the younger of the two, was sitting opposite them in a chair. On her knee was an old fox fur that she stroked constantly as she rocked back and forth.

"Make yourselves comfortable."

Mrs Fenton's voice resonated a deep rasping tone, what some would call a smokers voice.

"Perfect timing, the tea has already brewed. Back in a mo."

With Mrs Fenton gone the threesome were left alone.

Both Calvin and Bolly averted their eyes from Beth, Calvin because her toothless mouth with dried saliva in the corner made him feel a little queasy, were as Bolly's reasons where totally different. It was all she could do to prevent herself from bursting out laughing, especially when Beth kept kissing the dead fox on the lips.

Beth looked at Calvin. Her tight lips pulled back showing pink gums to the visitors as she spoke.

"Are you the plumber?"

Calvin refused to look at the grinning Bolly as he replied.

"No. Sorry."

Beth continued with the conversation, oblivious to Calvin's reply.

"Nips me bum."

Bolly trying to keep a straight face asked.

"What nips your bum?"

"Toilet seat." Beth replied.

Beth held out a small white paper bag.

"Like an almond? " Bolly declined the offer. The bag was then thrust under the nose of Calvin.

"Take one. Go on."

Calvin reluctantly took a nut and popped it into his mouth.

"Take another," she insisted.

Trying not to offend, Calvin took a second and popped the hard nut into his mouth, crunching them both at the same time.

Beth was trying to get Calvin to take a third when Mrs Fenton returned carrying a tea tray. Placing the tray on a small coffee table, Mrs Fenton immediately proceeded to pour her guests a cup each.

"Help yourselves to milk or sugar."

Her voice was warm, as were her manners to the guests.

Calvin was about to say no thank you. The only none-alcoholic beverage he took was coffee. When Beth offered Calvin another nut, Mrs Fenton instantly intervened.

"No, dear, the gentleman doesn't want one. Don't know why she buys them. Can't eat the nuts, not without any teeth. Once she has sucked all the sugar off them, they're wasted."

A smirk crept across Bolly face as she watched Calvin lunge forward to gulp down the piping-hot tea. Feeling physically sick, he tried to swill down the remnants of the nuts that were stuck between his teeth.

Mrs Fenton, shocked by Calvin's strange behaviour put it down to his being an American.

"You have called about the house?" she asked.

Bolly replied as Calvin poured himself another cup of tea.

"Yes."

Mrs Fenton stirred her tea with the spoon as she looked into Bolly's face before replying.

"I can only tell you what I told your uncle years ago."

"Uncle?" Bolly was surprised.

"Yes he called. Asked about its history."

With a sombre note Bolly asked her question.

"And does it have a history?"

Mrs Fenton let out a sigh before replying.

"If you are experiencing what we did, as I believe your uncle did also, then I am sorry to disappoint you. Yes, the house belonged to us before your aunt and uncle, but there was never anyone killed there, let alone murdered."

Now the last piece of nut had finally been dislodged from between his teeth, Calvin found his voice

"What did you experience?" he asked

Mrs Fenton looked at the strange American wearing sunglasses.

"You want to know about the children?"

Neither Bolly nor Calvin replied. Rising from her seat Mrs Fenton walked over towards a highly-polished sideboard. Opening one of its cupboards she removed a large cardboard tube; rolled up inside were several large sheets of paper. Handing the tube to Calvin, she sat back in her chair.

Calvin carefully unfolded the papers. Each one was a pencil sketch. Each one a sketch of children's faces.

Bolly took a deep breath as she instantly recognised one of the children, the little child at the top of the stairs.

"Oh, my God!" she whispered.

A small tear appeared in the corner of Mrs Fenton's eye.

"Beth drew them. She was always a sensitive soul, and a very good artist. As for who they are, and why this horror should be haunting the house, I have no idea."

Calvin slipped one of the bottom sketches to the top. It was a sketch of a man. Beth instantly stopped rocking and flung the fox to the floor, she rose to her feet and pointed at the sketch

"He's the devil! The devil! "

Mrs Fenton jumped up and tried to calm her sister, who was shaking and sobbing uncontrollably.

"The devil! The devil!" She continued to yell.

Mrs Fenton begged for both Calvin and Bolly to leave.

"Please go and take those dammed things with you. I should have burnt them years ago."

Without a word, both Calvin and Bolly left, taking the sketches with them.

Judge's House
Peel Kent England.
November 6th 1969

The soft red glow of the light gave the room a sombre tone.

Meynell carefully slipped the white sheet of paper from one tray of solution into another. His face was blank, expressionless as he watched an image slowly form in the liquid. Before the finished product could be removed from the developing solution a voice called out from the other side of the door.

"David."

At first he made no acknowledgement.

"David." The voice sounded again.

"Yes, Gran." he finally replied.

"Dinner's ready." she continued. "Be sure to bathe and change. Now hurry along and don't be late, you know how your grandfather hates tardiness."

"Right, Gran." He replied

Meynell carefully lifted the fully-developed photograph out of the tray and hung it on a line to dry. He smiled and hummed 'You may not be an Angel', as he examined each photograph in turn. Photographs of old churches, especially the cherubs that adorned them.

Calvin's Cottage, Litton Village, England. November 6 rd 1969

The heat from the fire made Christine's face glow red as she Bolly and Calvin examined Mrs Fenton's sketches.

The fire might have been hot, but nothing could warm the chill in their hearts, as Bolly held aloft two sketches of little children, girls. In fact, with the exception of two, all were of girls. Seventeen sketches in all, fifteen of them girls.

Calvin sat in silence as he watched the young women set aside the sketches of the children they had seen. Christine suddenly stopped when she came to the sketch of a man in his late forties, with thinning hair that flopped over one eye, eyes that were covered by wire-framed spectacles.

Bolly took the sketch from her sister and showed it to Calvin.

"Well, is that Meynell or not?" she asked.

Calvin's red eyes squinted without his sunglasses, even in the room's subdued lighting.

"It could be." he responded.

"What do you mean, could be?" Bolly retorted.

Calvin's face was expressionless.

"Meynell is a young man, and this man is at least twenty years older."
Bolly screwed up her nose, as was her habit when she knew she was wrong.

"Yes, but it is him."
Christine interrupted.

"What if it's a relative of his? He could be a descendant of the man in the sketch."
Calvin nodded in agreement.

"True, there is only one flaw in that theory. If he is a descendant of this man, then someone is lying."
Christine instantly responded.

"Well, we are not lying."
Calvin raised his hand in a pacifying gesture.

"Never said you were. It's just a statement of fact. The man in the sketch can't be Meynell because he's too old. And Mrs Fenton claims that no other family other than her own have lived in the house, prior to yourselves."

Bolly threw the remainder of the sketches down, causing them to spread across the floor. One of the sketches caught Calvin's eye as she spoke.

"That's it. Meynell wants the house back to cover up some family secret. And Mrs Fenton gave us these sketches to try to put us off the scent."

Calvin was oblivious to what Bolly was saying as he picked up one of the sketches from the floor. He held it with both hands and stared at the little face before him, the face of a young boy with large dark eyes and long black hair.
Christine was the first to notice.

"What is it?" she asked.

Calvin pondered over the sketch.

"This doesn't belong here," was the reply

Bolly was now as intrigued as Christine.

"Why?"

Calvin sat back in the chair, still looking at the drawing.

"Can't say just yet, but it doesn't belong with the rest. Have either of you seen him?"

Christine shook her head as Bolly looked at the drawing with a puzzled expression.

"Him? I thought it was a girl!" She exclaimed.

Holding the sketch in both hands, Calvin closed his eyes, only for a moment, and not long enough for either of the women to realise what was actually happening.

A vision stuck Calvin. A vision only he could see, of waves crashing against cliffs, against the entrance of a cave. Inside, the cave was dark and wet as the tide rushed in. The vision was over as quickly as it came. Showing no emotion, Calvin placed the sketch back on the floor with the rest.

"Fifteen girls, one boy and a man," he observed.

Bolly piped up as usual.

"Meynell. The man is Meynell."

Calvin shook his head.

"You don't know that. Before you interrupt again, let me finish. What I want you to do is phone the police, and show them the sketches."

Bolly stood up.

"Oh yeah. Hello, constable, sorry to disturb you but we have this house that's haunted. And well, here are the sketches of the children who have been murdered. Oh, and we have one of a man. He's the one we think is doing it. The only thing is, he's not dead, he's alive. But he still haunts the house."

Calvin placed the tinted glasses over his eyes. Even the mellow light from the standard and the table lamps were beginning to irritate his sensitive eyes.

"Okay, they take the piss, so what. If you want to put an end to it, just contact the police and let them take over."

Christine interrupted.

"What if they won't come?"

Bolly nodded in agreement.

"Good point."

Calvin looked at both women in turn.

"Contact the police force in Kent, they'll have to investigate. They have a dead child and others missing."

Bolly still wasn't convinced.

"And if they do, and they don't believe us, then what?"

Calvin removed his spectacles for a second or so to look at Bolly. His red eyes glowed brighter that the flames in the grate.

"If they don't, then I'll stay the night of the next full moon."

Adrian Hoff's House. Boston, America. November 7th 1969

The car wheels slowed to a halt outside Adrian Hoff's mother's house in a quiet suburban area of Boston. Two men and a woman alighted from the automobile and proceeded to walk towards the front entrance.

It had been several years since they had last met. In fact the last time all three of them were together had been in April 1945, at an informal party of Winston Churchill's. A gesture of acknowledgement for this most secret of services, and their contribution in bringing about the downfall of the Third Reich. A little-known fact and one that would be kept a close secret for many more years to come.

After all, who would believe that Hitler and his henchmen where practising occultists? Certainly not the general public, and certainly not the majority of the brave men and woman who gave their lives in the defence of their country and beliefs.

The truth of the matter was that Hitler had been an occultist and Churchill and Roosevelt, being no fools, had listened and understood what they were up against by forming their own deterrent to Hitler's elite group of occultists.

Former members of the Thule Gesellschaft and Vril Society had been instantly recruited into the Ahnenerbe SS. Himmler had appointed Richard Darre, the head of the SS race and Resettlement Bureau, himself a firm believer in the 'Blood and Soil' ideology.

Before the war the Ahnenerbe had conducted more legitimate scientific research, including archaeological, mainly research into Germanic pre-history, homeopathic medicine and the benefits of vegetarianism. The more sinister element had been involved in medical and racial experiments on concentration and extermination camp prisoners.

And then there were the pure occultists. Men and women dedicated to the development of psychic abilities and magical rituals involving what can only be described as the dark side, or Satanists. A sinister sect with secrets and goals so dark it would be many a year before they would unfold.

Professor Rubin Abraham, accompanied by Marie Blaine, allowed Dr Vogel to knock upon the door of the house.

A small dumpy, woman opened the door.

"Yes?"

Vogel removed his Homburg before speaking.

"I am Doctor Hans Vogel and these are my associates. I believe Mr Hoff is expecting us."

The woman stared at the party without replying. Vogel looked at his companions before continuing.

"This is the house of Adrian Hoff, is it not?" The woman nodded her head. "Then may we come in?" he continued.

Without uttering a word, the woman stood aside to allow the party to enter. All three entered the house, Professor Abraham being the last. Once they were inside the woman closed the door.

A faint sobbing could be heard coming from a room upstairs. The woman nodded in the direction of the sound.

"My son. If he's not crying he's playing Wagner or screaming and shouting in German."

Marie Blaine looked into the troubled woman's face.

"You know it's German?" she asked.

"Of course." The woman replied.

"Why of course?" Marie asked.

The woman looked at a photograph of her late husband hanging on the wall.

"My husband's father was German; in his home as a child German was spoken as much as English."

Vogel interrupted.

"So, I take it your son upstairs would be familiar with the German language?"

"Yes. He speaks fluent German," she replied.

Suddenly a loud scream, followed by shouting in German, brought the conversation to a halt. The woman burst into tears as she implored the trio to help her son.

"Please help him! Go quickly!"

Despite his age Abraham was the first to rush up the stairs, two at a time, followed by Vogel and Marie Blaine.

Throwing open the door to the bedroom, Abraham stopped in the doorway and watched in amazement. There, in the middle of the room, stood the naked figure of a young man of nineteen years. His body shook as if in a fit, yet he did not fall to the floor.

Tentatively the party entered the room, with the mother choosing to remain in the doorway. Adrian Hoff remained rigid as his eyes rolled around in his head. White saliva emanated from his mouth. To everyone in the room it looked like a fit of some kind, the only difference being that despite the attack Adrian Hoff was laughing. Laughing like a hyena. A sinister uncontrollable laughter that chilled them to the bone.

Suddenly the fit ceased and the young man fell to the floor. Quickly, Abraham, who was a large, powerful man, lifted Hoff onto the bed to cover his nakedness with a sheet.

As he laid him down he felt wetness on his hand. Looking down, he saw that the cuff of his shirt was stained crimson and the stain was growing larger, as though it were blotting paper soaking up spilt red ink.

Removing his arm from under Adrian Hoff's body, his eyes widened as he watched the sheets on the bed turn red with blood, blood that flowed from an invisible wound, out of the young man's side. His mother burst into tears.

Dr Vogel nodded for Marie Blaine to lead the woman away from the room, allowing the two men to examine the young man, who was slowly coming out of his trance.

The door behind them opened allowing Marie Blaine to rejoined her companions having managed to calm the woman down.

Using part of the bed sheet, Vogel wiped Adrian Hoff's side.

The blood had ceased to flow and there was no visible wound mark or scar. Yet the sheets where awash with blood, so much so that he must have lost at least a pint.

Adrian Hoff sat up on the bed. Realising he was naked he instantly covered his body with the blood-stained sheet; an act that was quickly reversed as he jumped from the bed, eyes wild with terror at the sight of the blood.

To save his embarrassment, Rubin Abraham instantly removed his overcoat and gave it to the young man, who covered his body with it. Vogel looked into Adrian's eyes.

"Mr Hoff. I am Dr Hans Vogel. You contacted me, yes?"

Adrian Hoff took in several deep breaths before replying.

"Yes, Doctor Vogel. I recognise you."

"Are you well enough to talk?" The young man nodded.

"Would you care for a drink of water?" Vogel continued.

The young man shook his head as he flopped down in a chair next to the window.

"No. No thank you," he replied, before almost bursting into tears. "Oh my God!" he shook his head. "I am so pleased to see you! Help me please. I think I'm going crazy or I'm..." His voice cracked as he hesitated afraid to say the word. "Possessed"

He grabbed Vogel by the coat and pulled him to him. Their faces almost touched as he spoke.

"I have seen the horrors."

Vogel felt uncomfortable being so close to the young man's mouth. And tried to pull back a little before replying, but Hoff's grip was too tight.

"Horrors like you have never seen," he continued.

Marie Blaine gently took hold of Adrian Hoff's hand and coaxed him to release his grip.

"Please tell us about them. Perhaps we can help."

Adrian Hoff slowly relaxed his grip on Vogel until he was completely free.

Marie Blaine removed a notepad and pen from her bag and waited for Vogel to continue the introductions.

"Allow me to introduce my companions. Professor Abraham is an archaeologist and expert in esoteric studies, not unlike myself. Madam Marie Blaine is a renowned psychic and clairvoyant from your beautiful city of New Orleans. Now, Mr Hoff, we have just witnessed something. What, at this moment in time we, are unable to ascertain, so if you could enlighten us a little more we would be obliged."

Adrian Hoff straightened his back as he spoke.

"What did you witness, Doctor?"

Vogel looked at his companions. He was surprised at the change in character of the young man. He was now quite restrained; in fact he was almost arrogant in his composure.

"We where hoping you could tell us what it was you were witnessing." Vogel replied.

Adrian Hoff rose from his seat straightened his back and stood tall and straight. He buttoned Abraham's coat to the top before replying.

"You wish for me to tell you. Considering the distance you have travelled I will."

Hoff's accent changed he was now speaking English in a broken German accent.

"I saw a fat man with a red-and-purple-veined face in the uniform of a officer of the third Reich with a gun. He and I were shooting at a group of women and some men. The women were screaming and begging for mercy."

Hoff looked Vogel in the eyes.

"No mercy was given."

Hoff suddenly stopped speaking and turned to look out of the window. Vogel, Abraham and Blaine waited for him to continue.

"Please what happened next Mr Hoff?" Vogel eventually asked.

Hoff turned round to look at his guests.

"I killed him.

"You shot him?" Vogel asked.

Hoff walked over towards Vogel and placed his hands either side of Vogel's head.

"No. I clasped my hands, like this. And he died."

Vogel recoiled. Suddenly Adrian Hoff slumped to the floor in a dead faint.

Vatican City, Rome, Italy. November 7th 1969.

The eyelids flickered before opening, to reveal eyes of ice blue that rolled around the sockets and twitched until the dilated pupils grew accustomed to the dimly-lit room.

The narrowing of the eyes was not so that they could become accustomed to the light. The squint was caused through rage.

The Archbishop rose from his seat and walked over to the ornate desk. Removing a hidden key that hung around his neck, he preceded to open a locked drawer. A small plain red book was removed from its hiding place by slender fingers. Manicured fingernails flicked through page after page until it found the required leaf.

Raising the telephone to the ear, he instantly dialled the number. It took several rings before a voice on the other side answered. A male voice, that held a feminine trait.

"Yes?" was the response.

"Muller?" the Archbishop asked. The voice was slow to respond. "Muller?" he repeated the question.

"Yes," it replied.

"Do you know who this is?" The Archbishop speaking in German.

"Yes," was the single response.

The Archbishop smiled as he spoke.

"Good. It has been a long time, has it not?"

Muller's voice on the other end of the line, slowly warmed as his guard dropped.

"Too long,"

He hesitated before asking the next question.

"Is it time?"

The Archbishop paused before answering.

"It was not intended to be so, but shall we say events seem to be dictating the pathway."

"And?" Muller asked.

"I wish to call a meeting of the council," was the response.

Muller's voice grew in pitch as he found it difficult to hide his excitement.

"You wish me to arrange it?"

Unlike Muller's, the Archbishops voice was soft and calm.

"In time. First we have a problem to take care of. Someone has awakened the master, and the time is not right. I wish for you to take care of the matter. But first we must see what damage has been done."

Muller's voice took on a sinister tone. Even over a telephone he could send shivers down most men's spines. Only the man he was talking to was not like most men.

"What do you want me to do?" Muller asked.

The Archbishop slowly traced the outline of his lips with his tongue before replying.

"I wish to meet you, and you alone, one day from now in Boston. Full details will be transferred to you by the usual channels."

"In the meantime you will find as much information as you can about our legacy. The rest will be discussed in person. Good evening, Dietrich."

"And you, Wulff," Muller replied.

The Archbishop replaced the telephone. His blue eyes held a stare so icy it would have chilled the heart of a saint, or killed him, just as he had killed his commanding officer all those years ago in the Austrian border town of Feldkirch.

New Scotland Yard, England. November 7th 1969

Ray lit another cigarette, drawing the air deep into his lungs.

A knock on his office door caused a large cloud of grey smoke to emanate from his mouth as he called out.

"Come in."

The door to the office opened wide, allowing the long slim figure of Detective Sergeant Max Harland to enter. He was in turn followed by the more rounded frame of Detective Constable Ted Doran. Both men stood opposite their boss. Harland was the first to speak.

"You wanted us, guv?"

Ray eyed both men up and down before replying.

Harland was smartly dressed in the latest fashion. His hair was a reasonable length and well groomed, whereas Doran's appearance bordered on the scruffy. His brown leather jacket had seen better days; as for the seat of his corduroy trousers, they were so threadbare and shiny it was only a matter of time before the cheeks of his backside would be visible.

Ray ignored the fact that both men were still standing.

"Got a little job for you."

Neither man responded.

"Fancy a little trip up north?"

Harland, being the senior, replied.

"How far up north?"

Ray took another long pull on his cigarette.

"Durham," he replied

Harland and Doran looked at one another as they waited for Ray to continue.

"Look, lads. I'm sorry to have to pass this on to you, but Banks has kicked it into touch. So I thought we might as well take it up."

Doran reached into his pocket and removed a Polo mint before popping it into his mouth. Harland moistened his lips with his tongue before asking the question.

"What's wrong with it?"

A faint smile flickered across Ray's face before he replied.

"Two sisters think they may have some information regarding the missing children."

Harland was confused.

"Then why haven't the other lot covered it?"

Ray drew his lips tight across his face, in what could only be described as an apologetic grimace, allowing the smoke to filter its way between the gaps in his teeth.

"Ghosts," he half-whispered.

Doran crunched hard on his polo as he spat out the words.

"Ghosts?"

"Yeah. Ghosts," Ray continued. "The girls claim they have seen a ghost murdering ghost children only he is not a ghost; and is a living being."

Harland cocked his head to one side.

"Am I missing something or is this the Twilight Zone?"

Ray raised his hands in the air.

"Look, lads, I know it sounds like a load of bollocks, but whatever Banks misses, we pick up. Just go up there and see the stupid bitches. At least we'll been seen to be doing our bit."

Doran smiled.

"Mightn't be that bad. Good beer up north."

Ray smiled.

"There you are, Max. Ted doesn't mind. Just go up and take a statement. You never know."

Harland ran his hand in frustration through his well-groomed hair.

"You never know? Don't tell me you believe in all that crap?"

Ray's face hardened as he looked at his junior.

"I had an experience, some time ago on a murder investigation. Some bloke, a medium, contacted us. Told us where to find the body, the lot."

Harland looked at his boss.

"And?"

Ray's expression was serious as he answered.

"The body was where he said it would be. It took us no more that a hour or so to eliminate him from the enquiry, and three years to catch the killer."

"Why so long if you had an all-seeing eye on the job?" Harland asked.

Ray shrugged his shoulders.

"Because my governor didn't believe him or his alibi. For six months and fifteen days we hounded that poor git day and night. Broke up his marriage, lost him his job"

"Eventually we found him hanging from the back of   his bathroom door. Poor bastard couldn't take any more. Just go up there, Lads, and do your job. Okay?"

Neither man replied as Ray lit another cigarette. The fresh smoke sent him into a fit of coughing. With a wave of his hand, he ushered the men out of the room.

Christine's House, Durham, England. November 9th 1969.

Calvin, with legs straggling his Harley Davison, patiently waited outside Christine's house for the policemen to leave.

The first to come out of the house was Bolly, who instantly spied Calvin and called him over.

"Shit!" he whispered under his breath.

The last thing he wanted to do was meet the police, but if he had refused then it would look even more suspicious.

Reluctantly he made his way along the path, and joined the rest of the party, who were by now all standing outside the house, Bolly, Christine, Doran and Harland.

The policemen turned and took a double look as they watched the huge frame of Calvin make its way towards them. His appearance emphasised by his long white hair flowing in the light breeze and his eyes covered by sunglasses.

Bolly was the first to speak.

"This is Mr Dane."

Calvin's head nodded a greeting to the policemen, as Bolly continued to speak.

"It was Mr Dane who suggested we contacted you."

Harland viewed the American with his usual quizzical expression.

"How very conscientious and public-spirited," he sarcastically remarked.

Calvin looked at the two policemen through the filtered lenses that covered his eyes. He smiled as he held out his hand to Harland, who reluctantly took it. Once the hand was taken, Calvin's grip tightened.

"You don't believe, it then?"

Harland straightened up, trying to appear taller than he was, which was still five inches shorter than the stranger before him.

"No. In fact I think it's a load of balls."

Calvin smiled as his grip tightened

"A load of balls, yeah. Still, if I were you I'd look under the passenger seat of your car, before your wife does."

Calvin allowed Harland to pull his hand free.

"What?" exclaimed Harland.

Calvin continued to smile.

"There's a gold coloured lipstick case there and it's not your wife's."

A shocked Harland was about to walk away when Calvin caught him by the arm.

"Think about what the girls have said. It just might not be a load of balls."

Harland made no reply as he walked away followed by a confused Doran. Before they reached the gate Calvin called out once more to the policeman.

"Sergeant. The blonde you were with. She placed it there on purpose."

Reaching the car, Doran turned to Harland.

"What the fuck was all that about?"
Harland unlocked the car.

"Fuck knows," was he response.
Doran glanced back at Calvin who was still looking in there direction.

"He's one hell of a spooky bastard."
Harland whispered under his breath.

"How the fuck?"

Flora Carlton's House, Boston, America. November 13th 1969.

Flora Carlton was the wealthy widow of property tycoon Darius Carlton who, although never pushing himself to the fore, had been a known sympathiser of the Klu Klux Klan, secretly providing the movement with substantial financial backing. Upon his tragic and unexpected death, due to a cerebral haemorrhage, Flora, the sole heir to the estate, took over.

Instantly, she cut all ties to the Klan and proceeded to reform the company. The last thing she needed was for her past to be investigated, being the former lover of Reinhard Heydrick and a devout believer in the master race theory. It was therefore inevitable that the Klan had to suffer, regardless of her feelings.

She had been born of the finest German stock, and for the first eighteen years of her life had lived in Pittsburgh, Pennsylvania. Her father, a staunch Nazi sympathiser and admirer of Hitler, had sent her over to Germany to study economics at the University of Heidelberg. It was there that she had taken her first lover, Rudi Rhom a relative of Ernst Rohm, leader of the brown shirts.

For ten years she had lived, studied and worked in Germany, until 1940, when she crossed the border into Switzerland to take up a position in one of the Swiss banking houses.

To the majority of the staff in the bank she had been an enigma; no one outside of the upper hierarchy knew what her position was or whom she worked for. All that they knew was that she had stayed in Switzerland throughout the whole of the war and for five years after it. She had handled one group of accounts that only herself and the manger knew anything about.

She had been introduced to Darius Carlton, who was ten years her senior, by a Catholic Monsignor at a party held by the French ambassador in Rome. They instantly hit it off and were married a fortnight later by the same Monsignor. In a twist of fate, if you believe in fate, one year later, on their return to Rome, Darius Carlton died in his wife's arms while the Monsignor looked on. It was the same Monsignor who was now an Archbishop and whom she was waiting anxiously to greet.

Later that evening after dinner Flora Carlton and her five guests retired to the drawing room for brandy and a smoke.

The atmosphere was congenial, as all six guests passed the time exchanging pleasantries; meaningless discussions meandered on, concerning the state of the country or the world in general. They were all on their guard not to speak of the past just in case a slip of the tongue were picked up by one of the servants.

With the servants now out of the way, the six could relax. It had been several years since they had all been together in one room. There should have been seven for dinner, but one of the party was unable to make it. He was keeping his head low, as they say.

The Israeli secret service was very active in his part of the world, and high-ranking Nazis, especially geneticists, were top of their list. One of the six present was Dietrich Muller an assassin and former officer in the Gestapo. The slight limp he carried was the result of a bullet shattering part of his ankle one night on the Austrian-Swiss boarder. Another was Oswald Weiss Professor of Archaeology, and Mythology specialising in European cultures. He was now based in Toronto Canada, but before and during the war he was part of the Ahnenerbe SS which had been sent off in search of the Shroud of Turin and other religious relics and mystical artefacts. He was especially interested in the Knights Templar, also the Grail legends, and their connection to Joseph of Arimathea and Great Britain.

It was his ambition to excavate specific sites around Britain in search of his goal, including the chapel at Rosslyn in Scotland. He felt sure there was something hidden deep in its foundations. If it meant he had to tear down the chapel stone by stone to find it, or simply to satisfy his curiosity, then he would.

The third was Franz Keitel, now known as Frank Kane, a resident psychologist at the Memorial Hospital Chicago also former member of the Ahnenerbe SS, where he had been head of research into parapsychology. Although he was not a surgeon, he was responsible for the program that had experimented on patients who showed psychic ability. His main research had been to try to isolate the part of the brain that was responsible. He had also initiated tests involving drugs injected into different sections of the brain to see if they could stimulate or enhance the patients abilities. Unfortunately, the mortality rate had been high and the experiments inconclusive.

The only other woman was Ida Kroll. Although mature in years, she still carried herself with a poise that oozed sex appeal. The men's eyes, with the exception of Muller's who's preference was for a different gender, never left her body as she sauntered over to the drinks table to pour herself another brandy.

Finally there was Archbishop Vol, the leader of the little group, and a former major in the Ahnenerbe SS. He was without doubt the most dangerous man among them, a true Aryan; tall blue-eyed, hair blond flecked with silver, the perfect descendant of the Herrenvolk. His psychic abilities were phenomenal, as was his genius. He had been one of Himmler's main strategists, entrusted with overseeing his master plan. It had been his duty to ensure that the Third Reich continued for a millennium, as the Fuhrer had predicted.

The exchange of the children with the Americans for cash and passports had been all his doing. He had never intended to keep the money for himself, which is why all but Muller and Kroll where assassinated. Flora Carlton had also been part of his long-term plan. She had been sent to Switzerland and placed in a bank with the sole purpose of accounting for all of the money filtered out of Germany by whatever route or means and to transfer it into accounts throughout the world. Money that would one day be used for the great dawning, the day when the descendants of the Herrenvolk would inherit the earth.

Vol lit himself a cigarette and waited for the rest of the group to settle down.

"Well, gentlemen and ladies, as nice as it is for us to meet and reminisce, there are more important issues on the horizon. Several days ago, while relaxing, I was drawn into a vision. Not one of my own choice, but one instigated by another. The vision first led me to a restaurant. I saw myself outside, looking in at a man having dinner. You are probably wondering what is so sinister about that. The problem is the man was Hans Vogel. He saw me and dropped his soup spoon back into the bowl, spilling the soup over himself.

At first I was baffled. Why would I have a vision of Vogel. Although he was someone I know of, I have personally never met the man.

Over the next few days I experienced several of these visions, including one of our secret vaults. The other was as strange as the first. This time I saw myself at the railway station in Linz, the town where our Fuhrer grew up. In each of these visions I felt the presence of more than one person.

Then, the other night, while meditating, I felt myself being, what is the word, tapped into."

"There was someone else was with me, who? I don't know. The feeling I got, and the direction, especially in the earlier visions, was strong, possibly one of my descendants. The second presence I have no idea other than, he or she may be a receiver and is subconsciously attuned to my wavelength.

I requested Ida, who still has some input at the centre where our legacy is based, to try and find out what experiments are currently being undertaken. Ida, if you would be so gracious."

Ida Kroll, stood up so she could have centre stage, to address the party.

"Beside the usual telekinesis, remote viewing, etc. it seems that our Mr Quint has allied himself with a former colleague of ours, Gerhard Herff, now better know as The Great Konrad. A stage magician. Those of you who remember him will know of his dabbling in the black arts. A dangerous man with a large ego and little natural talent."

Vol interrupted.

"Because of this side-show magician the whole of the program will have to be brought forward. We will have to make the necessary preparations for the return of our legacy."

Weiss interrupted. "Is it that serious?"

Vol stubbed his cigarette out in the ashtray.

"The receiver, the one who is either consciously or subconsciously tapping into me has become a threat. He is obviously attuned not only to me but also to whoever it is Quint is using for his experiments. According to Ida, it will more than likely be one of my own offspring; that is why I am automatically linked."

"As for this receiver, just before my last vision ended, through his eyes I saw three people in a bedroom. Hans Vogel, an unknown woman and Rubin Abraham, a Jew I should have exterminated some time ago back in Munich

Therefore gentlemen and ladies you will appreciate the seriousness of this situation, knowing two of the three-mentioned and who they are involved with.

Tracking them down will be no easy matter. If I give this receiver more than he or she has bargained for, hopefully it will lead us to our quarry. I am sure once we locate them Dietrich," Vol looked at Muller, "will be more than happy to oblige. As for our showman, unfortunately he has taken a vacation, so, until his return, we will not be able to find out exactly what he was up to. Ida will keep a close watch on all that is happening at the centre; who comes and goes, plus anything that may cause a stir. The time has come for our Mr Quint to dance to the piper, and our legacy to be returned."

Christine's House, Durham, England. November 27th 1969.

Calvin was sitting on the sofa in the centre of the room, facing the fire. His red eyes felt rested in the soft comforting glow from the firelight and the one standard lamp hidden behind the television set, positioned where all televisions are positioned in a place of authority with all of the chairs turned to them.

Bolly and Christine were occupying the chairs either side of him. He acknowledged neither of the women; instead, like a surveillance camera, scanned the room inch by inch.

In the opposite corner to the television next to the window was a large rubber plant standing five and half feet in height, with polished dark green leaves, Aunt Ivy's cherished possession.

Perched in the centre of the mantle in pride of place, was a large ornate clock in a glass case, with a white marble base and a gold frame and a pair of golden cherubs holding the clock face.

Calvin slowly rose from his seat and stood before the fireplace. Noting the time he turned towards the young women.

"Time to say goodnight."

Christine looked at her sister, then at Calvin.

"Are we all going to bed?"

Calvin's eyes were glowing in the strange light, and for once Bolly was in a less argumentative mood.

"Come on Chris, We asked him here, so let him do the job."

Bolly led Christine out of the room. Standing in the doorway, she turned to Calvin.

"You going to be all right?"

Calvin gave only a slight nod of the head in reply. Once Bolly and Christine were out of the room, Calvin switched off the light before making his way to the window.

The moon looked cold and sinister as it peeped through a cloud, tentatively waiting for the right moment to fully show itself.

Calvin whispered to himself and watched the moon slip out of its lair, bathing the room in its mirrored light.

"The Hunter's Moon."

Making his way back to the chair he sat down, hands clasped in front of him and slowly closed his eyes.

Almost fifteen minutes elapsed before the clock on the mantle chimed the hour, eleven o'clock. As the last chime faded away in the semi-darkness Calvin was aware that something was happening. Gingerly he opened his eyes, afraid to startle whatever it was he sensed in the room.

The first thing he noticed was a strange odour. The smell of ether mixed with perfume. He sat upright in the seat. A strange shuffling noise could be heard behind him near the window.

Rising from his seat, he made his way towards the direction of the sound.

The room was plunged into darkness as the moon ran for cover, retreating behind a cloud. Even the glow from the fire seamed to dim and fade away as darkness engulfed the room.

As suddenly as it had beat a retreat, the moon returned, brighter and bolder in the sky, illuminating the room like a huge arc light. Calvin looked around him with eyes like those of a robot taking in all they could before swiftly transmitting the images back to the brain so they could be analysed.

He was no longer standing in the same room. Gone was the old television, in its place was a large flat screen-digital monstrosity with a built-in video. The furniture in the room had also changed. Everything was different, everything except the ornate clock in a glass case.

He was aware of something beside him. Where the rubber plant had stood was the shadowy form of a man.

Calvin made no movement; he even controlled his breathing, afraid to break the silence, as he watched the man make his way towards the sofa.

A faint sobbing cut through the air with an icy chill, the sobbing of a little child. The man gently picked up a cushion off the chair and held it behind his back.

"Hush now, my sweet, angel. Hush." The phantom whispered.

The child continued to sob. Calvin's body was rigid, motionless like a window dresser's mannequin as he silently watched.

"Hush my precious," the ghostly voice continued." Soon you will join the rest of my angels, safe in the arms of God, where no one will ever be able to harm you."

Before the child could utter a reply the man pressed the cushion into her face. She struggled in vain as he held the cushion firm until the last drop of breath was drained out of her little body.

Kneeling down he gently stroked the hair of the lifeless child before him and smiled. Lifting his head, he turned, and looked in the direction of Calvin, before removing his glasses to wipe the lenses with his handkerchief.

Calvin drew in a small gasp of air, the first sight of emotion he had shown throughout the whole macabre scene. The face before him was undoubtedly that of Meynell. Not the young Meynell that he had met, but an older, mature version. Suddenly the vision vanished and the room was plunged once more into darkness.

Calvin, relying more on his psychic than physical abilities, made his way towards the door that lead out into the hallway.

Standing in the moonlit hallway, he watched and waited. It was there again, that awful sickly smell of perfume and ether, a horrid surgical smell that overpowers and turns the stomach. The instant the sickly smell appeared the sound of heavy footsteps could be heard slowly climbing up the stairs.

His eyes followed a bodiless sound as it made its way towards the first landing under the stained-glass window. Particles of dust danced in the moonlight, congregating in a mass to form the shape of the man carrying a different child up the stairs.

Calvin silently followed the phantom up the stairs to the first landing, and watched all that Bolly had described. The child's begging and pleading as she hung onto the door handle for grim death. Her hands been wrenched away from the bedroom door by the man as he carried the child unceremoniously along the corridor towards the bathroom at the far end, next to the stairs leading to the next floor.

A shaft of light illuminated the first floor corridor. It came from Christine's room as Bolly popped out her head.

"What's happening?"

Calvin's annoyance was made clear.

"Get the fuck inside." He hissed.

Bolly was quick to reply.

"Only asked. Miserable git."

The figure vanished the instant Bolly opened the door.

"Shit." Calvin rounded on her. "Get back in the room and fucking stay there."

Bolly reluctantly retreated back into the bedroom, with the whispering voice of Christine asking her what was happening.

The corridor was once more plunged into darkness. Calvin made his way towards the bathroom with its tiled white walls making it look like a hospital morgue. To his disappointment the bathroom, was empty with the exception of a large white claw-foot enamel bath that stood in its centre.

Calvin left the bathroom closing the door behind him and was about to walk away, cursing Bolly under his breath, when he heard a faint noise coming from the other side of the door. The noise grew and grew it was the unmistakable sound of water being splashed about in a bath. Gently pushing the door open to enter, his body grew rigid. In the middle of the room was the man, his face twisted in anger, as his long slender hands fought with a tiny pair of hands that thrashed and clawed at the fiend above.

Calvin rushed at the figure to pull him off and save the helpless victim struggling for her life under the water. The instant he touched the figure of the man, the bathroom was plunged into darkness, illuminated only by the light of the moon outside.

Calvin fell to his knees, slamming his fists hard against the side of the bath.

"You bastard," he cried out, the tiled room amplifying his cry of frustration. " You stupid bastard.

With hands still clasping the side of the bath his mouth twisted in a snarl he turned his head towards the direction of the door, before rising to his feet to make his way out of the bathroom and into the corridor once more.

The sound of footsteps could be heard once again, only this time from the floor above. Rushing to the stairs that led to the top floor of the house, Calvin ascended them three at a time.

With no windows, the long corridor was immersed in darkness. Although Calvin's eyes found the semi-darkness comforting, in total darkness he was as blind as the next man.

Feeling along the wall with his right hand until it found a door, he turned the handle to enter a room filled with toys.

A train set was laid out upon a table and obviously cherished by its owner. Beyond it, a large rocking horse stood in front of the window next to a table full of toy soldiers, all neatly lined up ready for battle.

Calvin took his time as he tried in the faint light to make out all that the room held. One thing did catch his eye. Framed on the wall were several pages of a newspaper.

Carefully making his way towards them, Calvin squinted as his eyes strained in the semi-darkened room to read what they said. He dared not touch for fear of them disappearing; instead he did his best to read the headlines on the one closest to the window.

'Eminent Couple Die in Suicide Pact.'
The rest of the print was too small for him to make out. Curiosity satisfied, he left the room and returned to the corridor, feeling his way as before until he came to another room and entered it.

It was a bathroom similar to the one on the floor below, only this one smelt dank and dirty. In the corner of the bathroom were several small sacks of white plaster. In the pot basin against the wall was an enamel bucket and a large stick, obviously for mixing the plaster. Calvin left the room, bemused at its contents.

He was about to continue to feel his way along the corridor when a strange red glow emanated from under a door in the room at the far end of corridor. Feeling his way along he reached the door. Tentatively gripping the handle, he opened it and silently slipped inside the room.

The room was engulfed in a red glow. He scanned it in his usual manner. The red glow was coming from a solitary bulb suspended from a socket in the centre of the room, or to be precise the darkroom.

In one corner were the developing trays and in the other a large high-backed leather chair facing the wall. Making his way towards some photographs and negatives hanging from several lines that criss-crossed the room, he examined them with his eyes, afraid to touch.

Carefully picking his way among them, he stopped only briefly to let out a sigh of disbelief and sadness at images they held.

Reaching the chair, he glanced at the wall it was facing. The wall was filled with framed photographs of children, children naked from the shoulders upwards at any rate it was only the upper part of their bodies that were showing.

Children, all girls, all aged between three and thirteen and all with their eyelids stitched together and a hideous grin, a toothless grin that stretched across the face, as if the teeth where covered by a grotesque boxers gum shield.

The smell was back, the sweet sickly smell. Slowly he turned his head. Sitting in the chair behind him was the man, his cold blue eyes admiring one by one the framed photographs on the wall, like a proud parent looking through his family album.

Rising from his seat, the man walked over to the corner of the room and crouched down. His hands grabbed hold of a sack and began to drag it towards the door.

His face grimaced in pain as he held his back, rubbing it with one of his hands before continuing with both hands to pull the sack to the door and out into the now-illuminated corridor. Calvin the ever-silent observer continued to watch and follow.

Calvin's attention was distracted by an open door leading to a room he had not entered. The room was ablaze with the flickering light of candles. At the far end of the room was a small altar with two large wooden statues of kneeling cherubs painted gold.

Returning to the corridor, Calvin watched the man who continued to head towards the stairs at the far end of the corridor. Suddenly he vanished.

Calvin quickly made his way towards the stairs, lead by his ears instead of his eyes, as they followed the rhythmic sound of one dull thud after another.

A shape began to materialise. Below him was the figure of the man dragging the sack down each stair one by one, thud after thud, downwards to the entrance hall before pulling the sack in the direction of the kitchen.

The sickly odour vanished. Calvin had learnt that no odour meant no man.

His intuition was verified when he rushed into the kitchen to find no sign of either the man or the sack.

Opening the door leading out into the garden, he stepped outside. The night was cold and damp while the sky above threatened rain.

Calvin looked about him. Something, something over in a corner of the garden caught his eye. At first he thought it a trick of the light that was until he heard the unmistakable sound of someone digging.

In the far corner of the garden was the man, digging a hole no more that three feet long, and three feet deep. Not a big hole, but then it was large enough for his purpose.

The hole dug to his satisfaction, the man gently laid the sack inside and carefully shovelled the earth back into place. Patting the final shovel full of soil onto what was now his latest victim's resting-place.

Calvin stood motionless and watched the final act unfold as the figure knelt down over the shallow grave to say a prayer before finally melting away into the night.

He was about to return to the house when a strange sensation stopped him. A damp chill ran through his body, a chill that numbed his bones. Instantly he knew this was different. Different to the monthly ritual he has just witnessed.

The silence was broken by an eerie sound, like the distant cry of a vixen calling her mate. Calvin remained as still and as quiet as possible, while the cry on the wind drew closer and closer, until it called out his name.

"Calvin."

Something grasped hold of his hand, something that should not be able to hold on to living fingers. Something cold, wet and lifeless was tugging on his fingers, like a maid milking a cow.

"Calvin." It called out to him again.

Looking downwards, his red eyes meet large, dark, begging eyes. Eyes that pleaded with his, as the mouth below the eyes opened and called out his name, once again.

"Calvin. Help us, Calvin."

Calvin stood transfixed as the little hand released its grip. With arms outstretched the tiny figure slowly glided backwards into the shadows.

Calvin raised his fingers to his lips and tasted them.

"Salt," he whispered to himself.

Large drops of rain fell from the skies. As if on cue, the heavens had decided to have their say. Calvin stood in the rain, staring vacantly into the night.

A shaft of light cut into the garden, followed by Bolly's voice.

"Calvin. Calvin, what are you doing?"

Without replying, Calvin turned and walked back towards the waiting Bolly.

Christine's House, Durham, England. 1.30am November 27th 1969.

Calvin lifted a welcoming cup of coffee to his lips. A drop of water dripped from his hair and plopped into the steaming liquid.

"Shit! " he moaned.

He brushed his hair backward from his face before settling back in the chair, ensuring to tuck the towel that was around his waist between his knees. The only piece of cloth between him and complete nudity.

Christine had offered to run him a bath after his drenching in the garden, but knowing what he now knew he declined the offer. He was more content to sit in the chair and drink his coffee, watching his clothes dry before the fire.

"Well, come on. Tell us what happened." Bolly's patience was running out.

Calvin took another sip of his coffee, deliberately keeping them waiting.

"Jesus, what did you see?" Bolly's impatience was growing.

Sitting upright he finally answered.

"Well it wasn't Jesus. But I did see the man and the children."

Christine closed her eyes and tightened her lips before speaking.

"Then the house is haunted?"

Calvin once again pushed his hair back from his face before replying.

"Yes and no," was his reply.

Bolly was becoming annoyed.

"Fucking hell, it's like pulling teeth. Just tell us what you saw."

Calvin smiled at Bolly.

"Ever the lady. I told you. I saw the man and the children. As for the house being haunted in the true sense, no, it's not."

Christine was puzzled.

"If it's not haunted, what is it?"

"Images," was his reply.

Bolly drew closer.

"What do you mean images?"

Calvin looked at both young women.

"Visions. We all saw visions. That's why the mediums couldn't pick anything up. This is not a true haunting. It's a prophecy. You, Mrs Fenton, your aunt and myself have all been witnesses to a prophecy, a glimpse into the future, a time portal. Bolly suspected Meynell of being the man, but how could he? Meynell is far younger than the phantom murderer of little children that haunts this house. The answer is that Meynell was older because it hasn't happened yet. I don't know the reason for these visions. And that's exactly what they are, visions. The full moon is undoubtedly one contributory factor and the other -well-" Calvin hesitated. " I believe it was Christine."

Christine was quick to retort.

"Me! Why me?"

Calvin took another sip of coffee before answering.

"With the exception to the full moon, the only time this haunting occurred was when young children lived here or, as in the case of Mrs Fenton's sister, a sensitive soul. Christine's sensitivity is only other factor. There was no haunting when Simon was not at home so. Sorry, Christine, it has to be you.

"But what about me? I saw it as well," Bolly interceded.

Calvin laughed at Bolly's observation.

"You sensitive! You're about as sensitive as a wooden condom."

"Very funny," she retorted.

Calvin continued.

"That's why the mediums couldn't pick anything up. They would have had to be here when the moon was full, and with Christine or someone like her."

Bolly and Christine sat in silence as they tried to absorb the findings.

Looking into his empty coffee cup, then at Christine, Calvin asked.

"Could you make me another coffee?"

Christine eyed him suspiciously.

"You're not trying to get rid of me, are you?" she asked.

Calvin smiled.

"Don't be so suspicious. All I want is another coffee."

Christine reluctantly took his cup and left the room.

The instant she closed the door, Calvin leant closer to Bolly; drawing her nearer to him, he whispered.

"I saw something else. Tonight."

He held his hand up, preventing Bolly from speaking.

"A boy. The boy in the sketch."

Bolly was puzzled.

"What's so strange about that? Between us we have seen most of the children in the sketches."

Calvin sighed before answering.

"This one is different. Remember, I said he didn't belong there. When Mrs Fenton's sister drew him he was the future. Not any more."

Bolly looked for the first time directly into Calvin's eyes. Eyes that pulsated like the fire in the grate.

"You mean he is really dead?"

Calvin nodded his head.

"Fresh kill."

Bolly drew in a deep breath as a tear appeared in the corner of her eye.

"Meynell?"

Calvin broadened his chest as he placed both hands behind his head before replying.

"That's what I intend to find out."

Bolly was quick to intercede.

"You mean, we."

Calvin shook his head and sighed.

"What's the point? Okay. We."

An Old Derelict Churchyard, Near Weaton, Kent, England. 1.30am November 27th 1969.

Shafts of light from the police torches flitted from headstone to headstone like luminous moths.

Two lone figures sat huddled together in the rear of the police car, patiently waiting and praying for a voice to call out

"We've found him, he's okay."

Their wait was in vain; no call came. The only sound that greeted them was the apologetic, monotonous drone of the police inspector as he returned to the car, accompanied by the dejected faces of his colleagues

Christine's House, Durham, England. 3.55am November 28th 1969.

The last embers of the fire struggled to give out what heat or light they could. Calvin, his body curled in a foetal position on the sofa, twitched and moaned as he slept.

His sleep was filled with a solitary dream, only this was not a normal dream, or a nightmare. It was a dream in reverse form, black was white and white black, like a negative.

Calvin saw himself at the rear of his cottage. The ground was full of snow as he climbed in slow motion over the rear wall and fell into the churchyard behind. Scrambling to his feet, he stumbled from gravestone to gravestone, accompanied by the rapid beating of his heart.

Behind him a large shape mounted the wall, taunting, laughing at his terrified fumbling figure. He could see himself as if he were a third party. There was something covering part of his face, but he couldn't make out what it was.

The figure jumped down from the wall and drew closer, causing the pain in his chest to grow as an unseen hand griped his heart, forcing him to fall to the ground, clutching his chest.

The clock in the churchyard cranked itself up ready to chime, as the pain in his chest caused his heart to pump faster, louder until it felt as if it would explode inside his ribcage. He let out a scream, just as the clock on the mantle struck four.

Still shaking and covered in sweat Calvin immediately began to dress. He was wearing his under-shorts when the door opened. Bolly and Christine rushed in.

"What's wrong? What happened?" they asked in unison.

Calvin ignored them and continued to get dressed, with Bolly as usual the first to respond.

"What are you doing?"

"I'm going," he replied.

"Was it the boy?" Bolly asked.

Christine interrupted.

"What boy?"

By now Calvin was almost dressed.

"Just leave it, and go back to bed."

Bolly drew closer to him.

"If it wasn't the boy, then what the fuck was it?"

Calvin pulled on a boot.

"Look, I've done all I can."

Bolly snatched the remaining boot and glared at him.

"You've done all you can? What about the future?" she snapped.

Calvin snatched the boot back. His voice was angry.

"The future is all I'm interested in. My future."

Bolly looked at him and for the first time his red eyes no longer looked demonic. They looked more like an Easter bunny, more pink and frightened.

"You're afraid, something's put the shits up you, and you're running away," she retorted.

Calvin rose from his seat and brushed passed the silent Christine and out into the hallway, closely followed by an infuriated Bolly.

Calvin opened the door to leave. The sound of Bolly's rebuke rang in his ears as he closed the door behind him.

"Go on, you shity bastard! Piss off!"
Her back slumped against the panelled wall in the hallway as she gently slid down, crying.

Flora Carlton's House, Boston, America. November 30th 1969.

A black limousine drew up outside Flora Carlton's house. Muller was the first to alight, followed by small squat man with a bald head. The roundness of the face was emphasised by round black-framed spectacles that made him look like a cuddly panda. Gerhard Herff, or, as he was now known, The Great Konrad.

A third person climbed out of the car and followed behind Muller and Konrad. His name was Sommers, a mean, cold calculated killer who took great pleasure in garrotting his victims, and a member of the Stasi, East Germany's secret police. As far as Sommers was concerned, killing was a pastime, and a sexual fix. If he had not taken it up for a profession, then he would undoubtedly have become a serial killer. At least this way he was paid for his enjoyment, plus the bonus of not having to worry about covering it up.

Konrad was led into a small study and offered a drink. His hands shook, causing the ice to tinkle against the glass. The shock on Konrad's face at the sight of Muller in his dressing room at the Emerson Majestic Theatre Boston sent more than butterflies racing around his stomach.

He knew Muller only slightly, having met him on two previous occasions. They had both been amicable enough. What Konrad feared most was his reputation; in the Gestapo Muller had been known as a ruthless perfectionist, feared even by his colleagues, a close friend of Himmler who shared not only his dream but his passion for the occult, and would stop at nothing to please his master.

Konrad made no protest as he was led out of the theatre by Muller and the younger Sommers. Had he known Sommers or the extent of his reputation, then he would have filled his pants. If the two men's presence in the room wasn't bad enough, then the next face he would encounter would shake him to the core.

The door to the study opened, and in walked Vol. Konrad's glass shook, spilling part of the drink on the floor. His heart raced at the sight of the smartly-dressed six-foot tall man, his grey blond hair cropped short in a spiked flattop, and ice-cold blue eyes. Konrad knew all too well that he was in deep shit.

Vol was not just a major in the SS or a psychic. He was an occultist of the highest order. As for Konrad's party tricks and occult offerings they were no more than cheap games in comparison to the man before him.

As for Konrad's coven consisting of ten women and two other men, it was no more an excuse to have sex. Dressing in their robes accompanied by arcane ceremonies, were great to watch, but, compared to the man who now towered above him, they were depraved parlour games no more.

Vol was a Satanist of the highest order; therefore being a bishop in the Church of Rome was to him the greatest of ironies, allowing him to indulge his blasphemy to the extreme, for Vol was the epitome of evil.

"Gerhard, how nice to see you."

Vol held out his hand. Konrad, still shaking, took it. Vol smiled as held on tight, glaring into Konrad's eyes. A moment or two, no more, just enough to make the frightened Konrad almost vomit with fear.

Vol released his grip before speaking.

"Your drink, it is almost empty; allow me to refill it for you."

Vol removed the glass from Konrad's hand and walked over to the drinks cabinet.

"Whisky, is it not? "

Konrad nodded his head. Returning to his guest, he nodded for the other two men to leave the room.

"Please take a seat."

Konrad obeyed, Vol remained standing.

"Gerhard, Gerhard what have you been up to?"

Konrad remained silent as Vol continued to speak.

"There I was relaxing, and the next thing I knew I was drawn into your little game."

Vol clasped both arms of Konrad's chair as he leant down, his face almost touching his.

"You have been a very silly man, You have awakened someone who was not ready to be awakened and now all of our plans have been, shall we say, affected. Do you understand?"

Konrad shook his head. Vol continued.

"No, of course you would not. You are only an insignificant louse, an irritant. Still, irritants can sometime cause distress, and that is what you have done."

Konrad's breath came in short gasps; he thought he was about to die, and closed his eyes in anticipation. Suddenly Vol straightened up.

"No time to dwell on the past, we must look to the future."

Konrad slowly opened his eyes, to see Vol lighting a cigarette.

"Now, because of your, shall we say unintentional interference with our plans, we have had to bring our timetable forward. Still, nothing in life ever goes according to plan, even mine. So, my friend, I wish to know all about your little experiments. Especially what the outcome was, and who was involved. You see, I was not the only one who was drawn into your game; you opened the gate for an enemy to become involved."

Konrad spoke for the first time.

"You mean the freak?"

Vol looked at him. The choice of word was not one he was expecting.

"Freak? " he asked.

Konrad's voice grew in power as he spoke.

"Yes the albino, the one who fled the centre."

Vol straightened himself up.

"I was informed he was dead."

Konrad's voice stuttered as he replied.

"That's what Quint thought until we held one of our meetings and Karl went into a trance."

"Karl?" Interrupted Vol.

"Yes," Konrad continued." He was the psychic we were using. He is one of the most powerful psychics in the centre."

Vol waved his hand.

"Continue?"

"As I said, we had Karl all wired up and he tapped into the freak."

Vol sat down.

"Tell me, was there anyone else you may have tapped into?" he asked.

Konrad thought for a moment.

"No, not that I am aware of, why?"

Vol did not reply to his question but asked one of his own.

"What was your involvement in this? If Karl is a powerful psychic, why would they need you?"

Konrad shuffled in his seat.

"Quint thought that the use of the occult, coupled with a psychic, might bring results."

"And what were the results?" Vol asked.

Konrad gulped down the drink before replying.

"He was hoping to draw out someone from his past, someone he feared. He said that he and the centre would never be safe as long as this group existed.

At first he tried to quiz me. Obviously, knowing my background, he thought I might know of their existence."

Vol pursed his lips before speaking.

"And what group is this?"

Konrad was no fool; he knew whose clutches he had fallen into. The clutches of the very group Quint sought.

"The keepers of the seal," he replied.

Vol rose from his seat.

"And what does Quint know of them?"

Konrad's stomach went into a cramp as his tongue fumbled for an answer.

"He heard there was a mystical sect formed by Himmler, who were given a task so secret only the inner core knew exactly what it was."

"It was thought to be myth, but Quint believed in their existence, and has for some months. Ever since he had a dream he has been in fear of his life."

Vol lit another cigarette.

"And what was this dream?" he asked.

Konrad fiddled with the glass in his hands before replying.

"You will probably laugh, but Quint had a recurring dream about a white horse. On its back was an angel with burning eyes, and the angel to him meant death."

Vol pondered a moment before responding.

"You will resume your experiments with Quint. I will expect you to report all that happens directly to me. I need not warn you of the consequences should this meeting ever be disclosed."

Konrad assured him of his discretion and how proud he would be to serve. With a wave of his hand Vol had Konrad dismissed and taken back to the theatre by Sommers. After Konrad had left, Ida Kroll and Muller joined Vol in the study. He turned to his companions.

"It seams there is more to this little episode than we thought." He looked at Ida Kroll. "The albino, the one who escaped."

"Yes, he is believed to be dead." was her reply.

Vol's face was smug as he replied.

"Not according to our magician. So we now have a situation where Vogel has a receiver tapping into this Karl, and myself. "

Ida Kroll interrupted.

"Karl. Yes I should have realised it would be him. Then that answers it all. Karl is one of your offspring, as is Wolf."

The instant she said it she knew she had made a mistake.

"That freak is no offspring of mine." Vol's temper erupted like a volcano. "His mother's blood was tainted."

Ida Kroll apologised profusely.

"I'm sorry, I did not mean to imply anything, I am so sorry."

Vol, although angry at the implication that an albino could have sprung from his loins, continued.

"You, Dr Kroll, will provide us with a plan of the centre."

Ida Kroll interrupted.

"If I may speak. I have secured Quint's second-in-command to help us."

Vol look at her suspiciously.

"Second-in-command?"

Ida Kroll continued.

"Yes A man called Culver, he believes Quint has become paranoid, and is losing his mind and is a liability to the state. Also, this Culver is hungry for power; he hates the centre and all it stands for, believing as he does in old-fashioned greed as the best way of obtaining results. Plus the fact that the Americans are embarrassed about having twenty-nine pure-bred Aryans on their hands. If it were to get out about the centre and how the students, as they are known, were acquired, the repercussions would be astronomical."

Vol sat down.

"And has this Culver been involved in any of the experiments there?"

"No," she replied. "He is not interested."

Vol stroked his chin.

"Good. Then he has no idea what he has."

Ida Kroll smiled.

"As far as he is concerned he has a collection of Hitler's misfits, the result of a madman's dream, and the Americans, fell for it. Obviously, not all the of the children have psychic abilities. We knew that, but the Americans didn't, myself and a couple of aides covered up for the others by altering results. As they got older we schooled them ourselves. "

"They were the children of physicists, biologists, writers; a collection of the finest brains that the Fatherland could produce. And the Americans nurtured, schooled and allowed us to secretly hone their abilities right under their noses. Quint was only interested in the psychics and Karl was undoubtedly the star, he was guarded night and day by Quint's personal bodyguard. No one was allowed to talk to him or ask him questions.

Ever since Wolf escaped Quint has been paranoid, living in fear, God knows why. He sees Karl as his protector, against what I don't know but the rivalry between Wolf and Karl was intense, and Karl hated him with a passion."

Vol turned to Muller.

"And what of Vogel?"

Muller interrupted.

"He has gone to ground, along with a young man called Adrian Hoff. Obviously he is the receiver."

Vol controlled his temper.

"Why was he not killed?"

Muller was one of the few people who were not afraid of Vol. His eyes locked on to his inquisitors without blinking.

"I sent two men to take care of it. It was on the news no more than ten minutes ago, that a car with two bodies inside has been pulled out of the river."

Vol took a long pause before speaking.

"We will let events unfold while we prepare for the return of our legacy. Dr Kroll, you will gain the confidence of this Culver, no matter what it takes. We will need him at a later date. As for that side-show magician he will do as he is told. And once his usefulness has expired, then so shall he. Our friend Dr Vogel is a little different. He will re-emerge, and, once he does, he will be eliminated."

Dukes House, Albridge Kent, England. December 1st 1969.

The pathetic figure of Mr Duke stared out of his window, watching the children play football in the street. His mind drifted back to the time, only a few days ago, when it had been his boy who was kicking the ball against the wall and upsetting the neighbours.

An unmarked police car pulled up with four men inside. The doors of the car opened, allowing three of the men to get out. Duke moved away from the window and sat down in a chair.

There was a knock at the door as Duke drew his hand lengthways down his face and let out a sigh. He was in two minds whether to ignore the callers or not. His mind was numb; he could neither think rationally or irrationally. The past few days had been the most traumatic in his life. His son had gone missing and his wife was so sedated she had no idea what week it was, let alone what day. And to top it all he had been the prime suspect in the police investigations. Now another collection of policemen was outside, all waiting for their piece of him. He was so depressed he felt like ending it all.

The knocks on the door grew louder, followed by a voice calling through the letterbox.

"Mr Duke, it's D.S. Cool, I have two detectives from Scotland Yard. They wish to speak to you."

Duke opened the door to allow the three men to enter his little terraced house with its small cosy front room and single window that looked out onto another row of terraced houses opposite.

Duke flopped down in his chair without any customary greetings.

D.S. Cool broke the ice.

"This is D.S. Harland and D.C. Doran from Scotland Yard."

Duke made no response as Harland looked round before speaking.

"Sorry to bother you sir, I understand you have had a rough time."

Duke looked up at him and gave a slight laugh.

"Rough time. My boy's missing, possibly dead, and my wife's gone insane, refusing to have anything to do with me, through your lot accusing me of my own boy's disappearance. Rough time. Fuck you and fucking rough time."

Harland felt sorry for the man before him, but the questioning he would have to go through was customary in these cases.

Suddenly Duke jumped up and rushed to the window, yanking the net curtains to the floor.

"See them kids out there, kicking a ball around. My boy should be out there, laughing, fighting and getting dirty. Why isn't he? I'll tell you why, because some fucking pervert's got him. Some sick bastard's got my little boy."

Duke fought back the tears.

"My little boy who went out to play like all kids do every day, only, only...."
Duke finally broke down and began to cry.

All the time while Duke was talking Doran was looking around the room. He noticed a framed photograph on the sideboard. Nudging Harland, Doran pointed to the picture.

"Guv."
Harland had no idea what he wanted him to look at.

"The photo." Doran nodded in its direction.
Harland looked at it.

"Yes."
Doran lifted it up to examine it closer before replying.

"It's the same boy, the one in the sketches."
Harland frowned.

"What sketches?"

"The ones at Durham," Doran replied.
Harland examined it closely.

"Are you sure?"
Doran shrugged his shoulders.

"Not a hundred percent, but..."
Harland held the photo up.

"This your boy, Mr Duke?"
Duke looked up at the photograph.

"Had it took at school, a week before he..."
Before Duke could finish the sentence D.S Cool took it from Harland.

"He looks totally different here compared with the photo you gave us."

Duke rose from his seat and walked over to the sideboard. Opening a drawer, he removed a pack of four photographs, all the same as the larger one.

"Here's some copies. Take what you want."
Harland took one and placed it in his pocket as
Doran continued to stare at the face of the child.

Calvin's Cottage, Litton Village, England. December 1st 1969

The bedroom was sparsely furnished with a wooden floor and a low-beamed ceiling. There were no items of luxury. Functional was the word, with a wardrobe in one corner and a chest of drawers in the other. The only luxury item, if it could be termed a luxury, was a cheval mirror in the corner of the room. Still, the room managed to maintain a welcoming feel to it.

Calvin lay on his side in bed and slowly closed his eyes. For the first time he was afraid of sleep, afraid of the dream in Christine's house and the fact that it might recur.

The night outside was still and quiet, allowing the winter frost to make ice flowers on the inside of the bedroom windowpane, as Calvin slowly drifted off into a light sleep.

His slumber was soon disturbed as a blast of cold air rushed passed his face. Without lifting his head he opened his eyes. Nothing could be seen in the dimly-lit room, as a strange noise emanated from the foot of the bed. Scratching.

Gently raising himself up. He looked around the room. The scratching stopped. He was about to lie back down when a cold blast of wind, mixed with a fine spray of water hit him in the face.

Startled, he once again looked about the room, the tall mirror in the corner catching his eye.

A liquid face began to form in the glass, followed by the body of the young boy. The body slowly emerged from the mirror and glided towards Calvin, who remained motionless.

The child's mouth opened.

"Help us, Calvin, help us."

Four other faces appeared in the mirror. Each face was as white as alabaster, eyelids stitched together and a sinister grimace more than a smile. The same grimace he had seen on the children in the photographic room that night in Christine's house.

The faces in the mirror melted back to where they had came from as the young boy, arms outstretched continued to plead. Before drifting back into the mirror, and disappearing into the glass.

Calvin switched the bedside light on and looked around. The sound of the wind could be faintly heard outside as he swung his legs out of bed and stood up. Suddenly his feet felt something wet. On the floor beside the bed where the boy had stood no more than a second ago, was a pool of water. Calvin touched it with his fingers before tasting it. Salt. It tasted of salt.

Christine's House, Durham, England. December 2nd 1969.

Christine and Aunt Ivy were busy packing when there was a knock at the door, Bolly volunteered to answer it. Standing in the porch were Harland and Doran. Bolly instantly folded her arms and leant against the door jamb.

"Yes?" she enquired.

Harland scratched the side of his cheek; a nervous reaction before an anticipated apology.

"May we come in?"

Bolly refused to budge.

"Got a search warrant?"

Harland disliked apologising at the best of times, but he could be a diplomat when he needed to be.

"Please, Miss, we would like to have another word with you and your sister."

Bolly slowly stood aside, allowing them to enter. Both men were shown into the sitting room and awaited the arrival of Christine and their aunt.

Harland stood to greet the older woman.

"We haven't met. I'm...."

Bolly cut him short.

"This is the arsehole who accused us of being on drugs."

Their aunt made no comment as Harland shuffled uneasily where he stood.

"I've apologised for that. Please could we start again? We have called about the sketches, the ones you say the old lady gave you. We would especially like to see the one of the boy."

Bolly walked over to the cabinet where they were kept.

"He's dead, isn't he?" she said.

Harland looked at her quizzically.

"Dead. Why do you say that?"

Christine interrupted.

"Because Calvin said."

She never finished the sentence as Bolly's glare cut through her like a knife.

Harland instantly picked up on it as Bolly handed him the sketch.

"Why would he say the boy was dead? As far as we know he is only missing."

Doran held the photograph up against the sketch. It was undoubtedly the boy.

"Well?" Harland continued.

The three women looked at one another before Bolly answered.

"Because he is a psychic. He stayed here the other night and the boy appeared to him."

"You're saying he saw a ghost?" Harland exclaimed.

"Yes." she replied.

Doran rolled the sketch up to take it away, allowing Harland to continue the questioning.

"So this Calvin claims he's also seen ghosts?" Christine tried to explain but only succeeded in confusing the issue about them not actually being ghosts but visions from the future."

Harland had heard enough. He was more interested in the fact that Calvin had claimed that the boy was dead. Before he had chance to continue Bolly intervened.

"Look, Calvin didn't do it. He was with us most of the time, and if it's the boy who is missing in Kent, then it would be impossible for him to have got down there and back up here, unless he had a jet. Anyway, did you find that lipstick?"

Harland made no reply to her question.

"We would like this American's address." he insisted.

Bolly shrugged her shoulders.

" Okay. But if I were you I would treat him with respect."

"And why is that?" Harland gave a little laugh.

"Will he put a curse on us?"

Bolly returned the smile.

"You'll soon find out if you don't."

Public House,
London, England.
December 2nd 1969.

Calvin could not sleep after the second visit of the boy. His mind fought with itself; he knew what he had to do, but he was afraid. If he helped, then his own life would be in danger. In his own words.

"What the fuck."

Climbing aboard his Harley, he drove non-stop to London. December being the time of year most people are winding down and preparing for Christmas, he knew that if he hung around the American embassy long enough he would see a maggot or two as he called them, slither out. And his judgement was proven right. In fact the maggot that emerged later that day was as if he had been hand picked.

Calvin followed a party of three men and five women as they made their way on foot to a public house not far away from the Embassy. The maggot Calvin was interested in was a man called Angelo. Calvin had met him while at the centre. He was one of Quint's lackeys, and someone who knew about the work there and Calvin in particular. Angelo was a dangerous man and not to be underestimated, but Calvin figured he would at least have respect or frighten him enough to do what was asked. As for the repercussions, he would face them when they came.

Calvin sat unnoticed in the corner of the almost empty pub, patiently sipping a pint of Guinness, watching, waiting for the moment to strike. Finally it presented itself. Angelo rose from his seat and made his way to the toilet. Instantly Calvin followed.

Standing in front of the trough Angelo unzipped his flies. Out of the corner of his eye he noticed someone standing next to him. The man wasn't having a pee, he was looking straight at Angelo.

The first thought that ran through his head was, fucking pervert. He was about to tell him to fuck off when he realised who it was looking at him.

His mind raced back in time, back to the centre, to the laboratory. On one side of the table sat Karl, tall and blond, similar in features to Calvin, only he was not an albino, and on the other side, Calvin. They were stripped to the waist and both had wires connected to their bodies, especially the head. In the room was Quint, a male doctor, and Ida Kroll. Karl and Calvin where both concentrating on a rat in a glass tube. The rat went one way towards Karl then back towards Calvin. Both men forced the rat towards the other. The loser's bell would ring if the rat broke their ray. The rat squealed in pain as it went one way, then the next. Finally a bell rang. In a fit of temper Karl smashed the tube with his hand, crushing the rat.

The thoughts that ripped through Angelo's mind had caused him to pee on his shoes. Calvin laughed. Coming out of his daydream, Angelo instantly went for a gun inside his coat. Calvin grabbed his hand and kneed him in the groin. Angelo fell to the floor, allowing Calvin to remove his gun and toss it into the trough.

The door opened and in walked one of Angelo's friends. Before he had time to help, Calvin was upon him. Once he had a grip on his flesh Calvin used his power. The man began to convulse. His eyes rolled upward in their sockets as blood poured out of every orifice. Within seconds his lifeless body slumped to the floor.

Angelo had recovered and tried to retrieve his gun from the trough, only to be kicked in the face, sending him flying across the toilet floor.

"Listen to me, roach," Calvin snarled. "The only reason you're still alive and not dead like your friend is because I need you to do me a favour."

Angelo tried to rise to his feet.

"They'll get you. You freaky bastard. Once they know you're alive they'll kill you."

Calvin smiled at his threat.

"And who'll tell them, not your buddy over there."

Angelo cried out in pain as Calvin grabbed him by the hair and ripped a large piece of it out of his head.

"You know what I can do." Calvin held up the clump of hair in his hands. "With this I can come to you any time in your dreams, on the John, or when you're having a jerk."

Calvin reached inside his pocket and gave Angelo an envelope.

"Inside is a name and address. Check him out and I want to know anything you can find out about who lives there. Especially if they have any photographs. Look for a photographic room."

Angelo slowly rose to his feet holding his head.

"You want me to break into a house?"

Calvin smiled once more.

"You catch on quick for a Wop. Meet me in the pub next door, two days from now at noon. Make sure you have the information and don't even think of contacting Quint."

Calvin held the clump of hair up in his hand.

"Understand?"

Angelo nodded.

Croxton Bishop's Apartment, Oxford, England. December 3rd 1969

Lady Winspear rang the doorbell to what could be termed the penthouse apartment of an early Georgian house overlooking a small park.

A tall, slim man with grey-green-eyes and mousy-grey-flecked hair opened the door. He was dressed in a long black, silk, Japanese dressing gown and dojo slippers. A welcoming smile beamed across his face, partly obscured by a cloud of grey smoke that emanated from his mouth as he spoke.

"Eve, my dear, enter please do."

The flat was over-ornate to say the least, with treasures from every part of the globe, highlighting the flamboyant taste of the owner, who stood in the middle of the room puffing theatrically on his ivory cigarette holder.

"Do take a seat. Tea? "

"Yes please," she replied.

Lady Winspear sat in a chair and waited for Croxton to remerge from his kitchen carrying, as would be expected of him, a silver tea service and china tea set. Placing the tea tray on an ornate wood and ivory coffee table with carved elephants supporting the lower legs, Croxton began to pour the tea.

"Shall I be mum?" he asked.

Lady Winspear took the cup and saucer from Croxton.

"Calvin needs your help. The police think he's involved in a murder."

Croxton was about to answer when the telephone rang. Apologising to his guest he rose to his feet and made his way to the telephone.

"Croxton Bishop. Oh, hello. Yes. Not to worry, all is in hand. Must cut you short, you have telephoned at a rather delicate moment. Do you have a contact number? Can't talk now, must go, someone with me. Be in touch shortly. Ta ta."

Croxton scribbled a number down on the pad next to the telephone before returning to his guest.

"Now, dear heart, where were we? Ah yes, murder you say."

Lady Winspear continued.

"Yes it's all to do with that dammed house and the haunting or whatever it was."

Croxton took a sip of his Earl Grey with a slice of lemon.

"I anticipated your reason for calling and have already, shall we say, put the wheels in motion. Now shall we sit back, enjoy our tea, and you can tell me all you know about our friend."

She sighed before answering.

"I'm afraid it won't be much. If there's one thing Calvin's good at, it is keeping a secret, especially when it concerns himself."

An hour passed of pleasantries and reminiscing about the time they had spent together in Nazi Germany as spies. About comrades, still alive and those gone and almost forgotten. Eventually Lady Winspear bade him farewell and left.

The instant she had left, Croxton made a telephone call to the same person who had telephoned him only an hour earlier.

"Croxton here. "

A female voice answered.

"Hello. Have the arrangements been made on your side?

Croxton liked it when a person cut straight to the chase.

"Yes. I have everything in hand, and your side?"

"All taken care of," the voice replied.

"Good. You're sure they'll give him up?" he asked

"If he lives," was the reply.

Croxton hesitated before asking the question.

"Any reason why he shouldn't, after all he's already taken out three of your best?"

The voice on the other side gave a slight laugh.

"As the song says, the best has yet to come."

A Private Airstrip, Southern England. December 4th 1969.

Just off the tarmac, two black Jaguar cars sat waiting for the private jet to taxi to a halt.

Four men alighted from the plane and made their way towards the waiting cars. One of them was Quint accompanied by two bodyguards carrying the luggage. The fourth, a tall, blond, six-foot-six giant, wearing a long, black coat and a hood.

The drivers from the waiting cars climbed out to open the car boots for the bags. The two bodyguards climbed into the second car, while Quint sat in the back of the first, waiting for the tall blond man.

Karl looked around before climbing inside. It was the first time he had ever been out of Boston, let alone in a foreign country.

He sniffed the air like a predator.

"I can smell him."

His eyes narrowed as he lips drew tight across a row of peal white teeth forming what could only be termed as a snarl.

"You'll soon be mine, freak. All mine "

He whispered before seating himself inside the Jaguar.

Public House
London England.
December 4th 1969.

The pub was beginning to fill up ready for its lunchtime trade. Angelo sat nervously on his own in the corner, holding a large brown envelope. He glanced at the clock on the wall then checked it against his wristwatch. It was almost twelve. A hand on his shoulder made him jump. Calvin sat down beside him.

Angelo instantly handed him the large envelope and was ready to beat a hasty retreat. Calvin grabbed his arm.

"Whoa, hold your horses, let's see what goodies you've brought me."

Angelo's eyes widened as he glanced at the envelope.

"Goodies. What the fuck are you doing messing about with a sick bastard like that?"

Angelo spat the words out.

Calvin opened the envelope and examined the photos.

"These all the photos?" he asked.

"Aren't they enough? "Angelo replied." Fuck me, what else did you expect?"

Calvin pondered before responding.

"Dead children, none of dead children?"

Angelo's eyes opened wider.

"What?"

Calvin slid the photographs back into the envelope.

"Where did you get them?"

"From a drawer in the study," was the reply.

"What about the darkroom?"

Angelo shook his head.

"Nothing in there. Just photos of churches and stuff like that."

"You sure?" Calvin asked.

"Jesus Wolf, isn't it enough to have those sick fucking things?"

Calvin rose from his seat, taking the envelope. Angelo instantly grabbed hold of his jacket.

"Hey! What about my hair?"

Calvin smiled.

"I'd wear it in a parting. It'll suit you," he sarcastically replied.

"Fuck you," was the reply Angelo gave.

Calvin smiled once again.

"Insurance."

Placing the envelope inside his jacket, he left Angelo sulking in the corner.

"Son of a bitch!" he whispered under his breath. "You're a dead man walking."

Calvin's Cottage, Litton Village, England. December 4th 1969.

Later that evening Calvin was relaxing in his lounge, indulging in one of his favourite pastimes, warming his toes by the fire.

He was about to light a cigar when he heard a noise outside. Without hesitation he jumped up and removed a crossbow from the wall. Still in his bare feet, he grabbed the quiver that hung on the wall at the side of the fire and made his way into the kitchen.

The kitchen was in darkness as he loaded the bow and silently slipped out into the rear garden. He could hear the sound of voices on the road outside the cottage. A shape emerged from around the corner.

Calvin, crouching low, hid behind a bush, watching the figure approach the kitchen door. The figure's fat, stubby hand was about to turn the handle when it froze. Something sharp was sticking in the back of its neck, sharp like the point of an arrow.

Calvin's voice was menacing.

"Make one false move and I'll pin your fucking head to the door."

Doran was quivering in terror, as a man's voice called out.

"Jesus! Don't do anything silly."

"Who me, or Jesus?" Calvin replied.

Harland gingerly approached Calvin.

"Please, put that thing down and let's go inside. All we want is a little chat."

"Oh, I say. A chat. How frightfully English." Calvin sarcastically replied.

Bolly walked around the corner to join Harland.

"Shoot him Calvin," she cried out, almost causing Doran to faint.

"Just a joke. Put it down, Calvin, they're only here to ask a favour, nothing more."

Calvin did as Bolly asked, and reluctantly lowered the bow.

Inside the cottage, Bolly offered Doran a cigarette to help calm his nerves. Calvin's face showed no signs of emotion. Still holding the crossbow, he watched Harland, Bolly and Doran sit down.

"All right, William Tell," Bolly still found it amusing. "Put the bow away."

Calvin reluctantly did as Bolly instructed and replaced the bow on the wall before turning to look at Harland.

"What do you want?" he asked.

Harland sat back in the chair; with the bow out of the way he felt more relaxed and more in control.

"We know you had nothing to do with the boy's disappearance. We also checked out your story about the sketches, hard as it was to believe. But we still have the unsolved murder of the little girl found on the bonfire, and I was wondering if you could help."

"How?" Calvin asked.

"Bolly claims you are psychic. We were wondering if you would come back with us to Kent and see if you could pick anything up."

Bolly intervened.

"You don't have to go if you don't want to."

"She's right. It's up to you." Harland agreed.

Calvin thought for a moment before replying.

"Okay."

Bolly was in quickly.

"Can I come?"

Harland instantly replied.

"It's not a family outing."

Calvin sat down to pull on his socks and boots.

"If she doesn't come, then I don't."

Harland reluctantly nodded his head.

Catholic Church, Boston, America December 4th 1969

The gothic-looking church had a warm ambience to it. As Culver made his way down the centre isle he passed bowed heads clicking their way through the rosary as they whispered in private prayer.

Culver was an ambitious man. In his early thirties he had ruthlessly climbed to a high position in the CIA, creating a lot of enemies on the way. The game he was about to enter into, and the back he was going to stab, and the position he would inherit, were the greatest challenge yet.

A young priest spied him walking down the isle. He was easily distinguishable from the handful of people who were in the church. With his crisp white shirt, dark blue tie, navy overcoat and leather gloves, complimented by his perfectly groomed silver hair. Some would say his appearance was distinguished for a man of only thirty-three.

The young priest led Culver to a confessional box. He entered, and knelt down. The small partition slid back to allow the priest to speak. Only this time it wasn't a priest but an Archbishop.

Culver sarcastically began.

"Bless me father for I have sinned."

Vol's voice on the other side of the screen whispered.

"And what are your sins?"

"None," was the reply "I'm perfect."

Vol had no intention of entering into trivial banter.

"Where is Quint?"

Realising that the man on the other side had little if any sense of humour, he instantly replied.

"He's in England."

"With whom?" Vol asked.

"His bodyguards and another." Culver replied

"Who is the other?"

Vol's voice was menacing and showed no respect. Culver suppressed his anger as both men entered into a quick-fire round of questions and answers.

"One of the students."

"How interesting." Vol took a second or two before continuing." Do you know the reason for the visit?"

Culver's voice remained calm throughout the whole of the interrogation; and for the want of a better word that was what it was.

"A loose end that should have been tied up a long time ago." Culver replied." The one they're after is known as the freak. Strange though Quint seems afraid of him."

"And the one with Quint. I take it he is capable of tying up this loose end?" Vol asked.

"They reckon he's the best, so if anyone can do it, he can," was the response

"Excellent." Vol's voice grew excitable. "It should be an interesting contest."

Culver was uncomfortable kneeling down.

"Look, I only came here to make sure you keep your part of the bargain. As for this group of so called psychics, I don't care what you do with them."

Vol interrupted.

"Of course you don't. You're a greedy man Mr Culver. Greedy for power, greedy for money. That is why we are doing business. We can give you both providing you give us what we want."

Culver pushed his face close to the confessional.

"You can guarantee that Quint will die?"

Vol's voice rang out melodically as he answered.

"Oh that much I can. Whether it be by the hand he now feeds or another. But I can guarantee that Mr Quint will not return to these shores unless it is in a coffin. Good day, Mr Culver, the bargain has now been struck and will be kept by both parties."

The partition slid back into place as Culver rose from his kneeling position and left the confessional box. It was the first time he had met this man, whoever he was, all of the arrangements having been made by Ida Kroll.

One thing did worry him; he was not in control of the situation. Why these people should want a bunch of Nazi offspring was beyond him. Coupled with the fact that he was still not sure whom he had just made a bargain with. A silly thought crossed his mind. He felt he had just made a bargain with the Devil.

Culver left the way he had entered. Oblivious to him was the female figure, head covered with a scarf, kneeling at the front of the church. Silently the woman slipped into the same confessional. Once inside the confessional, Ida Kroll removed the scarf from her head as the partition slid back.

"I want you to go to England; you have made your connections over there?" Vol's voice whispered.

"Yes," she replied. "All in place."

A small tinge of excitement rang in Vol's voice, having patiently waited over twenty years for the scenario to unfold.

"It seems we have one of our legacy over there."

"What do you want me to do?" she asked.

Vol pondered for a moment.

"Keep a watchful eye on the situation. Take no sides; if he is the true heir then he will prevail."

"What if he doesn't?" Kroll asked.

"Then kill Quint. Take Sommers with you. Now there's a man who enjoys his work."

Police Mortuary, Tunbridge Wells, Kent, England. 4-am December 5th 1969

Harland pushed open the door to the morgue, allowing Calvin to enter. Bolly, with Doran to keep her company, stood outside in the corridor.

The room, ablaze with light, caused Calvin's pupils to pinpoint even through sunglasses. It was not only the light that was enhanced by bouncing off the white tiled walls, sound also reverberated around this natural acoustic arena.

Alone, in the middle of the room on a table, under a white sheet lay the lifeless body of the child. The mortuary attendant gripped the sheet like a civil servant about to unveil a work of art before the local mayor. Before he had chance to perform his civic duty, Harland raised his hand, stopping him.

"Wait outside, please."

The attendant's face held a puzzled expression as he obeyed without question.

The click of the door closing echoed around the room. Harland looking tired and pale, placed his hands on the sheet ready, to pull it back. Calvin drew in three deep breaths as he prepared himself, before nodding for Harland to continue. Pulling back the linen cover he slowly revealed the top half of the charred remains of what once was a little child. Calvin looked then motioned for Harland to reveal the whole of the body.

Calvin closed his eyes and let out a little sigh before speaking.

"Fire destroys not only the flesh but also the memories they hold."

Lifting up the child's arms, he finally found a piece of flesh that was untouched by the flames, a piece under the armpit. Offering the arm to the reluctant Harland, Calvin gently placed his fingers on the piece of unblemished skin.

Calvin closed his eyes once again. Suddenly his head jolted back, his breathing became heavy in short bursts as an intense vision exploded in his mind.

"It's almost dark, twilight," Calvin began to narrate his vision. "I'm in a field, in the distance, no more than five hundred yards away I can see the steeple of a church. I could be on the edge of a village. There are no houses in view, only the church. There's a large bonfire in the middle of the field with a ladder leaning against it. On the top of the bonfire is a chair. I'm climbing the bonfire. I can see the ground getting further and further away. I'm sitting in the chair. Someone is tying me in, I can't move or cry out but I can see three young boys below. They are looking up at me, and at whoever is tying me on the chair. I can see the top of the head as they descend. Fucking hell."

Calvin snapped out of his trance.

"It's a woman! A fucking woman!" Harland cried out.

"Are you sure?"

Calvin made no reply as he gently covered the little child's body with the sheet.

Harland ran his hand down his face as he expelled the air from his lungs; he was still sceptical, and would have been even more so except for the fact that Calvin had described the bonfire and location exactly.

"How could you describe the events so vividly, the ground disappearing as you climbed the ladder, and the children?"

Calvin looked at the policeman as his hand gently touched the sheet covering the dead child's head.

"Because she was alive. She was burnt alive."

"Jesus!" was the only remark Harland could make.

At the door, Harland stood aside to allow the mortuary attendant to return to his sterile world, and the result of a sick fucker's fantasy.

Bolly and Doran stood patiently waiting for the news. Harland was the first to speak.

"Looks like we got ourselves a problem."

"What's new?" Doran echoed

Harland continued.

"Calvin said he saw a woman put the child on the bonfire."

Doran looked at them both before replying.

"Oh no! Shit not another fucking Brady and Hindley."

Harland could feel his blood rising. The thought of the child still being alive knotted his stomach.

"You sure about the woman?" Calvin nodded.

"And the three kids?"

Doran interrupted his senior.

"Three kids?"

Calvin nodded.

"Yeah, there were three boys, young kids. Oldest about ten no more. As for the woman, all I could see was her dark brown hair."

Calvin shook his head as he looked at Bolly.

"I could have sworn Meynell was involved. How the fuck did I get the vision from him?"

Harland interrupted.

"Vision. What vision?"

Calvin poked his finger up behind his sunglasses to wipe a small tear away before it could roll down his cheek.

"I shook hands with him, the same as I did you outside the house in Durham. I got the vision of a bonfire and a body. Fuck me. I was sure."

Calvin let out a sigh. He was sure it was Meynell, but for the first time he was now doubting his own ability.

"I did pick up something else," he continued.

Doran held a white paper bag, full of almonds and popped one into his mouth as Harland asked.

"What was that?"

Calvin shrugged his shoulders.

"I don't know if it's significant; it was only a flash. I didn't get time to see much. But it looked like a small glass room. You know a sun room, a conservatory, something like that."

Doran popped another nut in his mouth and crunched hard despite a disapproving glance from Harland.

"Okay, we'll look into it." Harland's voice rang with disappointment as he continued to speak. "And thanks for coming down. I'll get a driver to take you back. By the way, we had this Meynell checked out. He's the grandson of one of the country's most senior judges"

Harland held out a hand to Calvin.

"I don't know whether to shake your hand or not."

"Then don't," Calvin replied.

They were about to leave, when Bolly smiling asking Doran.

"Get those nuts from Mrs Fenton's sister?" Doran nodded. "Why not offer Calvin one. Calvin loves almonds, don't you Calvin?"

Calvin for the first time was appreciative of her humour.

"I only like them coated in sugar."

Dr Vogel's Apartment, Edinburgh, Scotland. December 7th 1969

Hans Vogel, with suitcases packed, looked around the apartment that had been his home and sanctuary for the past fifteen years. Unfortunately, the series of events over the past days had put paid to that. Instead of it being a sanctuary, it had now become a liability. The two men pulled out of the river were only the start. He knew full well what he was up against, what he didn't know was who and why.

A large man appeared by his side and removed the last two remaining suitcases. Although he felt a little sad about leaving his apartment and his comfortable way of life, at least he was now living. All the old memories from the past came flooding back. The missions, the secret meetings, the adrenaline pulsating through the body, he was like a junkie having a fix. Secretly he was pleased that it had come early, and he was still fit and healthy enough to be involved in what he knew was the inevitable prophecy. A prophecy that would effect mankind and, if allowed, would destroy it.

He let out a deep sigh as a tall figure appeared beside him. A figure with long grey, dishevelled hair dressed in a white monk's habit, like an escapee from one of the early Frankenstein movies.

Brother Alaric placed his massive hand on the Doctor's shoulder.

"Time to go." He said, rasping the words in his thick Hungarian accent.

Brother Alaric had been sent by the Marquis De Jay, and was his trump card. Adept in all that was considered by the church to be the works of the devil. But if one is to fight one's enemy and win, then one must know the enemy's strengths and weaknesses.

It was Brother Alaric who had removed Adrian Hoff to a place of safe keeping, if there is ever such a place. He knew Hoff's importance, and also the fact that he was nothing more than an innocent, drawn in by a freak of time, place and nature.

Although he was no longer receiving, it did not mean he would not be in the near future. Things may have quietened down as far as he was concerned, but both Alaric and Vogel knew it was only the lull before the storm. A storm they must now prepare for as no other.

Durham Cathedral, Durham, England. December 7th 1969.

It was mid-afternoon. Calvin and Bolly had returned to Christine's house in Durham to ensure everything was in order before she handed the keys to the property over to the solicitor. She had no intention of staying in the house alone, and her aunt and Christine had no intention of returning to it, whether it was sold or not. It had been delegated that Bolly would oversee the removal and storage of the furniture. And that was what both her and Calvin had been attending to most of the morning, a precise inventory, furniture fixtures and fittings.

Calvin, bored with it all, suggested they paid a visit to the Cathedral. A grand piece of architecture that held the bones of St Cuthbert and St Aiden, men accredited as being the founders of Christianity in Britain. The Cathedral also held the tomb of the Venerable Bede an ecclesiastical historian who died in 735AD.

Calvin and Bolly strolled along the side aisle of the magnificent Cathedral. The stained-glass windows and architecture were a wonder to behold. As much as Calvin hated religion and all it stood for, buildings of this magnitude held all that surveyed them in awe, no matter what their beliefs.

He considered religion to be the crutch of the masses, and although he was no communist, he hated the church and its hypocrisy. How could a church claim to follow in the footsteps of a man of meagre means who never desired wealth nor sought it? A church that venerates a man who lived a simple life and believed in sharing all he had. A man who preached, lived and died by his beliefs. Yet they in his name have so much wealth and power, avariciously clinging to it no matter what pain or suffering it may cause.

They had paid the customary visit to the tomb of saint Cuthbert and were making there way towards a room at the opposite end to the altar, a room that housed the tomb of the Venerable Bede.

As the two entered the room, Calvin had just been giving Bolly a history lesson on the Culdees. They were a group of Christians, reputed to have been led by Joseph of Arimathea, who settled on this green and sceptred isle, bringing the true form of Christianity to the people. Not the bastardised version that was enforced upon the-then known world by the Romans three hundred years later.

Suddenly Calvin held out his hand to halt Bolly's progress. Bolly instantly realised why Calvin had stopped her. At the far end of the room, kneeling in prayer before the tomb of the Venerable Bede, was Meynell.

The pair remained silent and motionless as they watched Meynell rise and leave the room by the other exit. Calvin instructed her to wait while he followed.

Back in the main part of the Cathedral, Meynell halted at a large wood carving in commemoration of the miners lost in pit disasters. The woodcarving was decorated with cherubs.

Meynell began to lovingly fondle the carvings, tracing the outline of the heavenly beings with his fingers. Suddenly his right hand was whisked away from the carving and was held in a vice-like grip.

"Mr Meynell, how nice to see you."
Calvin held onto the stunned Meynell's hand.

Suddenly a vision sent a shock wave through his massive frame. He could see the body of a child being held before him. The naked body of a little girl, it was as if he himself was carrying her. The child's eyelids were stitched closed, her face white, waxen and the mouth open in a hideous grin as if she had a boxer's gum shield in it. Just like the children in the mirror and in the photographs.

Calvin snapped out of the vision and glared at Meynell

"Son of a bitch! It is you."
Meynell's body began to shake as Calvin grasped hold of both his hands. Blood began to pour from his ears and nose as his body convulsed.

"Hello, Mr Meynell." A woman's voice rang out from behind Calvin.

Calvin turned to see two young women and a man standing behind him.

"Fancy meeting you here," she continued.
Meynell slumped to the floor as Calvin released his grip, and walked away, leaving the bemused

party to attend to the unconscious body in the cathedral aisle.

Without looking back, Calvin hurried towards the cloisters and the rear exit, followed by a terrified Bolly, who had witnessed it from afar.

"Hang on a bit!" she cried out. "Give me chance to catch up." Calvin eventually slowed down at the exit of the Cathedral. "What the fuck was all that about?" she asked.

Calvin looked about him before replying.

"Listen to me and do exactly as I say. You were right all along. That son of a bitch is the murderer. The sick bastard takes pleasure in killing children, whatever he does with them before or after God knows."

Bolly tried to interrupt, but he placed his hand over her mouth. Calvin looking around in fear.

"Shut up and listen." He removed his hand. "I want you to stay here and see what happens, then, if you can, I want you to follow him and ring me back at your aunt's house. Give me the keys and do as you're told, no ifs, no buts, just for once, fucking do it."

"Okay. You only had to ask," she retorted.

Calvin took the keys off Bolly and made his escape.

Spanish City, Whitley Bay, England. December 7th 1969.

Having recovered sufficiently to walk, Meynell much to the amazement of his saviours, refused to discuss the incident or the tall stranger.

With Bolly carefully following, Meynell headed home. He lived in a semi-detached house not far from the city centre, ten minute's walking distance, no more. Although he constantly glanced behind to make sure Calvin was not following him, he paid little attention to a duffel-coated young woman in a university City like Durham. To him, one student looked very much like another.

Bolly stepped inside a telephone box on the corner of the road where Meynell lived. She waited for a minute or two, then decided it made no sense for her to wait outside in the cold when he obviously was sitting in front of a warm fire.

She tried to contact Calvin at her aunt's but there was no reply. She therefore decided to telephone a taxi, as a walk home did not appeal to her in the slightest.

As the taxi drew up alongside the telephone box, she spied Meynell, suitcase in hand, climbing into his car. Shit, she thought what was she to do? She had very little money on her certainly not enough for her to follow him if he intended to return to Kent.

The taxi driver was becoming impatient as she watched Meynell pull off, heading in their direction. A rush of blood, God knows, but she thought, sod it, I'll follow for a while, just in case he is going somewhere else.

The taxi kept its distance as it followed Meynell out of Durham, but instead of heading south he headed north, for the coast. With Bolly constantly looked at the meter in the cab. She had checked her money and was now getting down to her last few pounds when Meynell pulled into a small hotel car park about 20 miles from Durham in a place called Whitley Bay. And that was where she was now standing, outside the hotel.

Having spoken to Calvin on the telephone, she arranged to meet him approximately five hundred yards down the road, in the car park of an amusement park known as the Spanish City.

Bolly stood impatiently, waiting as she heard the roar of not one motorbike but several, as a group of Hell's Angels swept into the car park. It was then that she spied Meynell inside the amusement park; he had obviously left the hotel and was wandering around from ride to ride, mainly watching the children as they laughed and played.

The amusement park was not exactly busy, especially at this time of the year. If it hadn't been for the fact it was a weekend, it wouldn't even have been open.

Ignoring Bolly, the Hell's Angels made their way into the park. The last one turned to look back as a new motorbike roared into the car park. It was a large silver Harley Davison.

Calvin parked the bike up and made his way towards Bolly. One of the Angels glanced at the bike, then at Calvin, before joining the rest of the gang.

"Okay. Where is he?" asked Calvin.
Bolly took a long pull on the cigarette she was smoking before flicking it away.

"Thanks for the greeting." She pointed to the amusement park "He's in there."

Calvin's impatience to finish the job was evident. Without a word, his long legs strode into the amusement park, a predator intent on getting his prey. Meynell's death was the only thing on his mind; pleasantries were completely out of the question.

Bolly grabbed hold of Calvin's arm and pointed in the direction of a carousel.

"Look! There he is."
Calvin's expression hardened as Bolly held tight onto his arm.

"You're going to kill him, aren't you?"
Calvin looked down and remove her hand from his jacket.

"You bet your sweet fucking life I am."
He was about to head off in the direction of the carousel when a group of skinheads dressed in short jeans and braces with Doc Martin boots began to run riot in the fairground.

Before either Bolly or Calvin had time to blink the group of Hell's Angels rushed at them from all sides, as a bloody pitched battle broke out.

Calvin was desperate to find Meynell, with Bolly in tow he headed for the carousel where he had last been sighted. A skinhead saw Calvin coming towards him and tried to jump on him. Like lightning Calvin stepped aside, grabbed him by the arm, and threw him in a ju-jitsu move to the ground before stamping on his head.

Meynell had vanished, obviously fleeing from the fight along with the rest of the fairground customers.

Bolly spotted him once again.

"There he is!" she cried out.

Meynell was outside in the car park; with him was a little girl, he was leading her by the hand. Calvin gave the skinhead, who was trying to get to his feet, a kick in the stomach before running towards Meynell.

Calvin stopped in his tracks; as from the side of him a young woman rushed towards Meynell, crying and calling out. Meynell turned and smiled as he waited for the woman to draw near. The woman was obviously the child's mother, as mother and daughter gave each other a hug.

Meynell smiled and waved to the child as she was led away by the ever-grateful parent, all under the watchful eye's of Calvin and Bolly.

Suddenly Calvin felt a blow to the back of his head, his legs crumpled beneath him as he hit the ground. Large black boots rained blow after blow into his body and his head as two skinheads jumped, stamped and kicked the helpless Calvin.

Bolly tried to intervene, but was stopped by a tattooed fist that crunched into her face, sending her to the ground.

The blow to the back of Calvin's head had come from a beer bottle, and the skinhead who held it smashed it on the floor leaving only the neck and its jagged remains in his hand.

His attention was momentarily distracted as a group of Hell's Angels headed towards him.

With no time to lose, he plunged the broken bottle into Calvin's face, leaving it embedded in his temple and cheek. Bolly, crawling on all fours screamed out as blood like a fountain squirted out of the wound in Calvin's head.

The fleeing skinheads kicked over as many of the Angel's motorbikes as they could, hoping it would stop their pursuers.

Bolly cradled Calvin's head crying out for help, as a figure appeared beside her; without looking up she begged for it to call an ambulance.

The figure smiled as he removed his spectacles to wipe the lens with his handkerchief, before walking away whistling.

'You may not be an Angel'.

Hospital Ward, Newcastle, England. December 8th 1969.

Vapour from the cold morning air mixed with the smoke from the cigarette, drifted upwards into the slow break of day.

Bolly leaned back against the cold rough, bricks and drew once more on her Woodbine. Her mind drifted back to the night she stood outside her aunt's house to have a smoke, the night she saw for the first time what she now knew was a vision of the future, a future that must not be allowed to happen, no matter what it takes.

Her eyes were red and sore from crying, and the bruise on her cheek still throbbed. Twelve hours had elapsed since Calvin was first admitted, twelve hours of sitting in a bleak waiting room or popping outside for a quick smoke.

The cigarette finished, she strolled back to the now-silent waiting room, which had at one time been a stage of constant drama after drama. If you wanted peace and quiet, then the accident and emergency department was not the place.

"Excuse me."

A nurse's voice snapped Bolly out of her thoughts.

"Are you the young lady with the gentleman who was stabbed with a broken bottle?"

"Yes," Bolly instantly replied.

"Then could you follow me?" the nurse continued

Bolly let the nurse lead the way. Because Calvin was an albino with light sensitive eyes, after coming out of the operating theatre he had been placed in a side ward with subdued lighting to recover. It was in the side ward where the outstretched body lay of someone Bolly now called a friend.

She sat beside the unconscious figure of Calvin, and gently touched the left side of his face. It was wrapped in a bandage that wove around the forehead, covering one eye.

A doctor entered the room, along with a nurse, Bolly instantly stood up to make room for them to do their duty.

"Will he be all right?" she asked.

The doctor checked his pulse before motioning for the nurse to draw the curtains in the room.

"We will have to keep him in here, especially with the eye condition. Don't worry, we will do our best to make him comfortable, and subdue the light as best we can."

"Will he be all right?"

Bolly repeated the question.

"He will be badly scarred."

The doctor's voice held a distinct tone of annoyance at having been asked the same question twice.

"As for the eye, time will tell as to what damage has been done. There is no point in waiting; he'll be out for hours."

"Are you sure?" she asked.

"Trust me, I'm sure," he reassured her.

At that Calvin groaned.

Both the doctor and the nurse looked at one another.

"It's not possible!" he exclaimed.

Blurred images, mixed with a blinding light, filtered their way into Calvin's brain.

"Where am I?" he groaned.

The question was directed at no one in particular, as all he could see were shapes.

Bolly instantly took him by the hand.

"You're in hospital, Calvin. Hospital."

Calvin desperately tried to focus as he hauled himself up. The doctor instantly requested a hypodermic to give him a sedative, and was about to give him an injection when Calvin grabbed him by the wrist.

"Mr Dane, please release my hand!" The doctor pleaded.

Calvin gripped it tighter.

"No drugs! I want no drugs!"

"But Mr Dane!" the doctor protested.

Calvin pulled the doctor on top of him; his strength was returning as his adrenaline fought the drugs in his body.

"I said I wanted no drugs and I fucking mean it!"

Bolly tried to pull Calvin's hand off the doctor.

"Calvin, let him go!" she cried.

The doctor called out to the nurse.

"Get help quickly!"

Calvin's voice was hoarse as he called out.

"Stop them Boll! I want no more drugs in my body!"

Bolly pleaded with Calvin.

"Okay. Let the doctor go and I'll make sure they don't."

Calvin reluctantly released the doctor, who instantly began to rub his wrist. At that the nurse plus two porters entered the room and pounced on Calvin, pinning him to the bed.

Bolly hit one of the porters across the head.

"Get your fucking hands off him! If he wants no drugs, then it's his choice.

The doctor, hypodermic in hand, was about to inject the restrained Calvin, when Bolly cried out.

"Stick that fucking needle in him and I'll sue you for every penny you've got!"

The doctor instantly stopped.

"But-" he spluttered.

"No fucking buts! If he wants no drugs then, no drugs it shall be!" she continued.

The doctor motioned for the two porters to release Calvin who was obviously weak and still fighting off the sedation.

"Get me out of this place!" he begged her.

Bolly looked at the doctor.

"Get me a release form, we're leaving."

Calvin's Cottage, Litton Village, England. December 10 th 1969

Three days had passed since Calvin had been injured. Three days of excruciating pain, yet somehow he had managed to contain not only the pain without drugs, but also help the healing process.

Calvin was seated in his favourite chair before the fire, and was in his own words getting more and more pissed off. The cause of his annoyance was Bolly, who was fussing over him like a mother hen, constantly fluffing the cushion behind him.

"Will you stop fussing?"

"I'm only trying to help," she retorted.

"I preferred it when you were obnoxious," he snapped.

Bolly smirked as she removed a bowl of water and the old dressings from the room. Although Bolly was acting as his nurse, Lady Winspear had insisted the local doctor call in and check on his progress.

As he couldn't wear his sunglasses, the curtains were kept shut throughout the day. Calvin felt the bandage on his face and shook his head in disbelief. How could he have been so stupid?

The words kept ringing in his head as if his conscience were crying out loud to him.

He gave a sigh and allowed his body to relax. The heat from the fire was warm and comforting, coupled with a full stomach and clean bandages, he found himself drifting into a deep sleep, allowing him to dream.

He saw himself rushing out of the kitchen of his cottage. Behind him was a large shape. The same shape he had seen in the dream, that night in Christine's house. Once again, the dream was in a negative form and in slow motion. He then saw himself scramble over the wall and fall into the snow inside the churchyard. He could hear his heart pounding and felt a terrible pain in his chest. He saw himself turn round to look at the shape standing on top of the wall laughing at him as he scrambled on all fours, like an animal, from gravestone to gravestone. The church clock was cranking up to strike the hour. One, two, three, the chimes continued. He could see his own face; one of his eyes was covered, the pain in his eye made him cup it with his hand as he felt hot liquid flow from it.

With a scream, Calvin woke from his nightmare.

Bolly instantly rushed into the room, only to see Calvin clutching at his face as blood ran down from his wound.

She tried to help, but was pushed away with force.

"Leave me alone!"

"What it is, what's wrong?" she asked.

Calvin calmed himself down.

"Look you have no idea what you're dealing with. I, I want you to leave. Please. It's for your own good."

Bolly stood with her hands on her hips.

"Yeah, sure."

Calvin sat back allowing his head to rest on the back of the chair. His voice took on a more mellow tone.

"Bolly, please listen to me; I'm not being melodramatic, I'm trying to save your life. If they find you here with me, they'll kill you."

"Who'll kill me?" she asked.

"The people who want to kill me," was his reply

"Why would they want to kill you?" she continued to question him.

Calvin drew in a deep breath before answering.

"I'll tell you as much as you need to know, no more. And that's on one condition. "

"What's that?" she asked.

The last thing he wanted was to get her involved but he had no choice. He had to bring to a close what was becoming an almighty fuck-up.

"Deliver a message for me in London. Once you've done it, I want you as far way from me as you can."

Bolly pondered.

"You'll tell me everything?"

Calvin shook his head.

"Too much information would be your death warrant."

"Awe, fuck it. Nobody lives forever. Go on, I'm all ears," she said.

"And mouth, don't forget that," Calvin smirked.

Bolly made no reply as Calvin readied himself to explain to her a little of his history.

"First of all, I'm not an American at least not by birth. I'm German, a product of selective breeding, only in my case something went wrong. As far as I know there were thirty of us, all bred either for our psychic abilities or our brains. When the Nazis realised they were losing the war they made a deal with the Americans and we were smuggled out of Austria, and into Switzerland and then on to America.

"Why?" she interrupted.

"To stop us falling into the hands of mother Russian, although there was a rumour that the Russians did get hold of another group."

"What about the British?" she asked.

"Too slow," was the reply.

Bolly continued to question him.

"Who were your mother and father?"

Calvin shook his head.

"My mother died giving birth to me, my father I never met. I do know that I have three half-brothers and two half-sisters."

"Half!" she exclaimed.

He took a moment to numb the pain before continuing to speak.

"Same father, different mothers. Our parents were chosen for their special talents, some were psychics, and others academics. A couple of the group were bred for their athletic abilities. And of course we all had to be blond, blue-eye Aryans. Certainly fucked up on me. Well, in the eye department that is. Oh and all the males had to have twelve inch cocks."

Bolly's eyes widened. "Really?"

Calvin laughed

"No but I thought I would throw that one in. The Americans placed us in a large house so they could monitor our growth and help develop our talents. The head of the department was only interested in the psychics and left the tutoring of the others to his staff.

For 24 hours we were monitored, filmed, watched. We were nothing more than laboratory monkeys. As we grew older some of the staff who were of German or Austrian decent used to secretly teach us the values of the Third Reich, and how special we were. With one exception. Me. I was always left out, the freak. The Americans didn't treat me that way; some of them felt sorry for me. In fact it was an American guard that used to let me walk around the grounds on my own. That's how I met Maria, the girl in the sketch. She was the gardener's daughter. She didn't see me as a freak; at first I think she felt sorry for me, then later she fell in love. One day she told me she was pregnant.

"Jesus! So you decided to run away?"

Calvin ignored her interruption and continued.

"So we decided to run away. We joined a hippie commune, we thought it would be safer. Maria gave birth to a little girl, and we stayed there for about a year. Then, God knows why, Maria decided to confide in another woman about our past. The woman, trying to get into the so-called prophet's good books, told him. It was a Tuesday morning, the day of the week when the females of the group went to town to buy provisions. The prophet sent Maria along, fortunately I had our daughter with me."

Bolly watched Calvin wipe a tear away form his eye.

"I felt something was about to happen. For the past year I had deliberately shut down. It was my only defence to stop them finding me. But the power was so strong. I could feel them. I could feel their minds probing for mine. I knew we had to get away, so I took my daughter and ran towards the town. There was a little house adjoining an old school; the old lady who lived there had been the teacher for the past forty years before they built a new school on the other side of town. As she had educated the majority of the townsfolk, they allowed her to live in the house rent-free. I persuaded her to look after my daughter until I returned. I knew I had to get to Maria before he did.

But I was too late. I spotted a large limo parked in the middle of the main street, and then I saw that evil bastard sitting in the back with Maria."

"Who was he?" she asked.

"Quint," Calvin replied. "His name was Quint. The car sped off in the direction of the colony. I stole a truck and picked up my daughter and disappeared. It was a whole year before I returned to pay a visit to the so-called Messiah. Some Messiah he was."

Bolly was engrossed in Calvin's story as she continued to question him.

"What did you do?"

Calvin sat forward, looking her in the face.

"Do you really want to know?"

"Yes," she replied.

"Okay, I clasped my hands either side of his head like this."

Calvin clasped his hands around Bolly's head.

"Then."

A smile flickered across his lips as he savoured the memory.

"I burst his head wide open. I concentrated all my hate on him until every blood vessel in his head ruptured, popping his eyes out of their sockets like champagne corks."

She felt a cold shiver run down her body.

"You killed him?"

Calvin looked her in the eyes.

"What did you expect? After all, I am the ultimate assassin. When I kill it can only be recorded as death by natural causes. That's what Quint had been training us for from birth, to kill. Nothing more."

Bolly removed Calvin's hands from her head.

"What of Maria?"

"Dead." His voice grew sad. "I found out from one of the company's maggots. All he knew was that they'd killed her."

Bolly stood upright.

"What happened to your child, and how did you become a friend of Gran's?"

Calvin waved his hand, cutting her short.

"I've told you enough. Now, will you help me with Meynell or not?"

"Are you going to kill him?" she asked.

Calvin looked her in the face once again.

"It's your decision. The children or him?"

Bolly let out a sigh.

"Fuck it. I'm with you, Kemo Sabe."

Public House,
London, England.
December 11th 1969.

Angelo's mind was flitting from one thought to another. He had hoped he had seen the last of Calvin, but he knew he was misleading himself. The son-of-a-bitch had him running scared, and he knew it. Angelo had to make a decision; should he lure him to a remote spot and kill him, or should he inform his superiors? He had to make the choice between Quint or Calvin; both were equally bad for his health.

Staring blankly at the drink before him, he failed to notice a young woman standing beside him. The shock of someone so close made him jump.

"Are you Angelo?" she asked.

Angelo looked up at the pixie-faced young woman and replied.

"Who wants to know?"

Bolly smiled at him.

"I've message from the Wolfman."

Angelo motioned for her to take a seat. Refusing the seat, Bolly handed him the brown envelope Angelo had given Calvin. He reluctantly took it from her.

"Open it up," she insisted

Angelo noticed that this time it was sealed. Ripping it open, he glanced inside. The photographs were still there, plus a note.

"Read the note. Please." Bolly remained standing.

"I need a reply."

Angelo looked up at her.

"Do you know what's inside?"

"No," she replied.

"No?" he asked

Bolly's eyes locked onto his.

"I said no, didn't I?"

Angelo gave a little sigh and shook his head before replying. Keeping his voice low.

"He wants me to kill someone. Doesn't that bother you?"

Bolly's eyes never left his.

"Not if it doesn't bother you."

"Me. Why me?" he exclaimed.

Bolly whispered in his ear.

"Because you have nice eyes."

Angelo sat upright.

"What the fuck are you talking about?"

Bolly's eyes hardened as she locked once more onto his.

"He said if you don't do as he asks, he'll pop them out of your head."

Bolly had made that bit up and was quite pleased with the response as Angelo sat in silence for a moment.

"You know they'll kill him, and then you?"

Bolly never blinked.

"Yes or no?"

Angelo gritted his teeth as he forced the words out with venom.

"Fuck you both. Okay, I'll tell him no."
Bolly was about to turn and walk away. Angelo jumped up, grabbing her by the arm. He glanced around the pub. The last thing he wanted to make was a scene.

"Does he know the sick son-of-a-bitch's grandfather is a high court judge?"
Bolly made no comment as Angelo sat back down in his seat.

"Okay. I'll do this one, but this is the last."
Bolly still refused to show any emotion.

"Good. He said he'll send you the name of a good hairdresser once the job's complete."

She was about to walk away when she turned to look once more at Angelo.

"Oh, by the way, he knows you've told Quint, but he'll forgive you if you do this."
Fear was written all over Angelo's face.

"I've said nothing."
Bolly made no comment as she left the pub and Angelo. He watched her leave, picked the envelope up and walked over towards the other side of the pub where three men sat waiting.

One of the men stood up to give him a seat before quickly leaving the pub to follow Bolly. Angelo sat down at the table.

Quint smiled at Angelo.

"Well?"
He slid him the envelope Bolly had given him.

"He wants me to kill the sicko. The judge's grandson."
Quint took a sip of his Martini before replying.

"Do it. It will lull him into a false sense of security."
Angelo's voice trembled as he spoke.

"He knows I've told you. How?"

Quint made no comment, as Angelo leant forward to whisper.

"Are you sure he can't kill me in my dreams?"

Quint gave a small laugh.

"Would I be alive today?"

Angelo clenched his fist.

"The bastard."

Meynell's House, Durham, England.
5 am December 13th 1969.

With Calvin out of the picture, for the time being that was, Meynell felt reasonably secure in his two-up-two-down semidetached rented house.

The property was situated in a quiet suburb close to Durham city centre, a neighbourhood were people got on with their daily life, rarely interfering or prying into the lives of others. This suited Meynell as he had spoken only a couple of times to his neighbours since he moved in.

Meynell lay asleep in his bed. A deep, peaceful sleep, not the type of sleep one would expect from a man who is suspected of the most horrendous of crimes.

The door to the bedroom silently opened as a masked figure entered the room and made its way towards the sleeping form.

Quickly a hand was placed over the sleeping man's mouth and a gun pressed against his temple. Meynell opened his eyes with a start, with the whites of his eyes standing out in the semi-darken-room. Terrified like those of a trapped animal.

"Shush." The voice from behind the mask was menacing. "Make one sound and your fucking brains will decorate the wall."

Meynell heard the American accent and assumed it was Calvin. Without questioning he climbed out of the bed and stood rigid in his striped pyjamas.

"Very chic," whispered Angelo.

Meynell began to cry.

"Please don't hurt me! Take what you want."

Angelo pushed the gun barrel hard against Meynell's temple.

"Shut the fuck up.

Meynell stopped pleading, but continued stifle his sobs completely. Beside the bed were a pair of slippers. Angelo pointed to them.

"Put them on."

Meynell was puzzled.

"Why?"

Angelo prodded him in the ribs with the gun.

"Just do as you're fucking told. Put them on, don't want you catching your death of cold."

Once the slippers were on his feet, Angelo forced Meynell down the stairs into the kitchen and the door that led into the garage. Once inside the garage, Meynell was forced into the car. He sat terrified, not knowing what to expect.

Angelo placed the key in the ignition and switched the engine on before snapping the key off in the ignition. It hadn't occurred to Meynell where Angelo had got the key, but the reason was soon apparent.

Meynell's head twisted and turned as he looked around the car, as Angelo threw an envelope onto the passenger seat before slamming the door shut. He tried frantically for a handle but there was none. No door or window handles, all had been removed.

Meynell began to cough as the fumes from the exhaust filled the car from a hose connected into the boot and through a hole cut out in the rear seat. He had no idea where the fumes where coming from as he clawed and banged on the windows, clambering from the back to the front desperately trying to find an escape, while the fumes burnt into his lungs.

Angelo slipped out of the garage into the kitchen and out of the house. He was walking down the drive when he heard the car horn.

"Shit!" he said to himself.

He forgot to disconnect the horn, and was about to go back into the garage when the next-door neighbour's light came on. Quickly, he hid behind a wall. The neighbour and his wife were outside Meynell's house in their dressing-gowns, banging on the garage door. All the time the horn was sounding. Angelo leapt into his own car and sped off.

Calvin's Cottage Litton Village England. December 13th 1969

When Bolly entered Calvin's bedroom he was stretched out on the bed asleep.

Walking over to the bed, she gave him a little nudge to wake him up. He made no response. She shook him; he still made no response, in fact to her he looked lifeless.

"Calvin," she whispered.

My God she thought, he's dead. Terror gripped her mind, she shook him hard and held her hand next to his mouth to feel if there was any breath. Nothing. Terrified, she laid her ear upon his chest before placing her face close to his, desperate for a sign of life.

Calvin's eyelid drew back, revealing his red eye.

"Yes."

Bolly jumped.

"You bastard! I thought you where dead."

"Well, I'm not." He smiled. "What time is it?"

"Almost 10.30am," she snapped.

The smile on his face broadened.

"Good. Pass me the phone."

Bolly passed him the telephone.

"Do you think he will have killed him?" she enquired.

"He had no choice," was the reply.

Bolly sat down on the bed.

"How are you blackmailing him?"

Calvin smiled.

"The stupid wop thinks I can come to him in his dreams."

"Can you?" she exclaimed.

Calvin yawned before replying.

"I have a piece of his hair and he thinks I can tune in on him with it, even kill him."

Bolly was on one of her question-and-answer sessions.

"If you can do that, then why haven't you killed Meynell in his dreams?"

Calvin clapped his hands together.

"Give the girl a cupie doll. You figured it out, but he's a stupid wop."

"So you can't kill him at all." she continued.

"I can if I touch him," was the stern response.

"How?" she asked.

"Physics, nothing more. People make more out of it than there is. It's just physics. You have a tape recorder."

Bolly shuffled on the edge of the bed, making herself more comfortable.

"Yes."

Calvin sat upright as he spoke.

"You switch the tape recorder on, and place the mike next to whatever you want to record, and the sound is recorded on the tape. Put it away and bring it out twenty years later, switch on the tape recorder and what will you get?"

Bolly didn't see the relevance

"The song or whatever." Calvin continued.

"Exactly. And that's what I am. I'm a tape recorder. Objects, brick or even flesh act like a piece of tape, they store information. I am nothing more than the machine that plays it back. The tape is useless unless you have the machine to play it back."

"Yes, but how can you do that?"

Calvin swung his legs out of the bed and stretched his massive arms.

"If you switch a television on you get an image of some guy in London or wherever. To get that image, besides power, you need a transmitter and a receiver. You accept that because it's scientific, and everyone can see it."

Bolly nodded.

"I'm no different to that." He continued. "Only I am both the transmitter and receiver. The problem is my receiver is in my head and nobody else can see it. I am the only one who can watch my telly."

Bolly pondered a moment before answering.

"I think I understand, but how do you kill people?"

Calvin's mind drifted back as he remembered the last time he had had a similar conversation with Maria.

"I receive their brain waves then boost them up and return them. Receiving and transmitting, that's all it is."

Bolly was slowly beginning to understand.

"So the more psychic the person is, the easier it is?"

"Exactly."

Calvin pointed his finger at her.

"That's how I was able to upset the medium in the church and the one you had at the house. I didn't need to touch them."

Bolly was intrigued.

"So you could have killed the medium if you had wished?"

Calvin shook his head.

"No one's that powerful. I was pulling on the energy from the rest of the people, a nosebleed or dizziness. Anyway, enough of that. Pass the phone."

Calvin dialled the number and waited for it to answer.

Angelo was on the other side.

"Where the fuck have you been?"

Calvin ignored him as he calmly asked.

"Is it done?"

"Yeah," Angelo replied.

"How?" Calvin asked.

"Suicide," was the response

Calvin replaced the receiver.

Hospital Durham, England. 7-30 pm December 13th1969

A large fat man weighing at least 23 stones strode down the hospital corridor like a sergeant-major. His face was red as his blood pressure rose along with his temper. Following behind, and doing her best to keep pace, was his slip of a wife.

Throwing the door to the private ward open, he burst into the room. There were no pleasantries. No, 'how are you?' No sympathy.

"Well?"

"Well, what?" was the reply.

The judge stood next to the bed and glared at his grandson.

"Come on. Answer, boy."

Meynell shuffled himself up in the bed. His voice was horse and his eyes sore, red and weeping.

"What do you want me to say?"

Meynell's grandmother instantly fluffed up his pillow to make him more comfortable.

"Stop fussing, woman. Leave the boy alone," the judge rasped. "Come on, I want the truth. If it hadn't been for your next door neighbour you would have been dead."

"There's your answer. I tried to kill myself." Meynell replied.

The judge looked around the room before replying.

"All taken care of, your on sick leave."

Meynell took a sip of water.

"Sick leave?" he enquired. "Now why would they do that. I would have thought the last person they would want for a bank manager was someone with suicidal tendencies."

The Judge jutted his fat chin forward, moving it around in the collar of his shirt.

"All attended to. No one will know and the neighbour has agreed to keep quiet, for a price."

"Still running my life." Meynell sighed.

Meynell's grandmother dabbed his eyes with a clean handkerchief.

"Come along now, dear, your grandfather is only trying to help. Once we have you home everything will be fine."

Meynell's face grew stern.

"I must return to my house first," he croaked.

The Judge was not happy at the suggestion.

"No need. I'll send someone round to pick up your belongings."

Meynell glared at his grandfather.

"I said, I will return to my house."

The words hissed out through clenched teeth.

His grandmother instantly tried to defuse the situation.

"Of course you can call back at your house. Your grandfather is only concerned about your health. Aren't you, dear?"

The Judge made no reply. Meynell's only concern was to retrieve whatever was in the envelope that had been tossed into the car by Angelo. As luck had it, in his frenzy to escape, the envelope had fallen on the floor and was lost under the passenger seat.

Calvin's Cottage, Litton Village, England. December 14th 1969

The majority of the bandage had been removed from Calvin's face; all that remained was a large patch on his forehead and a padded patch over the eye.

The doctor had been that afternoon and was amazed at his recovery. Still, it was too early to know if he would ever regain the sight in his damaged eye. The smaller patch had at least enabled Calvin to wear sunglasses once again, even if they were a little uncomfortable.

He sat pondering the best course of action when the door burst open and in stormed Bolly, paper in hand.

"Read this."

Her finger pointed to the line in question. 'Man overcome by fumes while working on car, collapses on garage floor.'

"Good. When's the funeral?" Calvin smiled.

Bolly tossed the paper to him.

"If there is a funeral then it's premature. He's not dead but in hospital and expected to make a full recovery."

Calvin rose to his feet and walked over to the window. Twilight was descending as he removed his sunglasses to watch the setting of the sun. He had always felt a common bond with the Vampire in Bram Stoker's Dracula. In the night Calvin didn't need to protect his eyes. Like the Vampire the night to him was a welcome friend.

"Trust a wop to fuck it up," he sighed.

Bolly joined him at the window.

"Does it mean we will have to kill him?"

Calvin turned to look at her, she notices how his face looked waxen in the mellow glow of the setting sun.

"Do you have a problem with it?"

Bolly nodded her head.

"Yes. I've given it some thought and I think we should leave it to the police."

Calvin's voice grew angry.

"I've possibly lost an eye through this bastard, and you want me to let him live?"

Bolly snapped back

"Kill him, go on, and you'll be no better than he is."

Calvin gave a half-hearted laugh.

"He kills children for pleasure."

Bolly held his hand.

"Please, Calvin, let Harland arrest him. Then you can go away before they find you."

Muller's Apartment, St Louis, America. December 14th 1969

Muller was taking a shower when the telephone rang. Hearing it, still naked, he plucked a towel from the rail and walked out of the bathroom and into his lounge.

A young man of about twenty years, wearing a dressing-gown, was sitting on the large white sofa in the centre of the room. The telephone was on a small ornate table at the other end of the sofa.

"I could have answered it for you," the young man said.

Muller did not reply. The look was enough. He picked up the phone.

"Yes?"

The voice on the other end of the line was Vol's.

"It is time. Your skills are now needed."

"I will leave this evening," Muller replied.

Muller replaced the receiver and turned to the young man.

"Get dressed. You're leaving."

The young man tried to protest as Muller went to the bedroom to collect the young man's clothes before offering them to him.

"You will find I have rewarded you with more than the going rate."

The young man got dressed. Inside his jacket pocket was two hundred dollars. His face held an expression of astonishment.

"Leave now." Muller had no time for niceties.

"I will contact you in due course."

The young man tried to kiss him goodbye, but was rebuked, leaving alone. Naked, he walked over to a large mirror and admired his body. A body he had kept in trim as best he could. The bullet he took in the ankle left him with a distinct limp that obviously restricted him from taking part in any form of sport that involved running. Other than that, he trained each day, especially in the martial arts mainly Ju-Jitsu.

Muller ran his hand down the side of the mirror, and a click could be heard as it slowly opened, revealing a hidden room, measuring about ten feet square. Walking inside, he switched on the light. The room was full of all types of Nazi memorabilia, as well as every form of killing method, guns, knives, crossbows and poison. At the far end of the room were two framed oil paintings, one set in gilt, the other in silver. The gilt one was of Hitler and the silver one of Himmler. Embarrassed to be naked before his superiors, he lovingly removed the black uniform of the Gestapo from a hanger and put it on. It fitted as if it had been specially made for him and it had. A feeling of pride rushed through his veins, forcing him to inflate his chest as he stood to attention before giving the Nazi salute to the paintings.

Judge's House, Peel Kent, England. December 15th 1969

It was a lovely crisp autumn day, with a bite in the air that clears the lungs and generally makes one feel good.

Meynell was in the garden raking up the leaves ready for the small bonfire that steadily smouldered away. He was whistling as he pushed a wheelbarrow full of leaves towards it. Hidden beneath the leaves was a large silk cushion.

Holding it to his face he closed his eyes and smelt the fabric. Memories came flooding back, memories most people would not wish to store.

With a sad expression he laid the cushion on top of the fire. The leaves and bits of wood that had been smouldering embraced the combustible material with great flames that danced around until they engulfed and consumed the treasured possession.

Slowly he placed his hand in his pocket and removed what looked like a small medicine bottle and was about to toss it into the fire when he heard a noise in the bushes behind him. The sudden crack of a twig made him lose aim and the bottle rolled away from the flames onto the grass.

Meynell scanned the surrounding area. He could see nothing. He tilted his head one way then another in the hope of picking up a sound. He was about to return to the fire when out of the corner of his eye he thought he saw a large dark shape disappear behind a bush. Afraid of who it might be, he instantly left the fire unattended and returned to the house.

Looking back at the bonfire some hundred yards, away he shook his head and whispered to himself.

"Just your imagination."

Entering the house, he made his way into the kitchen. Opening one of the drawers, he removed a pair of rubber gloves and placed them over his hands. He then removed a small plastic bag from a cupboard where it had been hidden behind some tins of food. Casually, he made his way into the study humming to himself as he walked. 'You may not be an angel'.

The study was a large Victorian room with a huge desk in front of the window. Meynell instantly made his way to the desk and removed one of the drawers. Carefully lifting all the papers out of the drawer he turned it upside down to reveal the wooden bottom. He then removed the photographs from the plastic bag. They were the photographs Angelo had tossed in the car. Inside the bag there was also some parcel tape. Removing a fresh envelope from the desk, he placed the photographs and a small piece of jewellery inside, and taped it to the bottom of the drawer. Returning all the papers back into the drawer the way they were, he then shut it and left the room.

Field Kent England.
December 15th 1969

A small group gathered around a charred circle, the remnant of a huge bonfire that had took weeks to build from old doors, chairs, wood and other combustibles. All gathered and built ready for that big night, Guy Fawkes Night. All that the bonfire needed was the effigy of Guy Fawkes. Only this time it was not an effigy.

Harland crouched down as he spoke to the three young boys, the same boys Calvin had seen in his vision. Three young boys who had finally owned up to setting the bonfire alight that November evening.

"All I want you to do is tell the truth. If you do, then nothing will happen to you. Do you understand?" the policeman asked.

The parents who accompanied the children coaxed them to reply.

"It wasn't me."

The first to speak was the oldest; a freckle-faced boy of ten, with red hair, who answered to Tog.

"Yes it was."

The second boy, Martin, cried out.

"You had the matches."

Harland intervened before it got out of hand.

"Listen to me, boys. I'm not interested in who started the fire. What I need to know is, who put the guy on the bonfire?"

Tog replied.

"It was a woman, she came from over there."

He pointed to a small belt of trees that led into a neighbouring field.

"Go on," Harland coaxed him.

"She came through the trees. She had the guy over her shoulder."

"No, she didn't,"

Martin interrupted once again.

"She had the guy under her arm."

Doran lifted the smallest of the three boys up, placing him under his arm.

"Like this?"

"Yes, like that," Martin continued "She put it on her shoulders when she started to climb the ladder."

Doran replaced the boy on the ground, as Harland, still crouching, looked at the two older children.

"Now, think very carefully, what did she do when she climbed down the ladder?"

Tog looked at Martin.

"She got a shock when she saw us, then she smiled and walked away."

Martin nodded in agreement.

"Which way did she leave?"

Tog pointed to the trees.

"Over there. Through those trees."

The smallest of the boys, Jack, replied in a voice that seemed far too deep for a child his age.

"She lost her hair."

Harland looked at Doran.

"What do you mean, lost her hair?" he asked.

"It got stuck on one of the branches," Jack continued.

"Was she wearing a wig?" Harland asked.

Tog shrugged his shoulders, allowing Martin the chance to speak.

"It was a wig, her hair was short underneath, and it was a different colour." Harland waited for him to finish. "The wig was brown but the hair underneath wasn't."

"Can you remember what colour the hair was underneath?" he asked.

The boy screwed up his nose and shook his head.

Doran turned to the children.

"Can you take us to as near as you can to the place the woman got her hair caught in the branches?"

The three children, followed by the adults, headed towards a small belt of trees and bushes. After several minutes of deliberation they all agreed on a spot.

Doran took out his grubby handkerchief and tied it around one of the branches to mark the spot. Both of the policemen assured the parents and the children that the matter was now closed, and asked them to leave.

Once they were out of earshot Doran turned to Harland.

"Looks like Dane's been right all along. I don't know many women who could carry a child up a ladder and place it on a bonfire."

Harland had to agree.

"So you think it was a man dressed as a woman?

Harland looked at the trees.

"Looks that way. Get forensics out here tomorrow."

Doran scanned the horizon before pointing past the trees to the fields beyond.

"Guess who lives over there?"

Harland looked up to the skies.

"The chief will have our balls if we bring him in for questioning without any evidence."

Doran shrugged his shoulders.

"What are we going to do?"

Harland shook his head.

"Fuck knows. We can only play it by ear and see what forensics turn up. While were waiting for them we might as well make a few discreet enquires."

Doran removed a Polo sweet from his pocket and popped it into his mouth, an annoying habit as far as Harland was concerned, especially when he used to poke his tongue through the hole, waggling it about for all to see. Doran looked at his superior.

"There's always Dane."

Harland made no comment as he walked away.

Judge's House, Peel, Kent, England. December 15th 1969

The vehicle slowed down as it passed the entrance to the concealed driveway. Two faces peered through the windscreen as they searched for the best place to park unnoticed by the occupants of the house. Finding a small cutting in the trees to the side of the grounds, Bolly eased her Morris Minor through the opening.

It was dark; the moon had deserted them. The one thing that Bolly had grown to consider her enemy had now turned its lunar cycle against them once again. For the first time in the last two months, she wished it would shine its murderous face through the blackness of the night.

Calvin grasped her hand as he stumbled through the thick undergrowth; with his orientation less then perfect. A man with one eye may be king in the land of the blind, but it's bloody hard for a man who only a few days ago had two and now is reduced to one, especially in the black caldron of night.

"You all right?" she asked.

"Yeh," was the reply.

Through the trees the mellow lights of the big house cut into the darkness as Bolly and Calvin found themselves on the lawn at the far end of the garden, not far from where Meynell had held his little bonfire.

Calvin turned his head to one side as his right eye, as best it could, scanned the garden.

"What's that over there?" he whispered.

With her two eyes she could make out the shape of a small building. Taking a torch out of his pocket, he shielded the light away from the house so as not to attract any attention. Its beam carved a path for them to follow, towards the building which, as they drew closer, took on the recognisable form of a summerhouse.

Calvin held out his hand, stopping Bolly.

"That's it, that's the impression I got."

Bolly was about to move forward when Calvin stopped her. He spoke in a hushed voice.

"There's someone watching us."

Bolly looked around.

"Where?"

"I don't know, but I sense someone's presence." he whispered.

They both listened, but the garden held numerous sounds as small animals on their nightly foraging scampered and scurried their way through the undergrowth.

The loud snap of a twig made them both spin round.

"Did you hear that?"

Calvin didn't answer his co-conspirator, as he held out his free hand like a man feeling his way in the dark.

"Something happened around here," he whispered.

Bolly looked up at him, eyes wild and nostrils flared, with her breath coming in short subdued gasps as the adrenaline flowed in copious amounts through her body.

"He tried to kill her, not far from here," he continued.

The sound of a car pulling up on the other side of the trees made Calvin snap out of his trance. Voices could be heard breaking into the night, followed by the sound of a police radio as it crackled its messages over the air.

"Shit, it's the police!" she cried.

Bolly wanted to run but was stopped by Calvin, who grabbed hold of her arm and led her towards the summerhouse. Another car could be heard pulling up, followed by the voice of a man.

"Anything wrong, officer?"

"I think you have intruders, sir," was the reply. Calvin and Bolly hid behind the summerhouse, frantically looking for the best escape route to take.

"Well what are you going to do about it?" the first voice demanded to know.

"I've already radioed for assistance, sir," was the reply.

A bright shaft of light illuminated Calvin's white bandaged face as he crouched along with Bolly in what they believed to be a safe hiding place.

"They're over here!" a policeman cried out. Calvin and Bolly instantly jumped to their feet and set off in different directions. A second police car could be heard pulling up.

Bolly ran off, pumping her arms and legs as fast as they would go. Suddenly the ground raced up to meet her face as she was unceremoniously, crashed to the floor, brought down by a rugby tackle worthy of Twickenham.

The large frame of a sixteen-stone policeman, pinned her to the floor. Without any further resistance her hands were forced behind her back as steel handcuffs clicked into place around her wrists.

Rolling her onto her back, the policeman rose to his feet to examine his prize, by placing his size ten boot on her chest.

"Got one!" he called out.

Suddenly there was a figure beside him, a figure larger than his.

"Get your fucking foot off her!"

The words had just left Calvin's lips as a heavy wooden instrument crashed between his shoulder-blades with a sickening thud, sending him sprawling to the ground beside the incapacitated Bolly.

Police Station, Peel, Kent, England. December 15th 1969.

Calvin sat motionless, staring coldly at the man across the table. The detective lit up another cigarette, his seventh in the last hour. The stubs in the ashtray stood as witness to the ineffectiveness of his interrogation methods. The smoke from the cigarette was blown deliberately into the face of the man opposite. Calvin made neither a sound nor a movement, allowing his one red eye to unnerve the policeman. Even though the bright light hurt his eye, Calvin continued to hold the man in his gaze as the door behind opened. The policeman opposite tried to move, but couldn't. It was as if he had been hypnotised by the tall American. The young officer guarding the door stood aside to allow his superior to entry.

"That'll be all, Johnson."

A large fat man with a bald head and double chin ordered the detective to make way for him at the table.

"Johnson, I said that would be all," he repeated the order.

Finished with playing games, Calvin released his interrogator from his gaze. Johnson slowly rose from his seat, leaving the smouldering weed burning on the table behind.

The Inspector looked at him as he unsteadily made his way to the door.

"You all right?" Johnson nodded and left.

Inspector Beverley stared at the man before him. He was a seasoned detective who had interviewed and broken down more than his fair share of villains, thieves and murderers.

But there was something strange about the man opposite, something he had never encountered before. Perhaps it was his red eye; he certainly had never met an albino before, let alone interviewed one. No, it was the first time he had ever felt uneasy in the presence of a prisoner.

"I understand you are not being very helpful." Inspector Beverley said.

Calvin made no comment as he continued to stare at the inspector, just as he had done to the detective before, only this time he made no attempt to hypnotise the man. His ploy was to remain as impassive as possible.

"Do you know who I am?"

Calvin still continued to stare in silence, as Beverley continued.

"I'm the bastard who can have you put away for a very long time. Do you understand?"

Calvin made no comment. Not a flicker of an emotion showed on his face. Beverley was becoming annoyed, and narrowed his eyes as he spoke.

"I understand your little companion has been making accusations about a certain well-respected member of our community. Is that true?"

Calvin's one eye bore into him.

"We don't need evidence against you." The policeman's voice grew in anger. "See these?" He laid a large brown envelope on the table.

"Inside are unsolved crimes, crimes tailor-made for you, takes nothing for us to make them fit. Do you understand?"

A faint flicker of a smile wafted across Calvin's face as he let Beverley continue uninterrupted.

"We know you didn't just pick on that house by chance. Blackmail, is that what your up to?"

Calvin was so still he might almost have been cut from stone.

There was a lamp on a desk in the far corner of the room. Beverley rose from his seat and placed it on the table. The bright light cut into Calvin's eye like a knife. Calvin instantly dropped his head and covered his eye with his hand. Beverley smiled.

"A little German trick."

Calvin grabbed the policeman's hand. Instantly, Beverley's head rocked back as blood burst out of his nose all down the front of his shirt and over Calvin.

Calvin knocked the lamp to the floor and hissed at Beverley.

"Another little German trick."

Beverley waved his hand in the air, summoning the young policemen over.

"Take the bastard out, and bang him up. "

The Judge, waiting in the corridor, watched Calvin being led away before storming into the room.

"Well, what did he say?"

The Judge was straight to the point as usual. Beverley shook his head.

"Nothing."

The Judge stared at the policeman.

"What the hell!"

Beverley held his head back as he tried to stem the flow of blood.

"Did he hit you?"

Beverley shook his head, before trying to speak as best he could with blood seeping into the back of his throat.

"We're not going to frighten that bastard."

The Judge paced up and down, trying to restrain his temper.

"Frighten or not, you keep him away from my grandson."

Beverly held a handkerchief to his nose and looked at the Judge.

"Your grandson had better not be the one."

"What one?" The Judge was genuinely confused.

"The one who murdered that girl, the one on the bonfire" the policeman replied.

Beverley expected the Judge's temper to explode; instead he was calm and almost apologetic.

"No need to worry about my grandson. I have arranged for him to be transferred to the international side of the bank. They have several positions abroad, and I have been assured that one of them will be kept open for him."

Beverley looked the Judge square in the eye.

"The sooner the better. The whole thing's beginning to have a nasty taste about it."

The judge walked to the door.

"I understand, I certainly don't want him around either. I take it you heard about his little exploit in Durham?'

Beverley's nose had finally stopped bleeding.

"Was it attempted suicide?" he asked.

"Don't know," was the reply.

"You think someone tried to kill him?"

The policeman's eyes fixed on the Judge. The Judge walked back into the centre of the room before replying.

"I looked at the car while he was collecting his belongings from the house. Every window and door handle had been removed. Once inside he was trapped."

Beverley stood up.

"We need to have Dane checked out?"

"Already done it," the Judge continued. "He had just been released from hospital; some skinhead stabbed him with a broken bottle. They assured me he would have been in no fit state to move around, not for at least a few days."

Beverley stood motionless. When he spoke he picked his words carefully.

"I didn't mention it earlier, but two Scotland yard detectives have been sniffing around today, a D.I. Harland and a D.S. Doran.'

The Judged was shocked.

"Have they asked about my Grandson?" he asked.

"No, but it may be a good idea to get that grandson of yours shipped out of the country as soon as possible."

The Judge nodded in agreement.

"What about Dane? Can you keep him away until then?"

The policeman dabbed his nose one more time before answering.

"Shouldn't be a problem; I'll take care of that."

The Judge opened the door to leave the room, then turned to the man.

"Make sure you do. There's more than my grandson at stake here."

Calvin had been sat meditating in his cell when the door opened. A fat red-faced policeman with a swollen nose stood impatiently at the cell door.

"Right you, out."

Beverley's face looked as if he had just been scalded.

Calvin slowly rose from the bed and swaggered towards the detective until his face was no more than an inch or two away. Beverley's, who instantly recoiled before speaking.

"I don't know who's pulled the strings for you, but make sure I never see you or that little bitch in this county again. Stay in the North East, with your flat caps and whippets, well out of my way."

Calvin stared at him as he tapped him on the chest with his forefinger.

"Cancer has no friends."

Beverley stood in stunned silence as Calvin brushed past him to meet the impatient Bolly, who was waiting at the far end of the corridor.

Placing his arm around her shoulder, he looked back at Beverley.

"Does he have cancer?" Bolly asked.

A faint smile flickered wickedly across Calvin's face.

"No idea." he whispered. "But he'll have a heart attack worrying about it."

Bolly grinned as she looked back at the policeman who was looking down and rubbing his chest.

Calvin's Cottage, Litton Village, England. December 16th 1969

Calvin had been sullen during the journey home and sat, arms folded, in the car without once looking at his chauffeur.

Bolly had tried several times to make conversation, only to be rebuked or answered with a grunt. Being Bolly, she had to pursue the matter further.

"We should have run when we heard that twig snap."

Calvin replied without looking at her.

"Done no good. It wasn't the police."

Bolly took her eyes off the road to look at Calvin, who sat impassively beside her. His face of what she could see of it wore a worried expression.

"Who do you think it was, Meynell?"

Calvin snapped back at her.

"How the fucking hell should I know. For God's sake, shut up and drive."

Not a word passed between them for the remainder of the journey. The car finally pulled up outside the cottage. Calvin climbed out and strode up to the front door with Bolly tagging behind.

The door wasn't locked. Strange, he was sure he had locked it the night before, and it was Mrs Thirkell's day off.

He paused as he entered the hallway. Bolly was about to remove her coat when Calvin held a finger to his lips as he gently turned the handle to the lounge door. Next to the mantle was a figure. He had his back to them admiring Calvin's collection. Before he had time to turn, Calvin rushed at him.

The man swung around, sensing there was someone behind, but it was too late. A foot caught him under the chin as Calvin's karate kick sent him crashing over the coffee table, before hitting the floor with a sickening thud.

Pinning him to the ground, Calvin removed a gun from inside the man's jacket. Tossing it onto the sofa he dragged the stunned man to his feet. His hand cupped the man's face as a mean snarl twisted Calvin's features into a grotesque murderous mask.

Bolly stood transfixed; she had never seen him so mean. The man's body began to shake as Calvin concentrated all the venom of the past weeks into the brain of his unfortunate victim.

"Stop it, stop at once!"
The voice behind him screamed frantically. He paid it no heed.

From behind a pair of female hands tried to loosen Calvin's murderous grip. In desperation the hands slapped him hard several times across the face until his grip lessened, allowing the body to crumple to the floor in a heap.

"He's on your side, for Gods sake!" Calvin's eye glared wildly and meanly at the woman.

Lady Winspear demanded Calvin assist her in placing the man on the sofa. Calvin, without much effort, lifted the man's medium-sized frame as if it were nothing more than a mannequin, and, with just as much respect, threw it onto the sofa.

The sound of clapping from behind caused them all to spin round to see a tall thin elegant man, a little camp in his dress, standing in the doorway applauding the performance. His long overcoat, draped over his shoulders in a theatrical manner was topped off with a large fedora.

"Bravo, dear boy, bravo, absolutely first class performance, most impressed."

Lady Winspear nudged Bolly, who was still enchanted by the entrance of their visitor.

"Arabella, never mind Croxton, go and fetch a bowl of water and a cloth. Quickly."

The man on the sofa was slowly coming around as Croxton held out his hand, offering it to Calvin.

"Allow me to introduce myself. Croxton Bishop."

Calvin looked at his hand.

"How do you know I won't do the same to you?"

Croxton smiled as his green grey eyes flashed with admiration at the fine specimen before him.

"My dear boy, one does not bite the hand that feeds it."

Calvin ignored Croxton and turned to Lady Winspear who was still tending to the injured man.

"I see you finally called in your old boy network," he rasped.

Calvin's contemptuous words fell on deaf ears as Lady Winspear ordered Bolly, who had returned with the bowl, to continue dabbing the blood away from the man's face.

Eventually she stood up to face Calvin.

"Why did you call him in?" Calvin asked.

"If it had not been for Croxton you would still be in the police cell," she replied.

Croxton looked over the top of the sofa at his underling, who was still worse for wear.

"Yes," Croxton's melodic voice rang out.

"If it had not been for the poor chappie who has just received your rather unfriendly greeting, you would most probably now be facing some trumped-up charge.

Calvin looked at Croxton.

"How did you know? "he asked.

"Oh, we have been busy keeping an eye on you for some time."

Calvin leaned against the mantle. He still looked a strange sight, with half of his face covered in bandages.

Bolly interrupted.

"So, he was the one we heard in the garden."

Croxton shrugged his shoulders.

"Possibly, who knows. Shame, he is one of my best men. I do hope there had been no irreparable damage, I have become quite fond of him of late, in a fatherly way of course."

From his inside pocket Croxton took out a silver cigarette case. Offering one to Calvin, who refused, he removed a cigarette. After tapping the cigarette end on the case he placed it in a cigarette holder and lit it, blowing the smoke out of the side of his mouth as he held the holder between his teeth.

Moving closer to Calvin, Croxton looked him square in the face.

"Now, shall we get to the point? I am led to believe you have a few problems concerning our American cousins." Calvin stared coldly at the man as Croxton continued to speak.

"Nothing we..."

Calvin cut his next sentence short.

"Hey, let's get a few things straight. You can forget this we business for a start. I have no intention of working for M.I.5., M.I.6., the C.I.A,, or the fucking KGB. I've had a belly-full of you guys, with your covert operations and double dealing. No, I'm out of that for good."

Croxton smiled as he removed the cigarette holder from his mouth.

"I am sure I do not have to tell an intelligent man like yourself the facts of life, or should I say in your case death."

At that the man on the sofa pulled himself up into a sitting position. Croxton spoke theatrically.

"Ah, Lazarus has risen. Some brandy?"

Lady Winspear looked at Calvin.

"Don't look at me. I'm not your servant."

Bolly stood up to get the drink.

"Two glasses, my dear," Croxton called out.

"Two?" Bolly asked.

"I was thinking of myself, still the poor boy looks in need of a pick-me-up, yes make it two. Not too much now," Croxton teased.

"One must not under any circumstances spoil the peasants; revolutions have been started over lesser things."
Croxton's face took on a sinister expression.

"Remember this, my dear boy. Once a light is switched on, shadows have nowhere to hide and you, dear boy, have just switched on the light."
Calvin answered in his usual arrogant manner.

"And what if I decide to switch off the light?"
Croxton glared at him.

"You can't, but others can always extinguish it for you. My card, I would advice you take it, like it or not you will require my assistance."

Croxton flicked the card on top of the drinks cabinet before helping his underling to his feet and leading the way out of the door.

Lady Winspear looked first at Calvin, then at Bolly.

"Shall we leave Calvin to rest. I'm sure he has a lot to think about."
Bolly was reluctant to leave.

"I thought I'd stay and make Calvin and myself something to eat. If that's all right with Calvin."

Calvin gave a slight nod of agreement, as Bolly, smiling, picked up the bowl and left the room for the kitchen.
Lady Winspear stood before her tenant.

"She seems to becoming rather fond of you."
Calvin made no comment.

"Do not forget who you are."
Calvin looked to his feet before lifting his head up to look once more at the woman who was standing, hands on hips, before him.

"Calvin," she continued, "Accept his offer; this thing's getting out of hand. I beg you, do as I ask. And please send Arabella home; I will never forgive you if anything happens to her."
Calvin nodded.

"She's a good kid, plenty of spunk. If you're afraid we'll end up in bed then why not tell her the truth?"

Lady Winspear made no reply as she turned and walked towards the door.

"Just send her home." she pleaded.

Later that evening with the fire banked up with logs, a warm ambience embraced the room. Calvin was asleep with his head resting on the side of his winged chair in front of the fire, while Bolly lay curled up like a cat, hugging a cushion on the floor.

Calvin moved his head from side to side as he groaned in his sleep. The groaning slowly began to take on a sinister tone as it increased in volume, eventually rousing the sleeping Bolly.

Her eyes blinked as she tried to focus on the seated figure above her. Calvin was having a nightmare. The same nightmare he had experienced in Christine's house. Once again a large black shape chased him. The shape that slowly and relentlessly followed him as he fled from the cottage and into the nearby graveyard.

A scream ricocheted around the room as he jumped to his feet, trembling with fear. Oblivious to Bolly's presence, he rushed out of the room, throwing the front door wide open, before dashing out into the night.

Bolly was quick to follow, but stopped in her tracks at the sight of the Calvin's kneeling figure, head cupped painfully between his hands.

Her hand reached out for her friend as she led his trembling body back into the cottage.

Switching on the light, she sat him down in his chair. Her hands felt wet as she looked down at her palms. They were covered in blood. At first she instinctively went to wipe them on her clothes, then halted as she looked around for the source of the deep red fluid.

Calvin Dane sat silent in the chair, his face crimson and his bandages dripping in blood. Not knowing what to do, she rushed out into the kitchen to fetch a bowl with clean water to bathe or at least try to relieve the injured man.

Calvin pushed her away.

"Leave it."

"Don't be silly. It may become infected." she retorted.

"I said, leave it alone."

His voice was mean and angry. She instantly recoiled.

"Suit your bloody self."

She threw the cloth down into the bowl, causing the water to splash over the carpet, before storming out of the room and out of the house.

Calvin sat motionless for several minutes before whispering to himself.

"Come on, yer bastard, show yourself!"

Ten minutes had elapsed when Calvin heard the front door open. Bolly strolled in. His face was bare, the bandage removed. Bolly winced at the state of his face. Beside the bruising that encircled his eye, there was a deep red angry scar that traced its way from temple down to the lower part of his cheek. The redness of the scar was emphasised by large black stitches like spider's legs which held the flesh together.

As for the eye it was nothing more than a red blob. She had changed his dressing before but she had never seen his eye in such a state.

Calvin held the cloth to his face, covering the offending wound, which had finally ceased bleeding. At first she felt sorry for him. She just wanted to throw her arms around his neck and hug him. Then common sense told her what his reaction would be. Finally, her old anger rekindled itself as she turned her frustration and lack of understanding upon him.

"Just what the hell is it with you? One minute you seem to be human then the next..."
Calvin sighed cutting her sentence short.

"Boll, I'm sorry, I know you find it hard to understand, but it's best if you don't have anything to do with me."

Calvin wrapped a towel around his head to cover up the side of his face. Bolly shook her head as she moved next to him to help.

He was afraid, and much as he hated to admit it, he liked and needed Bolly's company. But looking up to her elfin face, he realised that he couldn't afford to be selfish.

"It's no longer safe for you to be here."
Bolly looked at him, her blue eyes softened along with her voice.

"What's happening?"
Calvin took her hand.

"I told you there were people who would like to see me dead. Well I think they've found me."

Bolly felt a shudder run through her body as she thought of poor Maria, was she to receive the same fate, a fate she obviously did not want? She had fallen in love with him, and her fate was now cast to the wind.

Impulsively she threw her arms around his neck. Her heart raced as she sobbed, clinging onto him like a limpet.

"I don't care, all I want is to be with you."
She lifted her head away just enough to kiss him on the mouth.

Calvin grabbed hold of her arms, snapping her hands apart.

"Stop, we can't!"

"Why not?"
She was shocked at his rebuff.

"Fucking hell, what a mess, what a Christ almighty mess!" Calvin rose to his feet and shook his head.

"I should have told you. I should have fucking told you."

"Told me what?" Bolly was bemused.
Calvin took her by the hand to lead her to the sofa. Sitting her down, he looked into her eyes.

"She'll hate me for this." he continued.

"But I've got to tell you. It may be the only way to save your life."

Calvin released her hand as he stood up and began to pace up and down in front of the fire.

"I told you that I was bred selectively. And that I am not an American."
Bolly with a knowing expression on her face, replied.

"You're German. I know, and I don't care. I love you."

Calvin tossed the towel onto the floor, leaving his face uncovered.

"What your Grandmother didn't want you to know was that I am also your first cousin."

"What! You can't be!" The words stuttered out of Bolly's mouth.

"Yhep," Calvin replied. "I'm what you call the family skeleton."

Bolly was confused; she thought she had known all there was to know about her family.

"I don't understand, I know all of the family and none of them are German. My God, how could they be? Two of my uncles were killed in the war."

"Perhaps, but the fact is that I am still your cousin. Not only that, your grandmother is also my grandmother. That's why I told you to ask her how we met."

Bolly shook her head in disbelief, while Calvin stood very erect and authoritative as he spoke.

"When I ran away from the centre, for insurance purposes I broke into Quint's office and removed all of the files on myself and the rest of the children. That's how I knew about your grandmother, our grandmother. Her real name is not Eve but Eva. She is the daughter of an Austrian professor of history whom your Grandfather was very friendly with before the war. As a young girl, no more than fifteen, she fell in love with a young student and became pregnant. The child, to save the family's blushes, was adopted by a friend from Berlin and was brought up as their child. She was my mother." The family who adopted her later became staunch supporters of the Third Reich and all of its policies, including the building of a master race, especially that. As the years went by my mother showed certain abilities uncommon in the majority of people. These qualities were recognised by Himmler himself, who was a friend of the family. She was admitted to a house in Vienna, a special house, unlike any of the other breeding camps throughout Germany and Austria. This was a breeding house of the gifted, women who displayed not just abilities such as your mediums. They had to have true psychic abilities, abilities that I have been able to master. And these women were covered like brood mares by the chosen stallions of the Third Reich. Blond, blue eyed, pure bred Aryan males, who like the women, also had incredible abilities. The rest you know. That's why this Croxton Bishop guy is so interested in me."

Bolly ran her fingers through her hair before taking hold of his hand and tenderly kissing the back of it.

"I understand why there can be nothing between us, but that still doesn't alter the fact that we are cousins and I hope friends."

Just at that moment the telephone rang.
Bolly smiled.

"Stay where you are, cousin. I'll answer it."
Harland's voice crackled down the line.

"Can I speak to Mr Dane?" It's Inspector Harland."

Bolly held her hand over the mouthpiece as she spoke to Calvin.

"It's Harland."
Calvin took hold of the receiver.

"Yes?"

"Sorry to hear about your little brush with the law,"

Harland began.

"No problem," Calvin replied.

"You were right about the woman and the three boys," Harland continued. "We had a little chat with them, only what you saw as a woman was, we believe, a man wearing a wig."

Calvin pushed Bolly's face away from the receiver as she tried to listen in on the conversation.

"And?"

Harland continued.

"Well to tell the truth we were hoping you would be able to help us some more. It would have to be strictly off the record, though."

Calvin paused for a moment.

"Why not? May as well finish what we've started."

Harland couldn't hide his pleasure.

"Great. I'd like to thank you; I know you must be sick of driving back and forth, but we thought you might pick something up in the field, where the bonfire was."

Calvin shook his head as he answered.

"Waste of time going there; I know where he tried to kill the child."

"You do, where?" Harland's voice grew excitable.

"Meynell's garden," Calvin replied.

The tone of anticipation in Harland's voice sunk to the level of, 'Fucking hell I thought it was too good to be true.'

"It would be." Harland sighed

"Well do you want me to help or not?" Calvin asked.

Harland didn't hesitate in his answer.

"Sod it, can you come down tomorrow evening?"

Calvin whispered to Bolly, asking her the name of the pub they had stopped in.

Returning to the phone, he gave his reply.

"Okay, see you in the Brown Ox, it's a pub in the village. Know it?"

"No doubt Doran will," was the response. "If not, he'll smell it out. Tomorrow evening then, eight pm."

Calvin replaced the receiver and turned to Bolly.

"Let's get some sleep, you've got another long drive ahead of you tomorrow."

Bolly smiled as she flung her arms around his neck and gave him a kiss.

"Welcome to the family."

Judge's House
Peel Kent England.
December 17th 1969

Knives, forks and plates, neatly set out, lay on the brilliant white tablecloth, waiting for the men of the house to take their respective seats. Meynell was the first to sit down and was instantly fussed over by his grandmother. Placed before him was his regular breakfast of scrambled egg, bacon, sausage and tomatoes. A full English breakfast cooked especially for him, just as he liked it.

"There you are, dear."
Her hand brushed his hair away from his eyes.

"The toast is in the rack, I will bring your tea in as soon as your grandfather sits down."

The Judge entered, allowing the woman to slip silently out into the kitchen to fetch his breakfast.

The Judge, before sitting, laid a cheap plastic child's watch down on the table.

"What's this? "
The judge took his seat after asking the question. Once again, as if from nowhere, his wife appeared with the breakfast. After placing it down she left the men to quickly return with the tea. Allowing the judge to repeat his question.

"Well, what is it?"
"A watch," was the response.

The Judge peered over the top of his half-moon glasses.

"I know it's a watch. Where did it come from?"

"Where did you find it?" was the reply

"I found it in the bathroom."

Meynell waited until he had swallowed his piece of bacon.

"Is that where I left it?"

The Judge looked puzzled.

"What on earth were you doing with a thing like that?"

Meynell looked at it without picking it up.

"I found it on the floor of the bank. A child must have lost it. I intended to leave it with one of the clerks in case it was claimed. Obviously, I forgot."

"What was it doing in the bathroom?" the Judge continued to question him.

"No great mystery. I felt a lump in my pocket and there it was. It's the first time I've worn the trousers since picking it up, so I laid it beside the basin. What's the third degree for, have I committed some terrible offence?"

The Judge looked up at his wife, who had returned and was hovering around like a vulture, anxiously waiting for the moment to clear the dishes away and bring in a fresh pot of tea.

"Leave us alone; I wish to speak to David in private."

His wife obeyed without question.

Turning to his grandson, he picked up the watch and dangled it before him.

"Do you know what happened here the other night?

Meynell looked a little confused.

"You mean about the prowler?"

The Judge closed his hand around the watch as he continued to play with it.

"Do you know who he was?"

Meynell shook his head.

"Should I?"

The Judge continued

"It was an American called Calvin Dane."

Meynell still shook his head.

"Who?"

"You met him," the Judge rasped.

Meynell pretended not to know what he was talking about.

"I did, when?"

The judge felt he was lying but was not sure.

"When you went to visit the house in Durham, the one you wish to buy."

Meynell's face changed as he finally pretended to recognise the name.

"Oh, so that's what they call him. So this Calvin Dane was our prowler. How strange, I only met the man once at the door for a few seconds, no longer. He was polite, we shook hands, exchanged the usual pleasantries, nothing more. And now you tell me he was our midnight visitor. How strange."

The Judge was used to watching people's reactions in court and always prided himself on his judgement as to whether a person was lying or not, but his grandson showed no such signs. He was either the best liar he had encountered or he was telling the truth.

"You are sure you have never met him since?"

"Not to my knowledge."

Meynell stood up without waiting for his second cup of tea.

"I think I will pop down to the cottage this afternoon."

The Judge also rose from his seat as he spoke.

"What for?"

"For a break, "Meynell snapped. "Why? Do I need a reason, or have I become some sort of prisoner?"

"No, no, not at all," The Judge calmly responded. "How long do you intend to stay?"

Meynell smiled at his grandfather.

"Just the day, should be back late evening, unless I decide to stay overnight."

The Judge turned, and walked out of the breakfast room, and called to his wife.

"Get my overcoat, I'm in a rush."

Once the Judge was out of the room, Meynell removed a handkerchief and used it to pick up the watch, before wrapping it up inside the cloth. He smiled as he listened to his grandfather complain to his wife.

"There's a button missing from my coat."

"Not to worry, dear, I have some spare. I can sew you one on if you take it off."

"No time woman, this evening will do." the Judge snapped.

Meynell took a sip of tea and grinned as he stuffed the handkerchief-bound watch into his pocket.

Judge's House,
Peel, Kent, England.
8-30pm December 17th 1969

Doran caught the seat of his pants on a thorn bush as they stumbled in the dark through the trees towards the summerhouse, at the far end of the garden.

"Shit, it's ripped a hole in them."

Harland and Bolly both shushed him. Reaching the summerhouse, Doran and Harland let their torches illuminate the inside of the building.

"Keep the torches down!" Calvin ordered.

The place was empty apart from a long wooden bench. Calvin asked them all to be quiet as he held out both his hands, like a blind man feeling his way. He stood, motionless, before drawing in several deep breaths. Suddenly his head jerked backwards.

"I see her, a girl, fair hair, about eight years old lying on the bench, fully clothed, as if asleep. There's a strange smell, a sweet sickly smell. There's a woman standing over her, she turns and walks over to a large dark green bag made of canvas. She's got her back to the child, and is removing a wig. It's not a woman, it's a man. It's Meynell. He's taking his jumper off. The son-of-a-bitch is wearing a padded bra.

He's now taking down his slacks. Wait, the child's moving, she's beginning to wake. Meynell hasn't noticed. His slacks are around his ankles, he is about to pull them off. He's still got his back to her and can't see her sitting up. The poor kids terrified. Go on kid, run for it. She's scrambling to her feet and rushing out of the door. The kid's unsteady, as if she's been drugged. Meynell's spotted her but his pants are half on and half off. He's pulling them up to run after her."

Calvin, followed by the others, made their way out of the summerhouse and into the garden, where he continued his narration.

"He's to fast, almost upon her, the poor kids still half-drugged. The bastard's got her next to the lilac shrub. They're both on the floor, the kid's screaming, Meynell's trying to stop her, his hand is over her mouth. He's looking around to see if anyone has heard.

The poor kid's terrified, her eyes are almost out of her head with fear. She's bitten him. She's sunk her teeth into his hand. It's bleeding. That's made him mad.

The kid's still on the ground, trying to scramble to her feet. He's got hold of her foot, pulling her closer to him. She's kicking, punching, fighting for her life. There's a large, thick, heavy branch on the floor. The kid's screaming, loud ear-piercing screams. He's lifting the branch up. The first blow to her head knocks her sideways but she's still screaming, two, three, four, he's hitting her one blow after another."

"She's stopped screaming. It's all silent. He's kneeling beside her, he tries to suffocate her with his hands, but she still has some fight in her yet. He's removing a thin cord like belt a from the woman's slacks he's wearing. The bastard's trying to finish her off.

He's strangling her. Her body's gone limp. No more fighting, no more screaming, even the faint gurgling sound has ceased. "

Calvin let out a sigh before continuing.

"Meynell's sitting beside her, he looks around him, then over to the house. No lights have come on, they can't have heard. The son of a bitch is now pulling her into his arms and he's crying, rocking her like a baby."

Calvin came out of his trance as he turned to the policemen.

"She bit him on the hand, there have to be teeth marks."

Harland looked at Bolly, who gave a shudder as she looked at the spot where the child was murdered.

"Anything else?" Harland asked.

Calvin held out his hands once again as he walked around the garden like a diviner searching for water, finally making his way towards the garden bonfire, or at least what remained of it.

Suddenly Calvin stooped to pick something up from the ground. It was a bottle, the same bottle Meynell had carelessly tossed into the fire and missed. Calvin clasped the bottle between his hands.

"I get the impression of the sea."

Harland looked at Doran.

"Yes, the sea, "Calvin continued.

"A house, or a cottage, overlooking the sea. I get the impression it's remote, no other houses around. It's definitely connected to Meynell. His presence is strong. Do they have a holiday home?"

Harland looked once again at Doran before nodding.

"We can check it out."

Calvin looked at the men.

"Find that and we'll find the missing link."

Harland nodded once again.

"Okay let's find a telephone."

"Angel tits?" smiled Doran.

Harland gave half a laugh.

"Angel tits it is."

"Who's angel tits?" asked Bolly

Doran smiled before answering.

"A friend of the guv's. If she's on nights she has access to information she shouldn't."

"She's on nights?" Harland nodded.

Meynell's Cottage, England. December 17th 1969.

Meynell had been at the cottage about ten minutes. The story of wishing to spend a relaxing day by the sea was a lie; he had other tasks to take care of first. That's why he had been so late in his preparations. The cottage, although only a holiday home, was well-furnished with as cosy appearance both outside, and in.

Meynell had always hated the place and the memories it held. Still, he had finally found a use for it now the Judge no longer used it for his private parties. From being a place, that had sent shudders through his body, at the mere mention of its name, it now provided Meynell with the perfect retreat.

He made his way over to the small light oak sideboard, removing his handkerchief from his pocket and carefully laying it out on the top. Unfolding the cloth, he smiled at the sight of the little child's plastic watch.

Picking it up with the corner of the handkerchief, he walked over to the sofa and removed one of the cushions before stuffing the watch down one of its sides and putting the cushion back.

The sound of a car in the distance startled Meynell, who quickly snatched up a large dark green canvas bag, the same one Calvin had seen in his vision, before switching the light off. Calmly and without any signs of panic, he made his way out of the house by the rear door.

Meynell made his way through a small but dense belt of trees high on a little hill towards his car, which he had deliberately parked out of sight. The rest of the place was open land with sea views.

Once safe, he couldn't resist spying on the figures below as he tried to make out who they were. The muffled voices of the four figures that congregated outside the cottage carried on the wind.

"Do you want me to open it?"
Doran's voice bellowed out into the night as he shouted, trying to compete with the noise of the waves crashing against the rocks below. Harland turned the car headlights on full beam so that the fat policeman could see the door and its lock. Meynell, still watching from above, smiled as he saw the figures below, instantly recognising Calvin and his female sidekick.

Suddenly a strange feeling came over him, as if someone was watching him. He rubbed the back of his neck as his skin became goosed, with the hairs standing proud in their follicles.

He jumped back as he saw a large black shape melt into the shadows, without a sound. Terrified and without looking back, he ran across the field to his car.

The door to the cottage clicked open as Doran, like some master thief, picked its lock.

Harland shook his head as the gloved hand of Doran, switched on the light to the lounge.

"I'm getting a little worried about you, Ted,"

Calvin looked around the room and held out his hands. Shaking his head, took the bottle from the fire out of his pocket. Clasping it in his hands, he stood motionless for a second or two.

"Not in here, outside somewhere, a stable or outbuilding. I'm getting an impression of a very cold place."

Calvin halted at the door and looked back into the room.

"He's been here recently. I can sense him"

The policeman and Bolly, found it hard to believe what they were witnessing, But there they were hanging onto every word, movement, that the American said or made.

Doran and Harland shone their torches on the floor as they made their way along the side of the house to a small group of stone outbuildings. Calvin stopped at the first, still holding the bottle in his hand. Shaking his head, he moved onto the next.

"This is it." His voice was calm.

Doran lifted the latch to the unlocked building. He was reluctant to enter, something about the place made him feel uneasy, but then he never was the bravest of persons when it came to the dark.

Standing to one side he shone his torch to show the way for the others to enter. All four crushed into the tiny room, too small for Calvin to work in with the others inside.

Doran was the first to volunteer to leave, followed by the ever reluctant Bolly, who was ordered outside by Harland. Standing in the doorway, Doran and Bolly watched as Harland, in possession of both torches, illuminated the room.

The floor was concrete, with a small circular drain in the middle with deep grooves spiralling their way out, so the water could flow more effectively towards it. There was a large pot sink fastened to the wall, with one cold water tap. The sink was so large, it was almost the size of a small bath. Coiled up beside the sink on a large stone slab was a hosepipe.

Harland turned to Calvin.

"I wonder what this place is used for."

Harland's voice echoed around the ice-cold room.

"Fish," interrupted Doran still standing in the doorway. "It's an old fish house. This is where they would fillet the fish."

Calvin looked around the room.

"This is no fish house. It's a death house.

Harland, torches in hand, so as not to be in Calvin's way, stood in the far corner. Calvin, with his hands outstretched, drew in several deep breaths.

"I see Meynell walking through the door. He's carrying a child, a little girl. He's laying her down on the stone slab. He turns and walks back outside. The child is either drugged or unconscious, she's still alive, I can see her breathing. He's back with his bag, I can see him changing, removing his wig and woman's clothes. Each article is carefully folded and piled neatly beside the child.

He is naked apart from his shorts, nothing else. He's reaching into his bag, pulling something out, it's large and round. It's a cushion. That's how the bastard kills them, the same as in the house, with a cushion. He's placing the cushion over her face, there's no struggle, the child hasn't made a move, no fighting, no tears, nothing. She must be drugged. She's dead. He's putting the cushion and his woman's clothes back into the bag.

He must be freezing, standing in only his shorts. He doesn't even have any shoes on. He's undressing the child. Her clothes have also been neatly piled up beside her. He's at the sink. There are some pots and a box of plaster filler, the type you fill small cracks or gaps in walls with. He's mixing it with the water, making sure that the mixture is just right. Oh my God! The sick bastard."

Calvin paused for a moment, as the three onlookers remained rooted to the spot, waiting for him to continue.

"This is one seriously sick son-of-a-bitch. He's filling her mouth with plaster. Son-of-a-fucking-bitch. I should have killed him when I had he chance"

Calvin snapped out of his trance. Bolly felt sick. Ignoring the others Calvin walked outside to take in a few deep gulps of bracing sea air. The other three looked on patiently, waiting for him to recover from an ordeal that had obviously upset not only them, but the ice-cold Mr Calvin Dane.

His large frame was silhouetted, inky black, against a turbulent sea that reflected the light from the moon.

"At first I thought he was a necrophile, but he isn't."

Harland moved closer to the American.

"What does he do, have sex with them before he kills them?"

Calvin shook his head.

"Sex as we know it does not come into it. This man is not murdering to appease his own sexual perversion, well, not one that's visible."

Harland was bemused.

"Well, what the hell is he murdering for?"

Calvin held out his hand to Bolly, who was shivering from both the cold and the thought of what had happened to the child. Wrapping his arm around Bolly, he pulled her to him before answering the man's question.

"To turn them into cherubs, statues. The man's obsessed with cherubs and churches, He's killing the children to turn them into statues."

Bolly looked up at him.

"You mean he covers them with plaster?"

Calvin shook his head.

"No, he fills up the openings in the body with plaster, then stitches their eyelids together."

Harland closed his eyes before asking the inevitable question

"And the bodies, what does he do with them? The one we found hadn't been tampered with like that."

Calvin shook his head.

"That was one of his mistakes. She tried to escape, and in panic he clubbed her, marking her face, making her of no use to him, she had become imperfect. That's why he was crying; he had destroyed the one thing he tries to preserve, the beauty and the innocence of childhood. Or, to him, a would-be cherub."

Harland was desperate. He wanted this man. It was like a hunger gnawing at his insides.

"Can you trace the bodies?"

Calvin stood beside the car. Resting his elbow on the roof, he pondered for a moment.

"Cherubs belong in churches. You have a map, you should find a church around here. That's where you'll find them, the children."

Doran got the map out of the car.

Calvin looked up towards the hill with the small clump of trees where Meynell had been watching them. Without taking his eye off the landscape he said.

"Look for a church or place of worship beginning with the letter O."

Bolly held the torch for Doran as he ran his finger across the map searching for the church.

"What makes a sick bastard like that tick?" Harland sighed.

Bolly lifted her head up to reply to Harland.

"I'm sure some do-good social worker will find a reason."

Harland called out to Calvin.

"I don't suppose you could be wrong?" Calvin made no comment, the look was enough.

"Yeah you're right, I've seen too much to doubt your ability." Harland sighed once again.

"Here we are!" Doran cried out, "St Oswald's, no more than a few miles inland."

Harland looked back at the fish house and shook his head. A lump appeared in his throat as a tear rolled down his cheek.

"What a place to die."

St Oswald's Church Kent England. 4am December 18th 1969

The beams from the car's headlights lit up the ruins of an old castle keep, as they made their way up the hill before descending, and halting outside the churchyard. Most churchyards look gloomy at night but this one was dark, oppressive, and sinister.

A fox ran past them, springing over the small rise before squeezing through the metal bars of the kissing gate. Doran watched the creature as it ran along the tree-lined pathway up what looked like, a long dark tunnel.

The tunnel was in fact rows of yew trees that had stood either side of the pathway for centuries, with their branches touching one another, bridging the gap to form the tunnel.

At the far end of the tunnel to the left was a small Norman Chapel, with its separate tower and stone ruin, the result of centuries of neglect after the turbulent period of Henry the Eighth's reign of reformation.

The churchyard, surrounded by a dry stone wall, had two small wrought-iron gates for an entrance. To the right of the main gate was a small kissing gate, the type of gate that will admit one person at a time by pushing the gate one way then standing to the side to let it swing back the other way before entering.

Doran looked over the gate; his heart was pounding. He hated to admit it, but the whole place, the cemetery, the yew tree tunnel and the chapel gave him the creeps. Even Harland felt a little uneasy about entering the place, especially at night.

Calvin was the first to enter, followed by Bolly, then Harland. Doran hung back and looked about him.

"I'll wait by the car?"

"Get your arse in here, Ted." Harland gave a command, not a request.

Calvin took the lead, with Harland close behind, his torch forging a path through the blackness, with the canopy of trees preventing what small amount of light the moon could shed to guide these most unwelcome visitors.

Doran's eyes were everywhere, darting in the direction of one noise to the next.

"Bloody spooky, isn't it?"

Doran was spooked. Having Calvin narrate an event was frightening enough. The possibility of him personally seeing something put the fear of God in him.

Harland whispered to Calvin.

"What do you reckon, buried in a grave?"

Reaching the end of the path and out of its yew tree tunnel, Calvin called the party to a halt.

To the left stood the chapel and the small arch that joined it to the old ruin tower. In the middle of the arch stood a low tomb, like an altar.

Calvin looked up at the moon as it hovered above. There were three days to go before it would be full; still it hovered ominously, positioned as if it were there by demand, directly above the stone slab, shedding cold unblinking light onto the dark stone altar. On the night of a full moon this tomb would be bathed in its silver glow.

Holding out his hands he went into a trance once again.

"This is his spot, his favourite spot. I see him carrying a naked child, her body has been sealed. In his mind she is now a cherub."

Calvin looked down at the tomb, at the child, as if he were actually there, as a phantom observer standing next to Meynell. Then all of a sudden it came to him, the mouth, the mouths of the children who appeared to him. The one large tooth like a boxer's gum shield. It was the plaster. That's why their lips were pushed back and deformed. Calvin shed an unnoticed tear as he continued to narrate.

"Meynell's taking a small bottle out of his pocket, not the one I had, another one, it contains a sort of oil. Oh, this man is sick. He's covering the child's body with the oil, rubbing it into her skin so it will shine in the moonlight. Now he's taking photographs."

Calvin came out of his trance. Turning to the others, he shook his head.

"He sits, he just sits and looks at them for hours. Once they're covered in oil he just sits and stares, doesn't masturbate or touch them, nothing. There's nothing outwardly sexual about these murders. It's all in the mind of one hell of a sick and twisted creature."

"This is his pleasure, this is what he is killing for. And he's revelling in it."

Bolly looked at the tomb, then at Calvin.

"What about dressing up as a woman?"

Calvin looked around him and hesitated before answering.

"To lure the children, nothing more. Children tend to trust a woman more than a man. Once they came close enough he would grab them and knock them out with chloroform. That was the sweet anaesthetic smell that you experienced. The smell of the perfume was to cover up the strong odour of the chloroform."

Harland turned to Calvin.

"Where are the bodies?"

Calvin pointed towards the chapel, which stood to their left. Harland tapped Doran on the shoulder. Who jumped.

"Try the door, Ted," he said.

Doran turned the large metal ring which was a handle, but to no avail. The door was locked.

"Don't look at me this time." Doran shrugged his shoulders as he spoke. "I've no chance of opening this one."

There was a small wooden peephole, like a cat flap. Calvin lifted it open and peered inside. Taking the torch from Harland he shone it around the inside of the chapel.

The chapel was tiny, with no more than seven rows of pews, seating a possible maximum of thirty people. On the far side of the church from the altar stood a tomb with the effigy of a knight lying in a death pose, gripping his sword. Calvin kept the beam trained on the tomb of the knight as he beckoned Harland to take a look.

"That's were they are, in there."

Harland let the flap swing back into place, before turning to Doran.

"Ted, go into the village, knock the vicar up and get the key."

Doran looked back at the trees and the pathway.

"On me own?"

Bolly grabbed hold of the torch.

"Come on shity arse, I'll hold your hand."

Calvin and Harland stood by the door to the church as the figures of Bolly and Doran disappeared from sight. They were almost at the gate when Doran was sure he heard a noise.

"There's someone following us."

Bolly shone the torch around; for one fleeting moment she thought she saw something, something large and black, but put it down to her imagination.

"Come on, let's get on with it," she said.

Harland lit himself a cigarette.

"Inside, are they?"

Calvin shushed him.

"What's wrong?" Harland whispered.

Calvin looked around.

"There's someone else here."

Harland shone his torch around the churchyard, sweeping it to and fro, straining his eyes as he followed the beam.

"You go that way and I'll go this," Harland whispered.

Calvin made no move. Instead of using his eyesight, he opened his psyche.

"Come on then, show yourself, or are you still afraid of me?" The words left his lips like the venom from a spitting cobra.

Harland's voice could be heard calling in the distance.

"Over here, quick!"
Calvin stumbled towards the policeman as best he could. Finally he caught up with him; standing on top of the dry stone wall.

"I saw something, big and black."
Harland's voice trembled as he spoke, partly due to being out of breath and partly due to fear.

Calvin looked at him.

"I believe you." He touched him on the shoulder. "Let's sit here and wait."

The two men sat, legs dangling over the wall, as they waited for the return of Bolly and Doran.

Harland had smoked his second cigarette when a set of bright beams searched through the night sky as they climbed the hill before dropping down towards the churchyard. Eventually the car drew to a halt. Bolly, Doran and a third figure alighted from the car. The third figure was the vicar, who refused to give Doran the key as he did not like the look of him.

The vicar stared indignantly at the seated figure of Harland as his legs dangled over the wall.

"I hope you have not got me out of bed on some wild-goose chase." He paused for a moment. "As a matter of interest, do you have a search warrant?"
Harland was quick to reply.

"Why? Do you have something to hide?"

"Certainly not!" retorted the vicar.

"Good." Harland was not in the mood for niceties." Then shall we get on with it?"

Harland stood up, towering over the rest of the party below. He looked around, but Calvin had already left heading in the direction of the chapel. Waiting for the rest to arrive, Calvin and Harland stood opposite one another.

"You saw something, didn't you?" Harland looked into Calvin's face as he asked the question. "What was it?"

"No one for you to worry about," Calvin replied. "Just a spectre from the past."

At that, the moaning voice of the vicar could be heard approaching. Still grumbling, he finally opened the chapel door. All of the party, with the exception of Calvin, filed into the chapel. Calvin called out without entering.

"In the tomb of the knight."

"What! You're not opening that!" The vicar protested.

Harland ignored the clergyman and examined the tomb, while Bolly lit as many candles as she could find.

The church was ablaze with the soft glow of candlelight; what should have been a comfort to the night prowlers made the place look even more eerie, as shadows hugged the stone walls, forming sinister images.

"Look, Ted it's been opened!"

Harland pointed excitedly to some faint marks where a tool had been used to slide the slab across. The slab should have been slid back into place, but obviously it had not. Instead it bore the tell-tale gouges of a crow bar.

Doran and Harland, with all their might, pushed the lid slowly across, opening the stone tomb no more than a few inches.

The stench made Harland wretch as he drew his head back. Doran also recoiled, calling out in the process.

"Shit!" Before apologising. "Sorry, vicar."

Harland took a deep breath before shining his torch into the gap. He saw what he wanted to see, yet hoped he never would. Three bodies of naked children, all hunched up in one common grave, already inhabited by a thirteenth-century Plantagenet knight.

The vicar jumped up from the pew and grabbed the torch from Harland. What met his eyes sent a shock wave through his body as he flopped backwards into one of the pews in a state of trauma.

"Ted, get in touch with head office," Harland ordered, "Get a squad down here. We've finally nailed the bastard."

Calvin remained at the door with Bolly, who having no intention of looking inside the tomb, moved out of the way to let Doran past.

"Coming?" he asked her.

"Give me a second."

She looked up at Calvin.

"You all right?"

Calvin nodded.

"Go on, go with him, he'll crap himself if he hears a noise. I'm all right, don't worry."

Bolly left with Doran as Harland joined Calvin by the door.

"Found them all."

Calvin shook his head.

"Not quite, there's still the boy."

"The boy, I'd forgotten about him," Harland replied.

Calvin let out a sigh before speaking.

"The boy was another one of his mistakes. In the dark he mistook him for a girl, what with his long hair, and the last thing a predator will do is ask, especially if they are within striking distance."

Harland had to ask him.

"Where do you think he is?"

Calvin shrugged his shoulders.

"I don't know, probably the sea, definitely something to do with salt water."

Judge's House,
Peel Kent, England.
7-00am December 18th 1969

The morning breakfast ritual was well under way as Meynell, buttering a slice of toast, hummed to himself. The Judge opposite was becoming more and more irritated by what he considered to be a tuneless drone.

"Do we have to listen to that?" he snapped.

Meynell smiled without replying, forcing the judge to snap at him once again.

"Be here this evening, I would like to have a word with you."

Meynell looked up from his breakfast.

"Important, is it?"

"Yes," the Judge gruffly replied.

Meynell smiled once again at his grandfather.

"If it's important, it would be better to tell me now."

The Judge peered quizzically over the top of his spectacles.

"And why is that?"

Meynell took a bite out of his toast before replying

"Because I am expecting visitors."

The Judge leaned across the table.

"Visitors, and who may they be?"

Meynell smiled once again, a smile that unnerved the judge.

"All in good time, you tell me what you wish to speak to me about. And I will tell you who my visitors are."

The Judge hated playing games. Controlling his temper, he looked across the table at his grandson.

"Enough of these silly games. I have arranged for you to be transferred to the overseas division. I thought it for the best, what with the trouble up in Durham and the fact that we don't seem to be, well, shall we say, on friendly terms."

Meynell took another large bite out of his toast, chewing loudly before asking,

"Where to?"

"Hong Kong," was the reply.

The thin smile that crept across his mouth turned into a positive beam.

"Excellent!"

The Judge was astounded. He had expected some form of resistance.

"You don't mind?"

Meynell watched as his grandmother entered the room with the tea.

"On the contrary, I couldn't be more pleased."

The Judge's face beamed with pleasure.

"Good, I am glad you are pleased. Now, who are the visitors?"

Meynell thanked his grandmother as she poured him out a cup of tea.

"The police," he replied.

The grandmother almost dropped the teapot.

"The police! Why on earth are they calling?"
The Judge was puzzled.

Meynell continued to play cat-and-mouse as he took a sip of tea before attempting to reply.

"Because I asked them to."
The Judge once again peered over the top of his glasses.

"What for?
Meynell deliberately kept them both waiting as he popped the last piece of toast in his mouth, only to take more time as he washed it down with a sip of tea before eventually answering.

"Because you're a murderer."
The Judge's mouth dropped open, while the grandmother equally stunned, sat down next to her husband.

"Murderer! Preposterous!" he snapped.
Meynell glared at him; his eyes became as mean as his voice.

"But you are, you've murdered five children."
The Judge lost his temper and screamed.

"You're insane!"
Meynell was quick to respond.

"Insane? On the contrary, five children have been murdered, and I have informed the police it was you."

"You what?"
The Judge spat out his words.

"I've murdered children, how could I, tell me? Five children, what about proof, alibis, have you taken any of those factors into account? You're a fool, boy, a complete fool. In fact you're more than a fool, you're a certifiable idiot. Who in their right mind would take your word against mine?"

Meynell rose to his feet as he leaned across the table, pushing his head forward. His callous eyes darted between the faces of his two grandparents.

"Certifiable am I."

He drew in a deep breath as his thin lips parted in a vicious smile, a treacherous smile.

"Ah, but it's not just a matter of my word against yours. The child's watch, you remember the watch, the one you picked up the other day. Tacky little plastic thing, you remember it, you had hold of it. Held it, fingered it, played with it in your hand. Shame the only finger prints on the watch are yours and the boy's of course. The one who went missing."

The Judge and his wife sat motionless.

"I placed it down the back of the sofa in the cottage where it will be eventually found, your cottage. And your missing button, also an incriminating piece of evidence.

Then there is a little locket belonging to one of the girls; I placed that where it will eventually be found, along with the photographs of the dead children and other children, children you were more than aquatinted with. Photographs now that is one thing you really do know about don't you?"

Saliva dripped from the corner of his venomous mouth as he leaned further over the table until his face almost touched the Judge's.

"Yes photographs. After all, it is your favourite hobby. Hobby. More an all-consuming passion. And little children, you love them so much you can't keep your hands off them, you're your own daughter, or should I say especially your own daughter. What a dutiful, caring father you were. How old was she when you first raped her? Three, yes, that was it, three.

You raped my mother from the age of three and continued to do so until she left home. When she killed herself, you dutifully took me in to live with you, and you couldn't keep your hands off me. As for you."

He turned his anger on his grandmother.

"You turned a blind eye to it all, living in your own little world of make-believe. Bitch. You're no better than he is. In fact you're just as much to blame for my mother's death as him."

"David," the Judge stuttered. "You don't understand."

Meynell cut him short as he grabbed the butter knife, pointing it at his face.

"Don't understand, You self righteous hypocrite don't understand. I understand only too well. She left a note. You didn't know that did you, no one did but me. A suicide note, and I kept it. I was too young to read it at the time, as I was only five, but I kept it. Hid it away until I was old enough to read it, until I hated you and what you did to her and what you were doing to me. I hated you with every breath I took."

His grandmother was crying with her head down. He grabbed her face.

"Do you know who my father is, do you? Well, I'll tell you. My father is my grandfather."

The woman broke down, letting out loud sobs, which had no effect whatsoever on Meynell.

"How touching, it's a pity you didn't shed a few tears for your daughter, and all the other innocent little children he defiled along with his friends over the years."

The Judge snapped back at him.

"I suppose murdering them is all right."

Meynell stood bold upright as he answered.

"Murder, I didn't murder them. I made them safe. I protected their innocence from creatures like you. My children are as pure in death as the day they were born. Like the cherubs in the paintings, alongside God, pure and untouched, living among the angels."

Several cars could be heard drawing up outside the house.

Meynell turned his head to look out of the window.

"Ah, here are our guests. I wonder what your friends from the brotherhood will think now about their esteemed member. Oh, and of course there's the list of members to your little club, your private club. The same little club that passed me around, like bag of sweets until I went away to boarding school. Being buggered there was like a Sunday school outing compared to what I put up with from you and your fucking sick friends."

Meynell rubbed his hands together like an excited child.

"Isn't it exciting, I'm looking forward to seeing you in court being judged instead of judging."

Meynell left the table and walked towards the door.

"Best not keep our guests waiting."

He left the Judge and his wife still seated at the table as he walked towards the main door.

Outside were a collection of police cars and men. Silently a black Jaguar swept up the drive and drew to a halt. Two senior policemen climbed out of the vehicle, Superintendent Gann and Chief Inspector Ray.

Meynell walked over to the two men. Before he had time to speak, a loud crack shattered the silence, followed by another, as both barrels of a shotgun erupted, one in the face of the grandmother and the other in the face of the Judge himself.

Meynell remained motionless as the policemen rushed towards the house. A thin smile of satisfaction expanded across his face as he removed his glasses to give the lenses a little wipe, while humming his favourite tune. 'You may not be an Angel.'

Calvin's Cottage, Litton Village, England. 8-35am December 19th 1969

Calvin scrambled over the wall, like an animal on all fours crawling in and out of the gravestones, searching for something or somewhere to hide. To hide from the shape that drew closer and closer, until it finally towered above him.

He awoke with a scream, the dream had visited his sleep once again, only this time it had been more vivid than ever before.

He lay motionless on his back as he felt the blood run down his cheek, as the room grew darker. So dark not even the bright light from the moon could penetrate the blackness.

Calvin sat upright in the bed. He needed no psychic powers to sense the coldness that was creeping over his body. At first he thought it was a shadow, a shape that had neither substance nor structure, yet he could see it. He stared at the thing, trying to make it out.

Using his powers he tried to probe whatever it was with his thoughts. The shape moved forward from out of the shadows. He drew it towards him, commanding it to show itself. Suddenly, as if on elastic, it snapped back into the dark. Back into the blackness, safe from prying eyes.

"So. You've finally found me." The words echoed around the room.

He was determined not to let it get to him; he must try to get some sleep. Settling down once more in the bed, he closed his eyes and tried to shut out everything, even the ticking of the clock.

A knock at his bedroom door awoke him from his fitful slumber as the cold light of the morning filtered through the window.

"Mr Dane." Mrs Thirkell called his name. "Are you awake?"

"I am now." he snapped.

"Sorry sir, but it's the telephone. An Inspector Harland to speak to you."

"Okay. I'll take it downstairs."

Although he had an extension in his bedroom, he was not stupid. Mrs Thirkell might be a good housekeeper but she was also, as Bolly would say, a nosey old cow.

Calvin dabbed the trickle of blood that still wept from his eye and walked downstairs, wearing only his shorts. Mrs Thirkell was not shocked to see him in a state of semi undress, as he often walked around the house on a morning in only his underwear.

She handed him the telephone.

"Yes?"

Harland's voice rang out down the line.

"Thanks for all the help, sorry we didn't nail the bastard."

"What's going to happen to him?" Calvin asked.

"Nothing, it's been accepted that the Judge committed the murders and shot both himself and his wife when found out."

"What about Meynell?" Calvin's voice was bitter.

"He's scott free." Harland replied, "Everything pointed to the Judge, fingerprints on the boy's watch, a locket, strands of hair from the wig on his jumper, a button from his coat found inside the tomb with the bodies, even photographs of the children and others, all his and in his study. The evidence against him was too much."
Harland paused for a moment.

"I don't suppose you could have mistaken Meynell for the Judge."

"No," was the curt reply.

"I didn't think so." Harland continued to speak.

"Anyway, the case is closed Doran and myself have been split up."

"What about the bite marks on Meynell's hand?" Calvin asked.
Harland sighed down the phone.

"Waste of time, they have a result, and they're not going to listen to me, and certainly not on the word of a psychic."
Calvin's impatience was showing.

"Not even on the word of the psychic who led you to the bodies. What you're saying is that you have no intention of finding out."
Harland refused to answer.

"Where's he living?" Calvin asked

"Forget it," Harland snapped down the phone.

"Don't even think about it. Anyway you're wasting your time, he's either left the country or is about to leave for Hong Kong. Sorry, Calvin, and thanks once again, you never know, we may work together again one day."

"Don't hold your breath."

Calvin replied as he replaced the receiver.

Calvin's Cottage, Litton Village, England. 9-55am December 19th 1969

Calvin walked to the window that overlooked the churchyard. Without turning around, he spoke.

"Bolly, I want you to do me a favour, and go away for a few days, well away."

Bolly held a puzzled frown.

"Why?"

Calvin turned to look at her. His face was stern.

"This time I'm deadly serious. I don't want you here."

"Can I help?"

She was sincere in her offer and he knew it.

"No, this is my problem, something only I can sort out, just do as I ask," he pleaded.

"Is it to do with your past?"

She began to walk over towards him as she spoke.

"Stop." He held up a hand. "I'm not asking you to go. I'm telling you"

Bolly halted as commanded.

"You really do mean it?"

Calvin nodded, and she for once agreed without an argument.

"Okay, I'll make myself scarce."

Calvin held up a finger.

"And not a word to your grandmother."

"She's your grandmother too," she replied.
Calvin turned his back on her, and gazed out of the window.

"Not a word."

Calvin's Cottage,
Litton Village, England.
10-45pm December 19th 1969

The aroma of cooking wafted through the house as Calvin tasted his latest gastronomic delight.

A sudden blast of cold air rushed into the kitchen. Calvin, without looking up, carefully sprinkled a few herbs into the bubbling pan.

"I've been expecting you." He spoke without turning round.

"Have you?" The voice came from behind.

Calvin finally turned to face the intruder. Standing in the doorway was a large man with blond hair, wearing a long black gabardine coat that almost trailed to the ground. The coat had a large hood that could be detached from the garment if required.

He smiled as he spoke.

"Hello, Wolf, pleased to see me?"

Calvin made no reply as he stared at the smiling figure, a smile that he knew well, the smile of treachery.

The man removed one of his black leather gloves before walking over towards the stove to dip his finger into the pan. The stew scalded the tip of his finger, and he quickly placed it in his mouth to cool it down, pretending to taste the contents.

"Mmm not bad, then you always were good at women's work."

Calvin still made no comment as he stared into the man's face, a face not unlike his own.

"Not a lot to say for yourself." The man's voice had a low, menacing whisper to it.

Calvin steadied the pan by the handle as he stirred the stew with a wooden spoon.

"What do you expect me to say?" Calvin's voice was calm. "Karl, what a surprise!"

Karl smiled as he responded.

"You were expecting me? Somehow I find that hard to believe. You see, I've been following you, watching just to see how you have progressed since you left our happy little family."

As they stared at one another, Calvin felt him trying to creep into his head. Unfortunately it was Karl who was winning. The pain in Calvin's eye was almost unbearable, as blood began to run down his cheek. Karl laughed aloud.

"Oh my! You seem to be bleeding. Paining you, I hope."

Calvin tried to concentrate on blocking out the power of Karl's mind. It was useless, the blood still flowed from his eye and dripped into the boiling stew.

Karl's face was fixed in a menacing grin.

"Quint has asked me to pass on his regards. He would of course have liked to pass them on personally but he thought I would be more suited to the task."

Calvin lifted his head.

"Okay, you've passed them on, now why don't you leave?"

Karl continued to grin as he removed his remaining glove, slowly pulling out one finger at a time.

"Now that's not very hospitable. Not when I have come all the way from America to attend your funeral in person."

Calvin tried to shut out the pain as he spoke.

"If it's the files you want---"

Karl cut him short.

"The files are of no importance to me. It's you I have called for."

Calvin lifted the pan by its handle and threw it across the room at Karl. Without looking to see if he had hit the target, he rushed out of the kitchen into the garden. His dream, his premonition, was about to be recounted all over again, only this time for real.

Large white flakes silently fell from the sky hushing the night, as Calvin scrambled over the wall of the churchyard, before falling into the soft snow on the other side.

His eye poured with blood that ran down his face before spattering a pattern of crimson dots onto the virginal carpet of white.

He turned to look behind, his face red with blood. Karl climbed on top of the wall. Standing, hands on hips, he laughed, with his long black coat flapping like the wings of a harpy.

The pain in Calvin's chest forced its way outwards as he tried with all his power to fight back, while frantically scurrying between the gravestones, searching for something, or a place of refuge.

The pains in his head and chest were too much. Finally he slumped to the ground between two gravestones.

Karl stood menacingly before him.

"You pathetic little piece of dog shit, crawling on all fours like a scalded hound."

Summoning all his powers of resistance, Calvin pulled himself to his feet, using the stones on either side as crutches. Holding on to one of the gravestones he glared at Karl who laughed aloud.

"You're not going to pit your pitiful powers against mine."

The venom in Karl's eyes bore into Calvin's mind.

"Look at you, four years of vegetating, brooding over your precious Maria, I don't know why you bothered, she was nothing but a whore. Still, she at least died after tasting a real man."

Calvin was about to make a lunge at him when Karl raised his hand, forcing Calvin to grip his chest in excruciating pain.

Karl continued to smile as he watched him suffer.

"Now where was I---. Let me think. Oh yes, six. Yes, that's it, six. Six times I let her feel what it was like to have a real man, and she loved every minute of it. I was in a very physical mood that day. That's why I snapped her neck like a twig."

Karl began to increase the pain in Calvin's chest. With his heart pounding like a jackhammer, it felt as if his ribcage was about to burst.

Unseen by Calvin, there was another figure hiding in the shadows on the other side of the churchyard. A figure watching, enjoying every minute of Calvin's torture.

Two figures were approaching the cottage. Instantly the man in the shadows drew his gun from its holster, but before he had time to raise it a wire garrotte was whipped around his neck. The gun fell to the floor as he struggled to free himself. The wire tightened and tightened until Angelo's body, slumped to the ground like a lifeless marionette.

Karl was about ten feet from Calvin.

"In pain?" Karl laughed aloud. "See how I've progressed, unlike you. You're so primitive, you need to touch to kill."

A voice cried out.

"Calvin."

Karl spun round to see who the intruder was.

Calvin seized his chance. Falling to the ground, he rolled behind the headstone next to where he was standing. Grabbing hold of the crossbow he let the bolt fly just as Karl turned round to finish him off.

As silent as death, the bolt winged through the air homing in on its target, crashing through the skull before penetrating the soft tissue of the brain, and forcing its way out the other side with a sickening splintering sound. Karl was flung backwards his arms outstretched as they clung to the nearest thing. Wrapping themselves backwards around a large stone cross, like a crucified Christ, who twitched and convulsed as the nervous system jerked to a halt, the final throws of life.

Subduing the pain in his chest, Calvin rose to his feet. The blue-faced clock was striking eleven as Bolly, accompanied by Croxton, called out his name once again.

Calvin paid no attention to them as he walked towards the crucified figure of Karl. Calvin pointed to the crossbow bold imbedded in Karl's skull.

"Who needs to touch to kill?"

He didn't notice Bolly and Croxton standing beside him, as he stared into the face of his would-be assassin.

"Who was he?" Bolly asked.

Calvin, without taking his eye off Karl's body, answered.

"My brother."

A car could be heard leaving the little lane to the side of the churchyard. Croxton tried to see who it was, but the car was in darkness as it sped away from the church with the dead body of Angelo in its boot. Once out of sight on the open road, Sommers turned on the headlights as Ida Kroll lit up two cigarettes and offered one to Sommers, who spoke.

"The Archbishop is not going to be pleased."

Ida Kroll shrugged her shoulders.

"He wanted to see if he was worthy."

Sommers looked at the woman beside him.

"I think he meant Karl, not the freak."

Bamburgh Castle, Northumberland, England. December 20th 1969

A lone black figure stood on the battlements of one of Northumberland's most magnificent castles. A relic of the past long before weapons of mass destruction dominated the earth. An era where men fought hand to hand in mortal combat.

The winter rain competed with the snow, eventually forcing the snow to retreat as the North East coastline stiffened itself for the onslaught that was to come, a formidable barrier to any would-be tourist, as formidable as the boiling oil of old.

Quint climbed out of the car, leaving his two bodyguards behind warm and dry. The driver looked up to the castle.

"You'd of thought he'd come down to meet us."

"You know what that crazy bastard's like and Quint will do anything for his pet monkey," his partner replied.

Quint dressed in a navy blue overcoat with the collar turned upwards, forced his way through the rain, to the agreed meeting place at the agreed time.

The black hooded figure continued looking out to sea as Quint spoke.

"Fuck me Karl did you have to pick such a Goddamned hellhole to meet."

The figure made no response.

"Well is it all over, can we get out of this frigging country?" There was still no reply. "Answer me for God's sake."

The figure slowly turned round to face Quint.

The two bodyguards in the car looked up once more at the castle.

"Do you think he'll be there?" asked the driver.

"Who?"

"Karl." The driver replied.

"Yeh." The second bodyguard smiled. "Not a chance of the freak winning. That big-son-of-a-bitch will have popped those red eyes right out of his head."

The men were startled by a tap on the window. One of the bodyguards instantly went for his gun, but stopped when he recognised the face looking in.

Ida Kroll and Sommers climbed into the rear of the car.

"Quint with Karl?" she asked

The driver of the car replied.

"Yeh gone up to meet him."

Before he could utter another word a wire garrotte was wrapped around the neck of the guard sitting in the passenger seat. As Ida Kroll thrust the silencer fitted to the gun barrel against the back of the drivers head, before reaching over and removing his gun from its holster.

The second bodyguard kicked and clawed with his hands as the wire cut deep into his throat until the final gasp of air was expelled from his body.

Sommers climbed out of the car and opened the front passenger door, allowing the body to slump to the ground. Removing his gun from the holster, he trained it on the driver giving Ida Kroll the chance to climb out.

"Outside and open the trunk." She ordered the driver, who instantly obeyed.

He knew his time was up and the only chance he would have would be outside the car. As he climbed out he instantly went for the spare gun fastened to his ankle.

A flash followed by single dull thud was engulfed by the howling wind, as a piece of lead ripped through the drivers skull, before embedding itself in the grey tissue it was meant to protect.

Sommers opened the trunk so he and Kroll could load both men inside before walking down the hill towards their own vehicle.

Two cars passed them on the winding road that led to the castle car park. In the rear seat was Croxton Bishop who touched his hat acknowledging Kroll and Sommers.

On the battlement Quint stood mortified as the hooded figure smiled at him.

"Morning Quint." The figure greeted him.
Quint's body froze as his mind had difficulty believing what his eyes were telling him. Regaining his composure he spoke.

"And Karl?"

"He's not coming."

Calvin tapped the centre of his forehead as he moved closer to Quint.

"Got a bit of a headache."

Quint's mouth was dry as he forced the word from between his lips.

"Dead?"

Calvin smiled.

"That would describe his medical condition."

Quint kept his eyes trained on Calvin; he knew he intended to kill him and had to pick the right moment to go for his gun.

"As a matter of interest, how?"

"Oh that would be telling." Calvin responded.

Quint unbuttoned his overcoat wide to show he wasn't carrying a gun, at least one Calvin could see.

"Only going to wipe my nose" he assured Calvin.

Quint slipped his hand into his trouser pocket to remove a handkerchief.

"It seams I underestimated you, Wolf."

Quint forced a smile as he spoke.

"Why continue this feud? Come back. There's no future for you without the group, living in fear, not knowing if the next day will be your last."

Calvin slowly moved closer keeping his eye on the man as he replied.

"That's were you have the advantage."

Quint wiped his nose once more, before replacing his hand inside his overcoat to put the handkerchief back.

"Advantage?" he asked.

Calvin moved even closer to his prey.

"Yes, advantage, because today is your last."
Quint's hand swiftly grabbed for the gun
fastened round his back on the belt of his
trousers.

Calvin had been expecting it, and pounced on
him like spider on a fly. His huge hand spanned
Quint's face while his other held the hand that
went for the gun.

Quint's body began to convulse as Calvin's
power surged unabated through his nervous
system. Quint's eyes, nose, mouth, ears all
began to bleed as his organs ruptured one by
one.

A voice called out to him from across the
castle courtyard.

"My, my what a temper."
Calvin swung round his prey dangling like a
lifeless effigy.

Croxton Bishop pulled the collar of his
overcoat up and around his ears.

"It seems that every time we meet you're
about to kill one person or another. We really
must stop meeting like this, it can get one a
frightfully bad name."

Calvin continued to hold onto Quint, whose
reprieve was only temporary as he once again
turned his attention to his former guardian.

"Don't try to stop me!" he hissed at Croxton.
He was like a wild animal, a predator prepared
to fight to the death to retain his prey, but unlike
an animal that kills for food, Calvin was about to
kill for revenge,

"Never had any intention of doing so."
Croxton waved his hand theatrically in the air.

"Please carry on, I find it all so frightfully interesting."

Quint's eyes rolled up into the top of his head as the whites turned red with blood. The convulsions stopped; his eyes swollen almost twice the original size, finally exploded like pressed grapes.

Quint slumped into a heap on the wet cold cobbles, cobbles that had seen more than their share of blood over the centuries.

Calvin took a few steps back from the body as Croxton looked down at the lifeless lump.

"There will be no questions asked. All he did was die of natural causes. Your brother now he is a different kettle of fish."

Calvin turned to Croxton.

"And in return for your services, you require mine."

"Precisely." Croxton smiled.

"And what if I refuse?"

Calvin asked as he kicked the lifeless body of Quint to ensure he was dead.

Croxton pulled his coat closer to him as the cold wind howled around the battlements.

"You're a free man until the magnificent British police force or the Americans catch up with you."

Calvin still not sure moved Quint's face with his boot reassuring himself that he was dead.

"What do you have in store for me different to what I left, unless it's a stately home?"

"Good God no!" Croxton exclaimed.

"Awful draughty places and far to costly to maintain. No we only keep those places for your fellow-countrymen and all those other ghastly foreigners. No dear boy, free as a bird. No bars metal or mental, live where you wish."

"And the catch?" Calvin asked.

Croxton placed his cigarette holder between his lips.

"If and when your services are required you will scratch our back, and we in turn will scratch yours. Quite a stimulating prospect, and highly a profitable one."

"To you that is."

Calvin still seething with anger kicked the dead body of Quint. Croxton raised his eyebrows at Calvin's show of anger.

"To both parties," was the reply.

"And if I don't accept?"

Croxton pointed to the lifeless lump of flesh Calvin had his foot on.

"You have the alternative at your feet."

Croxton tried in vein to light his cigarette fighting against the strong wind that that whipped across the sea and around the castle. Giving up he looked at his watch.

"Tempus Fugit, dear boy. Ten minutes, no longer."

He waved for a couple of his men to come over and remove the body. Carrying it down the ramp towards the portcullis they passed Bolly on her way to meet Calvin.

Without a further word Croxton turned and followed them down the ramp, nodding to Bolly as they passed one another.

Calvin was once again looking out to sea watching the waves tumble in a white mass, angrily attacking the beach like a marauding army of white froth, not unlike the turmoil that was at war inside Calvin's head.

Bolly stood beside him, her arm slipped around his linking with it. This warm gesture on a cold wet day was instantly rebuffed.

"Suit your bloody self," she snapped.

Calvin continued to stare out to sea without replying.

"Stop being such a bloody child. You know you need him. He told you where Quint would be and kept his promise by not stopping you kill him. Work with the Bastard."

Calvin continued to ignore her.

"Sod it I'm off what's the point? You're not interested in listening to my advice."

Calvin turned to look at her.

"And what is your advice?" he asked.

"Work for him," she replied. "Does it matter, who you work for, there's always going to be someone trying to kill you. So fuck it. Live like a man for once, out in the daylight and out of the shadows. Try it if it doesn't work so what, he's only another enemy."

"And friends. What of friends?" Calvin asked.

Bolly moved closer to him, her pixie like face looking up into his.

"You've always got me."

Calvin pulled the hood of her duffle coat down over her face.

"I think I prefer my enemies. Come on, let's swear an oath to the Queen."

The Centre,
Outskirts of Boston, America.
December 20th 1969

The centre was a large mansion set in twenty acres of land, with a lake, tennis courts and swimming pool. There were even stables with horses.

The security guard at the gate examined the passes of the lead car and coach. The fact that Culver was one of the occupants ensured that he let them pass with the minimum of fuss.

Once through the large electronic gates, the vehicles sped off round the bend and out of sight. The coach slowed down without stopping as two men jumped out and rolled over into the trees.

The driveway was about a quarter of a mile in length, leading towards the great house. Inside the car and the coach the occupants made themselves ready. All guns where checked and ready for use as the two vehicles approached the main doors. Two non-uniformed guards greeted the party in the car, while the ten gunmen on the coach lay on the floor waiting for the signal.

Culver, Muller and two other men entered through the double doors and into the hallway. Culver approached the reception desk.

The receptionist and the security guard sitting behind the desk immediately sprang into action, jumping to their feet. They knew Culver hated being kept waiting and was a stickler for the rules.

"Good day, Mr Culver. "

The receptionist put on her best smile as the guard stood erect waiting for whatever order might be given.

Muller swiftly glanced around weighing up the situation; two guards at the door, one on reception, and above on the spiral staircase he spotted two other men talking. He needed to know who they were before he gave the signal.

One of the men looked down at the party below and instantly removed a large black cross from his pocket and placed it on his jacket, much to the surprise of his companion.

This was the sign Muller had been waiting for. With only a look and a slight movement of the head the two other assassins with him positioned themselves so they could take out the guards on the door.

Culver was about to sign the register when he asked.

"Where is Doctor Bradley?"

"He's in the lecture room," the receptionist replied.

"And the students?" he continued.

"All with him, sir." was the reply.

That was all Muller needed to hear, the signal was given.

All three assassins drew their silenced pistols and opened fire on the unsuspecting guards.

The two by the door were the first to be taken out. Muller floored the one behind the desk in an instant with a single shot to the head. The man wearing the black cross had manipulated the guard at the top of the staircase so his back was to the action below.

Before he had time to react, Muller took careful aim and shot him in the back. He flung his arms upwards in shock and pain before falling over the top of the banister and crashing to the floor below.

The two assassins gave the signal to the others on the bus who swept into the house. The receptionist was hysterical, screaming at the top of her voice. Muller instantly took care of her, as a bullet struck her between the eyes. The rest of the men were dispersed to hunt down and kill anyone who was not wearing a black cross.

Like the angel of death in the bible they systematically went from room to room, rounding up secretaries, guards, teachers and doctors. All who did not have the cross on their jacket were killed. Once the task was completed, all of the alarms and cameras were disabled and their film removed and destroyed.

The next to die were the guards on the main gate, killed by the two men who jumped out of the coach on the driveway. The first guard had his throat cut while the other, begging for mercy with his hands in the air, was shot at close range through the back of the head.

The students had no idea what was going on as the doors to the lecture room burst open, and armed men entered and surrounded everyone in there.

Dr Bradley appealed for calm as Muller and Culver entered the room.

Muller raised his hands begging for them to listen.

"Gentlemen and ladies please remain calm. We are not here to harm you, quite the contrary."

A young woman of about thirty stood up. She was very attractive with bright blue eyes and long blonde hair.

She walked towards Muller, smiling.

"I remember you."

Muller looked at her.

"Do you?" he asked.

She moved closer to him. Muller instantly raised his gun.

"Now, my dear, not too close. I also have a good memory, and remember what you did to one of the guards in Austria, back in 1945."

She looked him up and down.

"So it is you."

"Yes," he replied.

"Why have you returned?" she asked.

Muller proudly straightened his back as he spoke.

"To give you back your birthright. All will be explained later; now we must leave, and quickly."

A tall young man stood up and called out.

"What if we don't want to go?"

Muller looked around the room. Twenty-five pair of blue eyes where all trained on him.

"If you wish to stay, you may. We will not harm you. The question I must ask is why you would want to stay. You are not laboratory animals to be caged, studied. You are of pure undiluted Aryan blood. You and you alone are the true descendants of the Herrenvolk. Soon mankind along with myself will be forced to accept your superiority and will bow down to your descendants in admiration. Stand up and be proud of your heritage, your ancestors. It is your duty to fulfil the dreams and ambitions of your parents, by fulfilling not only your destiny, but also the destiny of the Third Reich."

Muller turned his gun on two of the professors in the room who were not wearing a black cross, and shot them both between the eyes.

"Shall we leave?"

Muller bowed to the students then motioned towards the door.

The students all rose from their seats and followed Dr Bradley out of the room.

Croxton Bishops, Apartment, Oxford, England. December 23rd 1969

Croxton Bishop eyed the young man who accompanied Ida Kroll up and down, offering them both some tea, which was politely refused.

"Ah, down to business." Croxton rose from his seat and went into his study. He returned with a suitcase. Inside was a large bundle of files.

Ida Kroll motioned for Sommers to take them from Croxton.

"All unread?" she asked

"Of course," he replied. "Scout's honour."

She gave a little laugh as Sommers quickly flicked through the files. Sommers shook his head.

"There seems to be one missing."

"Really, which one?" Croxton asked acting surprised.

"I think you know," Sommers responded.

"The dear boy must have destroyed it. Not the most trusting of fellows, our Mr Dane, but an extremely interesting one." Kroll made no comment as Croxton continued.

"While we're on the subject, what of Calvin?" Ida Kroll's face showed no trace of emotion as she spoke.

"He's of no further interest to us."

Croxton lit a cigarette.

"I take it his life is not in jeopardy?"

"Not from us. He is no longer an asset. More a liability," she replied.

Without removing the cigarette holder from his mouth, he allowed the smoke to explode out of the other side as he spoke.

"Good; as long as we have an understanding, we are more than happy to underwrite his liability."

Ida Kroll opened a briefcase and passed over some documents to Croxton.

"Inside are the details of the airstrip where Quint landed and the people who met him. We have marked on the map where you will be able to locate their bodies. I take it they will be dealt with in the same way as Quint and his friends?" Croxton smiled.

"No need for the map. It's already been taken care of."

The surprised look on Kroll's face spoke volumes.

"Never underestimate the British. We have been in the spying game since Elizabethan times. And, by the way, do congratulate Culver on his little coup d'etat. How fitting that a dead man should take the blame."

Kroll rose from her seat and shook Croxton's hand, ready to leave.

"Quint always underestimated you. Something I will not."

Croxton smiled at her remark.

"Nor I you, my dear. Nor I you."

Solicitor's Office, Newcastle, England January 15th 1970

Meynell sat opposite a short, fat, bespectacled man. His sober dark blue suit had telltale traces of cigarette ash sprinkled on the lapel of his jacket. His hand doddered as he handed Meynell the document to sign.

Meynell neither read nor even glanced at the piece of paper, other than to find where his signature belonged.

The task completed, he immediately rose from his seat.

"You will take care of all the paperwork exactly as I asked?"

"Of course."

The man joined his hands together, interlocking his fingers.

"You can rest assured that we will handle your full estate and take care of the necessary documentation regarding the transaction."

Meynell was about to shake hands when he withdrew the gesture.

He had suddenly developed an aversion to the ritual of handshaking, courtesy of Mr Calvin Dane. Leaving the bewildered solicitor, he bade him goodbye.

A cold wind blew the snow around like confetti at a wedding, forcing the flakes to cluster together like a swarm of white bees. A creaking sound caused him to look up at the solicitor's sign, with its name swinging in the wind. Wilkins & Co. Solicitors.

He was so busy looking up at the sign that he failed to notice the little child running down the street, who accidentally bumped into Meynell knocking his briefcase out of his hand. Her mother instantly apologised to him.

"I'm so sorry, the little devil never looks where she is going."

Meynell smiled as he stroked her face with the back of his hand.

"Devil. No more an angel."

Removing his spectacles, he wiped the lenses with his handkerchief and watched the mother and child walk off hand in hand.

Replacing his glasses, he picked up his briefcase and walked of down the road, humming to himself, 'You may not be an Angel.'

Calvin's Cottage, Litton Village, England. January 31st 1970

Bolly handed Calvin a steaming cup of hot chocolate before settling herself down on the rug beside the roaring fire. Scattered around on the floor were the sketches of the children.

Bolly placed her cup in the hearth as she picked up one of the sketches and looked at the face of the child, before tossing it into the fire, to watch it burst into flames before forming a grey crumpled mass.

"Do you think it will ever happen?"

Calvin shrugged his shoulders and took a long pull on his cigar.

"Who bought the house?" he asked.

Bolly screwed up her nose as she tried to think.

"I'm not sure, Aunt Ivy did say. I know it wasn't Meynell. I think she said some man called Wilkins bought it. Strange though, he had a condition of purchase written into the transaction."

"Don't tell me." Calvin smirked. "You're not allowed within a ten mile radius?"

"Highly amusing," she retorted.

"You remember the clock in the room, the one on the mantle? You know the one you wanted to buy."

Calvin's face grew ashen.

"Well, under the terms of the sale, the clock had to go with the house. Strange isn't it?"

Calvin's mood grew darker at the mention of the clock.

Bolly picked up the final sketch, the one of the boy, and cried out.

"Look, it's sopping wet!"

Calvin took the sketch from her and looked at the face in it. Bolly tasted her finger.

"Ugh, it tastes salty."

An apologetic smile flickered across Calvin's face as he whispered under his breath.

"Sorry," before gently placing it among the flames.

South African, Embassy, New York. March 1st 1970

The Ambassador's wife struggled to fall asleep; the ticking of the clock beside the bed and the occasional grunt as the Ambassador turned over, were conspiring to keep her awake. She had lain there for the past half-hour or so, trying to get to sleep. It seemed that everything annoyed her, the clock, the grunts, the rustling of the sheets as the Ambassador kicked his legs. Eventually having had had enough, she was about to get up and go into the lounge. Her craving had finally got the better of her. She needed a cigarette.

As she swung her legs out of bed, a strange sound caught her ears. A clicking sound, like an animal's claws scraping across a polished floor. She paused a moment, not wishing to switch on the light for fear of waking her husband. The clicking sound drew near, she decided to turn on the light regardless. Suddenly the bed shook violently as if something large had pounced on it. She screamed and rolled out as her husband was lifted from the bed and pinned halfway up the wall. His arms and legs thrashed about in mid air as blood spurted from his throat.

Suddenly something hot and wet and heavy hit her in the face as her husband's body crashed back onto the bed in a pool of blood.

She screamed at the lump of flesh that had hit her and was still beating outside of the body in her lap. Screams that were drowned out by the crash of braking glass as the window in the bedroom was shattered into pieces.

Vatican City, Rome, Italy
March 3rd 1970

Archbishop Vol was about to leave to take mass when the telephone rang. He motioned his secretary to answer it.

The voice on the other side refused to give the man any information and insisted he speak to the Archbishop.

"Just tell him it's Louis Packard."

Once the message was relayed, Vol instantly dismissed his secretary.

"Louis old friend." Vol's voice rang down the telephone.

Packard's voice in response had a serious tone to it.

"We have a problem."

"A big one?" Vol asked.

"As big as they come," was the reply.

"And what may that be?" Vol was still in buoyant mood.

"An ancient one," Packard replied.

Vol stood motionless and pondered. He had heard of what Packard spoke of, but knew little of it.

Packard continued.

"We need your help. It's found a new ally, a protector. And like a dutiful servant, it's out to do its new masters bidding. Our men are out of their depth."

Vol was still pondering.

"Are you sure?"

"Yes." Packard's voice rang with fear as he continued.

"Do you know anyone good enough, as well as foolish enough to take it on?"

Vol tapped the large gold and ruby cross that hung around his neck.

"A predator can only be slain by another predator."

"Do you have one?"

"Yes I have one. A natural and expendable predator."

"Who is it "Packard asked.

A smile crept across Vol's face as the words hissed from between his teeth.

"A wolf, a red eyed wolf."

<u>The End</u>

SHADOW OF THE SHAMAN

By Billy Yull

Church of Our Lady, Ars, France. January 11th 1825.

The flickering flame of the candle illuminated a canvas painting of the Annunciation of the mother of Christ on the presbytery staircase. The priest stopped to carry out his nightly ritual. First he would bow his head in reverence, then he would say a small prayer and make the sign of the cross. Only this night he was unable to carry the ritual out, for his left hand held the candle and his right a pitchfork. Closing his eyes, he silently prayed and asked for protection from his heavenly mother before his weary legs gingerly climbed the remainder of the stairs to his place of rest.

Opening the door to his bedroom, his eyes scoured the room as he held the pitchfork in a menacing pose ready to strike at the first sign of movement. Satisfied the room was empty, he placed the candle on the small table beside his bed and slowly eased himself onto the straw filled-mattress.

The pumping of his heart slowly grew to a more respectable beat as he let out a sigh before leaning the pitchfork against the wall next to his bed. Swinging his legs up onto the bed he lay flat on his back and let out an even deeper sigh and closed his eyes.

His relaxed state was soon to be shattered. A loud crash that emanated from the floor below caused him to sit bold upright. Cocking his head to one side he listened, and waited; all was quiet.

"What could it be?" he whispered to himself.

Suddenly the bedroom door flung open with such force that it crashed against the wall, the handle gouging a piece out of the rough plaster.

Grabbing for his pitchfork, his eyes frantically scoured the room in a vain attempt to see what had caused the door to be so violently smashed against the wall.

Standing in the middle of the room, pitchfork held ready to strike he called out.

"Who are you? What do you want?"

Silence fell upon the room not even the old timbers dared to creak. His heart began to pound once again in his chest as the feeling of terror crept over his body.

"Who are you?" he repeated.

A strange noise met his ears, a noise he had heard over the past few nights. That was why he had the pitchfork, he was ready to defend himself from what he hoped were rats scurrying across his bedroom. Tonight the sound that greeted his ears was more intense louder, heavier that any rat could make, totally dismissing his theory.

It was a clicking sound, loud chilling, like an animal's claws scraping across the wooden floor. In fear he stabbed wildly at the invisible intruder gouging large chunks of wood out of the rough floor. Blow after blow was struck in vain, until the fork was thrust with such force into the floor it took all of his strength to remove it.

Out of breath and frustrated he flopped on to the bed allowing the pitchfork to crash to the floor.

The clicking sound had ceased. Gathering his composure he looked round the room. The flickering flame from the candle formed shadows in every corner causing his eyes to squint as they tried to make out who or what unseen force lurked among the shadows.

Sleep was no longer a priority. Sitting on the edge of the bed he crossed himself and began to pray. The first lines of the Our Father had not quite left his lips when a voice called out to him.

"Vianney. Vianney"

The priest continued to pray ignoring the taunts that followed.

"Potato eater. Potato eater. Do you not know who I am?"

He was not sure if the voice was in the room or in his head, but its guttural tones sent a shiver down his spine. His hands began to tremble and sweat as he clasped them firmly together in prayer.

"Thy kingdom come," he continued

The voice from the shadows let out a high pitched screech.

The priest clasped his hands over his ears, trying to block out the pain that sliced through the eardrums. It was to no avail; the screech was inside his head. Mustering all his strength and determination, he rose to his feet and cried out.

"Be gone, Satan! In the name of Jesus Christ our Lord I command you go!"

Suddenly the curtains were ripped to shreds by unseen claws, leaving them dangling from the pole in tatters. The same unseen claws gouged even larger chunks out of the wooden floor than the pitchfork leaving a trail of splinters out of the door and down the stairs.

Church of Our Lady, Ars, France. January 19th 1825.

Jean-Marie-Baptiste Vianney, Curé D'Ars, left the confessional. His body was weak and his willpower drained. The workload he placed on himself was more than any human would have been able to stand, without the extraordinary circumstances he now faced.

Over the years, Jean Vianney had gained the reputation of been a living saint; a spiritual confidant to those who sought redemption from their sins. The church had reluctantly been forced to acknowledge that this exceptional priest of genteel countenance possessed a gift. He could see into the souls of men and women alike. No sins or lies could be hidden from this man. He had what the church acknowledged as a gift from God. If this gift had been given to anyone outside of the church, then that would be a different matter, as the witch trials that swept Europe proved.

Jean Vianney was indeed a living saint, and, according to his friends and followers, that was why the devil or the Grappin as he named it, had singled him out.

For the past eight nights the Grappin had tormented the curé until dawn. Yet the curé still managed to meet his divine commitments by administering confessions to crowds that daily queued inside and outside the little church.

Closing the door to confessional, he glanced at the packed pews. Some people were praying, some asleep, intent on keeping their place in the queue. Others just wanted to kiss his hand as he blessed them before leaving for the presbytery.

As he made his way through the crowds, a young woman caught his eye. She was pretty, with features that placed her age at no more than twenty. That was until he looked into her eyes. He stopped and stared deep into her dark lifeless eyes. She made no movement to advance or recoil; she simply returned the stare.

Jean Vianney was momentarily paralysed, he had never felt like this before. It was as if she held him in her gaze.

A slow smirk appeared on the face of the young woman. A smirk that taunted him in the same way the grappin had, night after night. No words were exchanged between them, but he felt that there was an affinity between his tormentor and this female.

Without releasing him from her gaze, the young woman slowly melted back into the crowd of worshippers. His hand felt for his forehead as he fell into a swoon. A burly farmhand caught him, preventing him from hitting the floor.

"Make way!" he called out, "Make way!" Picking the priest up in his arms, he carried him to the presbytery.

The housekeeper opened the door and frantically led the farmhand into the living-room, where he placed the curé in a chair.

The farmhand in an attempt to revive the priest rubbed his hands, while the housekeeper fetched a bowl of water and cooled his forehead.

Slowly the Curé came round, his eyes glazed and weary from the encounter.

"Poor thing! Not had a wink of sleep for nights!" the housekeeper exclaimed.

"Why?" asked the farmhand.

The housekeeper was reluctant to reply. The farmhand repeated his question.

"Why?"

Placing her mouth almost upon his ear, she whispered.

"The devil."

The farmhand recoiled back. His expression spoke a million words. The housekeeper nodded, silently confirming her statement by mouthing the words.

"The devil.

Jean Vianney let out a long sigh.

"There is no need to whisper. I know what you are talking about."

The housekeeper bowed her head in guilt. The priest gently lifted her chin and smiled.

"Do not feel guilty for speaking the truth. It would only be a sin if it were a lie."

The farmhand, still kneeling beside the priest, didn't know why he did it; he simply acted on impulse.

"If you want someone to watch over you tonight, devil or no devil I will do it."

A radiant smile covered the face of the priest as he squeezed the man's hand.

"You would do this for me?"

The man nodded in reply.

"And you wouldn't be afraid? Jean Vianney asked.

"I never said I wouldn't be afraid, but I will do it," The farmhand replied

Jean Vianney placed his hand on the man's head.

"May the Lord bless you my son, for this night I do need a protector, afraid or not."

The next morning Jean Vianney rose refreshed. For the first time in almost a fortnight he had managed to get several hours sleep, safe in the knowledge that a guardian angel watched over him in the form of the big rough farmhand.

Before taking breakfast, he gave a private confession to his guardian, absolving him of all his sins. Although his heart was good, he had in his life been a man known for his temper and a love of the ladies. But he was about to be married and wished to change his ways.

As Jean Vianney placed his hand the man's head to absolve him, a vision flashed into his mind.

He saw the farmhand crushed beneath the wheels of a carriage. A spear of ice pierced Jean Vianney's heart as he looked at the man.

"Take my bed my son, rest in peace in the knowledge that your soul is as pure as the first snows of winter."

The farmhand smiled, thanking him before taking up his offer. Within seconds of lying on the bed he was asleep.

Jean Vianney gently closed the door and made his way down the stairs.

A foul odour emanated from below, causing him to retch. Halting at the painting of the Annunciation, he recoiled in disbelief. Shaking his head, he closed his eyes and called out in a low whisper.

"Is this what you have sunken to Grappin?" The painting was dripping in excrement.

Later that evening, after he had spent all of the day in the confessional box, he once again closed the door behind him, ready to retire for the night. His mind drifted back to the previous night, and the young woman who had never been out of his thoughts since their previous encounter.

As usual the church was full as he left and made his way towards the presbytery. In the distance he could hear the trundle of a carriage being drawn by several horses at great speed. Approaching him was the silhouetted shape of a carriage, with its coachman standing proud as he whipped the four coal-black horses that hurtled towards him.

He was rooted to the spot and his legs refused to move, no matter how hard his brain commanded them. The coach was upon him; suddenly he felt his body being lifted up and thrown out of the way.

A loud scream pierced his ears, as he lay helpless on the floor, watching the carriage wheels in turn crush the huge frame of the farmhand beneath them.

Before he had time to rise a figure appeared out of the shadows. She looked deep into the priest's eyes, before turning them towards the lifeless form of his would-be guardian angel.

A smile crept across her face as she slowly retreated back into the shadows where she came.

Church of Our Lady, Ars, France.
June 10th 1858.

For thirty-four years the nightly struggle between the devil and Jean-Marie-Baptiste Vianney, Curé D'Ars, had been relentless. The Grappin, as he called it, taunted him, bit him, clawed him, and threw him out of bed until one night, when the priest retired to his bed, carrying an oil lamp.

Placing the lamp beside his bed, he began to pray, as was his custom, and, as was the custom of the Grappin, it came to taunt him.

"Potato eater, why don't you join with me? Your body is weak and grows old. Join with me and I will give you eternal youth and power beyond your wildest dreams!" Jean Vianney sighed

"Why do ask the same question over and over when you know what the answer will be. Do you not tire of it Grappin? Are you so stupid that you cannot see I will never bend to you or your silly games?"

A loud roar shook the whole of the house down to its foundations. Pictures fell from the wall and chairs overturned as if an earthquake had struck. Suddenly the bed, which the priest sat upon, began to shake.

Jumping to his feet he grabbed for the lamp. For the first time in all these years Jean Vianney lost his temper.

"Enough!" he cried out.

At that he thought he saw something in the corner of the room. He had no idea whether it was a demon, or the devil. What he did know was that the creature was not from this realm.

Without thinking, he threw the lamp at it, causing the corner of the room to burst into flames. A loud shriek caused him to fall to his knees holding his ears. The shriek was followed by a crash as the glass in the window exploded outwards, showering the ground below.

The door to his bedroom burst open as the housekeeper and her young grandson rushed in. Tearing the heavy curtains from the shattered window, the grandson quickly beat out the flames.

Jean Vianney stood motionless, staring at the window.

"The Grappin has gone," he said "The Grappin has finally gone."

Crofters Cottage, Near Lahinich, Ireland. December 21st 1858.

The night was as black as pitch, with no moon to guide the lonely traveller who dared to venture on such a treacherous path.

The young priest followed a young child of no more than twelve along the path that skirted the rugged cliff-top. Below, the sound of the waves crashing against the rocks enhanced the deafening duet of sound caused by the howling wind and the raging sea. Fortunately the gale blew from the west off the sea, had it been from the East they would surely have been blown off the cliff and into the foam-white cauldron below.

The boy kept looking back to make sure that the priest was there.

"You all right father?" he asked.

"Fine," the young priest replied.

The lights to a small cottage could be seen glowing in the distance.

"Soon be there father," the boy reassured him.

The boy looked up at the black sky as the wind howled even more off the sea and across the barren landscape.

As they approached the cottage the priest halted; he thought he saw the shape of a young woman run past it. The boy also saw the shape and stopped dead in his tracks.

"The Banshee!" he cried, "She's come for Bridgett!"

The priest made no comment as they approached the door to the cottage. Reaching it, the boy quickly flung the door open and burst inside.

"We've seen the Banshee!" he proclaimed.

Two men a woman stood in silence as the waited for the young priest to enter. The priest, taking one more look round before entering made the sign of the cross.

One of the men, fat, bald-headed with a ruddy complexion, opened the door to the only bedroom in the cottage.

"She's in there father. God bless you and God save my child's soul."

The priest made no comment as he brushed past the man and into the room.

Three women stood around the bed. They were the child's mother, a nun and a woman from a neighbouring farm. It was her husband who was in the other room with the child's father.

No words were spoken as the mother motioned for her child of fifteen, Bridgett, to turn over and to lie on her stomach. Slowly her mother pulled back the covers to reveal the top half of her torso. Lifting the nightdress almost over her head she revealed her naked back.

Deep red weeping wounds etched their way from the shoulders down to the top of the buttocks. Each wound looked as though it had been caused by a three-clawed implement or by some creature. The young priest winced before motioning them to cover her up.

This was not the first time he had been to the cottage. He knew what to expect or at least he thought he did. The level of violence perpetrated against an innocent child was a new turn in the sickening scenario.

He drew in a deep breath before commenting.

"It will return tonight."

The nun looked at him before asking the obvious question.

"How do you know?"

The priest sighed

"You must all leave."

The child's mother was about to protest, when he held up his hand.

"Do as I say. Go with your neighbour. Leave the sister and me alone. Bridgett will be safe."

Bridgett's mother began to cry as she looked upon the gaunt, waxen, traumatised face of her child. The priest held the woman's hand.

"Have faith. By this time tomorrow all will be over. You will have your child back and this devil, will no longer be a threat to either you or your family."

The two women obeyed, leaving the priest and the nun alone in the room. In the other room they could hear the father protesting as the mother finally persuaded him to leave the cottage.

The slamming of the door caused the priest to make his way towards the window. Looking outside, he watched the party, carrying their lanterns, fade into the night. He was about to turn away when something caught his eye.

High on a hill looking down on him stood what looked like the shape of a woman. It was only for a fleeting moment, but enough for him to cross himself as a shiver ran down his spine.
He turned to the nun.

"Take the child into the other room and leave me alone."

The nun was about to ask why, when he held up his hand once again to cut her short.

"Please do not question me. Do as I ask. And under no circumstances enter this room, even if the devil himself is with me. And he may very well be."

The nun did as she was told and led Bridgett out of the room.

The priest knelt down and prayed, sweat poured from his brow and mingled with the tears that rolled down his cheeks.

Suddenly there was a scratching at the window. His heart missed a beat, he knew his time had come. Slowly rising to his feet, he walked towards the window. The wind howled relentlessly outside as he tentatively opened it, before backing away.

The thin curtains and covers on the bed flapped in the gale that now blew around the room. Without a word he slowly began to undress until he was completely naked except for the crucifix he wore around his neck.

A strange clicking sound drowned out the sound of the wind as the priest closed his eyes before crossing himself.

Suddenly his body began to convulse. He collapsed to the floor, then arched his back like a cat before crumpling into a ball in excruciating pain. Scream after scream echoed around the cottage with the terrified nun and Bridgett huddled together in a corner in the other room. Suddenly the screaming stopped; even the wind began to abate.

The door to the bedroom creaked open, in the doorway stood the priest. At first the two women were relieved, that was until they saw his eyes. The one thing about him was his bright blue eyes and how they sparkled in the light. Perhaps it was a trick of the light, the nun had no idea. All she did know was that they were now empty, as if the soul they mirrored had been removed.

As dawn broke the family returned; they never noticed the priest's eyes, or, if they sparkled, all they noticed was the change in their daughter.

A voice called out from outside. It was the neighbour's husband.

"Father! Father come quickly!"

The priest obeyed but without the haste, for he already knew what to expect. Slumped against the cottage below the window of the bedroom was the naked wizened frame of a woman.

Fort Detrick, Maryland, America. January 24th 1970

Marcus Painter burst into the laboratory, carrying a reinforced leather case under his arm. If eyes could show fear, then his had it embossed in his retinas.

A tall, thin, balding man was waiting for him.

"Well, have you got it?" he asked.

Painter, still out of breath not through running or any form of exercise, but through fear eventually replied.

"Yes, of course I have."

Painter was a man in his mid-forties, small, squat, with thinning dark brown hair. His eyes, if anything, were too close together, giving him the appearance of a squint.

He rubbed his hands in turn on his white laboratory coat, switching hands to hold the bag. The tall man moved closer to him.

"Excellent," he smiled as he held out his hands to take the case from Painter.

Painter recoiled, pulling the case closer to him.

"How much will we make from it?" he asked

"More than you will be able to spend in your lifetime," was the reply.

Painter smiled and was about to hand over the case when something in the far corner of the room caught his eye. Pulling back a little, he looked the man in the face.

"What about Lang? Shouldn't he be here?"

The tall man smiled.

"Lang. Oh, he's going to meet us at the airport."

Painter pretended not to care by shrugging his shoulders but he couldn't resist having another look in the corner of the room.

The tall man caught his gaze and the direction it took. Slowly turning his head, he glanced in the same direction as Painter.

A single foot could be seen sticking out from behind a tall metal cabinet. Shaking his head he turned round to face Painter.

"Sloppy. Very sloppy of me."

Painter's mind raced as he watched the tall man reach inside his coat to grab hold of a gun. Painter instantly reacted by grabbing the nearest thing to him, which happened to be a bottle of acid. He threw it at the tall man, spilling the contents over his hands and splashing his face.

The gun dropped to the ground. Painter was quick to react and ran out of the room, leaving the man writhing in agony.

With his heart racing, he quickly made his way towards his car and climbed inside. Carefully placing the case on the floor of the passenger seat, he was about to pull off when he realised he was still wearing his laboratory coat. Climbing out of the car, he removed it and threw it behind some bushes. Back inside the car, he made his way towards the front gate.

All the time he was driving the quarter of a mile to the gate he was expecting the alarm to sound. His mouth was dry, and he felt as if his heart would burst as he approached the checkout at the main gate.

The military police on the gate knew him well but still went throughout the usual procedure of checking his papers. The guard glanced at the case on the floor but paid no attention, thinking it was only a briefcase full of papers, written in some scientific gobbeldy gook, which was the norm with the scientists that came and went through this entrance to America's top secret biological research centre.

Painter let out a sigh of relief as he drove through the checkout and along the road towards the airport. All had been arranged for their escape. He had personally delivered his own suitcase and made reservations on a flight out of Washington under a false name and passport. The only difference was, there would be only him leaving and not the three as planned.

South African, Embassy, New York.
March 1st 1970

The Ambassador's wife struggled to fall asleep; the ticking of the clock beside the bed and the occasional grunt as the Ambassador turned over, were conspiring to keep her awake. She had lain there for the past half-hour or so, trying to get to sleep. It seemed that everything annoyed her, the clock, the grunts, the rustling of the sheets as the Ambassador kicked his legs. Eventually having had had enough, she was about to get up and go into the lounge. Her craving had finally got the better of her. She needed a cigarette.

As she swung her legs out of bed, a strange sound caught her ears. A clicking sound, like an animal's claws scraping across a polished floor. She paused a moment, not wishing to switch on the light for fear of waking her husband. The clicking sound drew near, she decided to turn on the light regardless. Suddenly the bed shook violently as if something large had pounced on it. She screamed and rolled out as her husband was lifted from the bed and pinned halfway up the wall. His arms and legs thrashed about in mid air as blood spurted from his throat.

Suddenly something hot and wet and heavy hit her in the face as her husband's body crashed back onto the bed in a pool of blood.

She screamed at the lump of flesh that had hit her and was still beating outside of the body in her lap. Screams that were drowned out by the crash of braking glass as the window in the bedroom was shattered into pieces.

Vatican City, Rome, Italy
March 3rd 1970

Archbishop Vol was about to leave to take mass when the telephone rang. He motioned his secretary to answer it.

The voice on the other side refused to give the man any information and insisted he speak to the Archbishop.

"Just tell him it's Louis Packard."

Once the message was relayed, Vol instantly dismissed his secretary.

"Louis old friend." Vol's voice rang down the telephone.

Packard's voice in response had a serious tone to it.

"We have a problem."

"A big one?" Vol asked.

"As big as they come," was the reply.

"And what may that be?" Vol was still in buoyant mood.

"An ancient one," Packard replied.

Vol stood motionless and pondered. He had heard of what Packard spoke of, but knew little of it.

Packard continued.

"We need your help. It's found a new ally, a protector. And like a dutiful servant, it's out to do its new masters bidding. Our men are out of their depth."

Vol was still pondering.

"Are you sure?"

"Yes." Packard's voice rang with fear as he continued.

"Do you know anyone good enough, as well as foolish enough to take it on?"

Vol tapped the large gold and ruby cross that hung around his neck.

"A predator can only be slain by another predator."

"Do you have one?"

"Yes I have one. A natural and expendable predator."

"Who is it "Packard asked.

A smile crept across Vol's face as the words hissed from between his teeth.

"A wolf, a red eyed wolf."

It has no eyes, no mouth no nose,

It has no sense of smell,

Yet still it stalks you from behind,

That faceless fiend from hell.

BillY Yull

Printed in the United Kingdom
by Lightning Source UK Ltd.
114971UKS00001B/40-102